"If one is very fortunate, a few books will fundamentally change their life. Such is the case for me and *Log Off*, an indelibly wise coming-of-age story crackling with humor and nostalgia. Felicetti will heal you, delight you, and make you want to hug your younger self; *Log Off* is an instant classic, a heartbreaker and a balm, and we're all the luckier for it."

T Kira Māhealani Madden, author of *Long Live the Tribe of Fatherless Girls*

"*Log Off* is a time machine, brilliantly evoking the Y2K era in all its LiveJournal glory. Kristen Felicetti's prose feels as real and intimate as making a friend on the Internet for the very first time and finding the key to her diary—I loved it."

Chelsea Hodson, author of *Tonight I'm Someone Else*

"*Log Off* is a brilliant and inventive debut with an unforgettable voice. Kristen Felicetti's writing is so off-handedly wise and instructive, I couldn't help but think of *Log Off* as a survival manual and by the end of my reading all other survival manuals were now obsolete."

Bud Smith, author of *Teenager*

LOG OFF

LOG OFF

Kristen Felicetti

First published by Shabby Doll House
June 2024
www.shabbydollhouse.com
@shabbydollhouse

Design and art direction by Tim Vienckowski
Cover illustration by Jinhwa Jang
Author photograph by Philip Pierce

Type set in Sabon and Circular

ISBN: 978-1-7379242-5-8

For P*pe's R*b*ll*on:
Colleen, Sue, and Caitlin

Time is never time at all
You can never ever leave
Without leaving a piece of youth

—The Smashing Pumpkins, "Tonight, Tonight"

Hello, people of the Internet. Let it be known that today, 9/5/Y2K, my legal guardian Brian finally joined the modern world and connected our computer to the great World Wide Web. I told him I needed the Internet for school, which was true, but my primary motivator was getting a LiveJournal. No way could I start one at the library. Whenever I logged on, there was always some old lady librarian hovering around, waiting for the inevitable moment I surfed my way to a big ol' porn site or downloaded some malicious virus that would crash the entire public computer system.

But now I've made an account, and from the comfort and privacy of my own home. Speaking of privacy, I don't want people from my real life reading this, especially people from school. I won't be using people's real last names and maybe I'll even change people's first ones if they're too unique. Though I guess my own first name is unique and I can't imagine calling myself anything else. Screw it, I'm calling everyone by their real first names. I shall change people's last names and the names of places at my own discretion. Whatever, I don't even know why I'm so concerned, the only four people who are going to read this are my friends from the Fiona Apple mailing list (hi!) that I added to my friends list here.

Tomorrow is the start of junior year. I can never sleep the night before the first day of school, because everything has so much potential to be magical and changed. By day three or four, it will all have dulled into the same old routine, but I live for that first day or two, where everything's sheer unfamiliarity radiates a glow of great possibility.

Current Mood: excited
Current Music: Ben Folds Five – "Jackson Cannery"

Wednesday, September 6th, 2000 | 4:51 p.m.

This year's English teacher, Mr. Krasner, has potential. I think the first thing to get out of the way about Mr. Krasner is how exceptionally hot he is. I don't mean hot for a teacher. I'm talking tall, dark, and handsome—movie star hot. The whole school knows it. So maybe my evaluation of his pedagogy shall be skewed, but I think his attractiveness has not completely corrupted his ability to have a personality or be a good teacher. We'll see. It's only been the first day.

He was sitting at his desk reading when we filed in, not saying hello to anyone, or even noticing that his students had arrived. When the bell signaled that class had started, he still did not do anything to indicate he planned to start teaching. We looked around at each other, wondering if someone should say something. Then he snapped the book he was reading shut, leaped over his desk, and in a very theatrical voice began reciting a poem as he walked to the front of the classroom: "America I've given you all and now I'm nothing!"

He roamed around the class reciting the rest of it, stopping occasionally to deliver certain lines with dramatic eye contact.

There were some swear words in the poem that he bleeped out, which made people laugh. We also laughed at a line about him going to the supermarket and buying things with his good looks, which felt like a little too much, like c'mon dude, we see your face. It was all honestly a little too much, I could tell he was really gunning hard for a movie-style Inspiring Teacher Moment, but he kind of pulled it off, because he was charismatic, and once again, absurdly attractive.

Plus, he calmed down after the poetry reading and became a real person. He said that the poem was by Allen Ginsberg, one of his literary heroes and the man he wrote his thesis on. We did introductions and went over the class outline and expectations.

The other thing worth noting was that Alice Sharpe was on the honors track now. At Parkview High School (not my town's real name), I'm in a lot of honors classes and the thing about being in honors classes is that if you are in one honors class, it's likely that you're in the others too. Your schedule essentially gridlocks with every other honors student and you have the same twenty-five people in all your classes from freshman to senior year. It's like a nerd school within the larger high school and the only time you interact with the Regents plebeians are in electives, lunch, and gym (where the tables are turned and many of the honors kids rather predictably perform the poorest).

While we waited for Mr. Krasner to start teaching, Alice sat down next to me, and said, "Hey. How was your summer?"

"Pretty good," I said. "How was your summer?"

I used to be best friends with Alice in third grade. We didn't say anything to each other for the rest of class, but I felt her presence the entire time. She didn't seem as awed by hot Mr. Krasner as everyone else. In fact, she looked like she was sucking a lemon during his whole performance.

Current Mood: curious
Current Music: Tori Amos – "Mr. Zebra"

Friday, September 8th, 2000 | 11:44 p.m.

Since school has started, that means I'll be working less hours at Earl's House, which is good for my sanity, but bad for my personal finances. Earl's House is a weird hybrid of fast-food joint and real restaurant that's actually the worst of both worlds, at least for the employees. It has a relatively complicated menu with a fast-food place's bad lighting. You run the orders out to people at their tables, but since everything is ordered at the counter, no one receives tips.

In summation: it sucks. But my summer job options were limited to places I could get to on my bike. I turned in a few applications, but Earl's was the only place that hired me, or even called me.

So here we are. Each shift I'm assigned to counter, runner, dishwasher, or floors. You have to be over eighteen to man grill or fry cook positions. Runner is the best because all you do is run the orders to people. I move fast and miraculously I haven't spilled anything on anyone yet. Sometimes I even imagine that it's the 1950s and I'm doing this on roller skates. Counter is somewhere in between. Most people like counter, but I find talking to so many people and getting their orders right difficult, especially during peak dinner hours when it's really loud. I often get yelled at and people are frustrated because I have to ask them to repeat things. Sometimes I don't know what's wrong with my stupid brain.

Tonight, I was on counter, and since it was Friday, it was packed.

An older couple came in.

"Hi, welcome to Earl's House," I asked. "How may I help you?"

They both ordered the fish fry special, but I forgot that since it was Friday that meant I needed to press a special button that gave them a discount on their fish fries, and so when I rang them up it was without the discount, and they accused me of "pulling a fast one" on them. I apologized and started the order again, with the discount, but this time they asked, "How old do you think we are?" To be honest, my answer would have been eighty, but you can't say things like that, so I said, "I don't know," to which they replied, "Old enough to get the senior discount, young lady," and I said, "Oh, of course," except you can't add multiple discounts to an order. I explained that to them several times, yet they kept saying, "Push it through, push it through" so I repeated that's not possible on these computers and they shouted that I should just do that for them because I had tried to "pull a fast one on them" with the whole fish fry business. It ended with me saying I was really sorry, but I literally could not add both discounts, did they want me to get the manager, and they said no but were very sour about the whole thing.

"Hi, welcome to Earl's House," I asked. "How may I help you?"

A cute boy from my grade came in with his mom who ordered for them both. Eye contact was avoided on both sides, obviously.

Next up was a man wearing what looked like a safari hat.

"Hi, welcome to Earl's House. How may I help you?"

"Where are you from?"

This has happened a few times. I had never experienced this until I started working with the public. But occasionally customers would ask this question, always men.

There were multiple ways this could go. Think of it as a Choose Your Own Adventure.

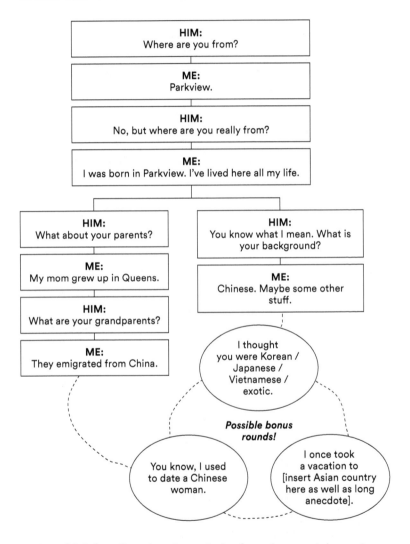

I couldn't handle going through the flow chart tonight, so I made it easy for myself.

"Where are you from?" he asked.

"China," I said immediately. "I'm Chinese. That would be from China."

But I sort of hated myself for it.

Current Mood: aggravated
Current Music: Fiona Apple – "Sleep to Dream"

Saturday, September 9th, 2000 | 5:01 p.m.

There's been three days of school and Alice still hasn't said anything to me since our initial rousing "How was your summer?" exchange. Not that I've said anything to her either. The two of us never had a falling out or anything, we simply drifted apart in fourth grade when we weren't in the same class anymore. That drift took us to different places as we got older. Cue the flashback, and allow me to explain:

In middle school, I enjoyed some moderate popularity with a clique of girls named Jenny, Jen, Kendall, and Naomi, until one day, halfway through eighth grade, Jenny called me up and ceremoniously informed me, "I don't want to be friends anymore."

I had been sorely friend dumped and the next day the other girls followed suit. Kendall repeated a variation of the same thing Jenny said, and Jen, the little coward, couldn't even tell me in person. She passed me a note folded like a fortune cookie that when opened read, "I don't think we should be friends. We don't have much in common. Sorry."

I don't know why it came as such a surprise. After all, I had participated in doing a similar excommunication of Naomi with them over the summer.

A small part of me felt relieved. I'd never quite fit in with them and the process of hiding that had been stressful. I didn't have the nice families and homes they had. And I spent a lot of time studying how they acted and what they talked about, so I could then go and do a similar thing the next time we hung out or sometimes even only a half hour later. An exhausting charade, but it was over now, and I could finally retreat into my head and fully obsess over what I genuinely liked. I had begun logging some serious Internet sessions at the library. I'd joined a Tori Amos mailing list and a Fiona Apple message board and started making friends on there.

The problem was I no longer had any friends in real life and that made my day-to-day eighth grade existence rough. Lunch period especially. Maybe that's why I went a little off the rails with my Fiona Apple presentation.

For Mrs. Gardner's social studies class, we all had to do a presentation on an important American historical figure in talk show format. Another classmate would act as the show's host and guide the interview. On the day of our presentation, we were encouraged to come to school dressed as our important American historical figure.

At first, I was stumped as to how I would dress as Fiona Apple. We didn't have any physical resemblance, me being Asian and all. Nor did she have any identifiable outfits. She mostly wore loose-fitting skirts and midriff-baring tank tops, the latter of which I was definitely not doing. Then I remembered a story I had read from her now infamous *Rolling Stone* profile. It ends with her talking about a fantasy she has, where she enters the school chapel and sprouts wings. Everyone who has ever teased her, or thought she was weird, is suddenly amazed that she has this extraordinary ability, and as she rises and flies away from them forever, they all whisper in awe, "Fiona has wings... Fiona has wings..." I bought some cheap costume angel wings and called it a day.

During the presentation, I talked about Fiona Apple's music, but after briefly touching upon her career successes, I mostly used the opportunity to portray Fiona's complex and troubled self. I quoted extensively from the *Rolling Stone* profile, which by then I had completely memorized.

I told my classmates to go with themselves, and how I ate nothing but split pea soup for my entire tour. I talked about how I was currently on psychiatric medication because I had wanted to die before. I talked about how in fifth grade I'd said, "I'm going to kill myself and take my sister with me," and how I used to stab the back of my closet because that was better than stabbing someone. I spoke about how when I read my first bad review, I scratched my arm until it bled.

And I saw Jenny, Jen, and Kendall watching this and thinking, "Wow, we really made the right choice dropping this crazy bitch." But in the moment of the Fiona Apple presentation, it was the one time I didn't feel bad about them dumping me.

Instead, I felt triumphant.

Yes, I was very proud of this presentation. I'd stayed in character the whole time. I'd also brought up serious topics that scared me to talk about, like rape and self-injury, but that I knew were necessary to mention as part of Fiona's personal history and important to discuss with my peers in general. And I could tell I'd held my classmates' attention. They had not been bored. If there was any flaw, it was maybe that I'd not done it with enough humor. The real Fiona Apple would have done this with a little more subtlety, a little more of a wink, like how she described her music video for "Criminal" as tongue-in-cheek. Overall though, it had been a great success.

Apparently Mrs. Gardner felt otherwise, because the next day she slid me a pass that said I had an appointment with the guidance counselor, Ms. Burke.

"Have you ever tried to harm yourself? Or had suicidal thoughts?" Ms. Burke asked. Her voice always sounded like she'd been sucking on helium.

"I wasn't talking as me," I said. "I was in character as Fiona Apple and communicating how she felt."

"Yes, about that," she said. "Mrs. Gardner told me the assignment was to present on an important American historical figure. Did you not understand the assignment? This means someone like George Washington or Susan B. Anthony."

My first inclination was to respond, "Fiona Apple *is* an important American historical figure," but I knew that would not go over well, so I didn't say anything.

Ms. Burke folded her hands in her lap. "Ellora, how are things at home?"

"Things are good."

"Well, it's interesting to hear you say that, because I already called home. I talked to your stepfather. He told me about your mom. That must be very difficult for you."

I was not going to talk to this airhead about my mom. "It's not a big deal. This has nothing to do with that. Oh, and he's technically not my stepfather, they weren't ever married."

She smiled like she pitied me, which I hated. I stared her down.

"I sense a lot of anger here," she said. "At me, and at yourself. I'm going to recommend you go to Group."

That got a reaction out of me. "No!"

Group was a program run by the drug and alcohol counselor Mr. Davis. It was almost exclusively populated by the Bad Kids, a clique of goths that loitered near the front entrance before and after school. My social standing at school was already abysmally low, so I really did not want to be seen as someone who went to Group.

But my sulky self had sealed my fate with Ms. Burke, and

later that week I was pulled out of class and forced to attend Group. Half the Bad Kids were there, sporting the latest Hot Topic fashions. Their most recent incident was campaigning for a Satanic Bible Study outside the Christian Bible Study Club. They sat around a table waiting for Mr. Davis to arrive.

And Alice was there. She wore a Nine Inch Nails t-shirt that was at least two sizes too large for her, a black choker with studs, heavy eye makeup, and black lipstick. I, on the other hand, wore a rainbow striped t-shirt with floral decals, which had been purchased from Limited Too. I picked the seat across from her.

"Hey," she said. There was some recognition of our elementary school friendship in her voice. "I heard about your Fiona Apple presentation. Did you really say you were going to kill yourself and take your sister with you?"

"Yoooo! That's tight," said a boy at the table wearing an Insane Clown Posse t-shirt.

"Yes. It's called acting," I said.

Alice didn't seem to care about that. "I like Fiona Apple too. Are you also into Ani DiFranco?"

"Yeah," I said, surprised. I hadn't met anyone at school who liked either of them, only people on the Internet. "Not as much, but I like *Little Plastic Castle*. It's a little front-loaded though. I think the better songs are in the beginning."

"What? Are you kidding me? 'Independence Day' is my favorite song ever."

But she wasn't mad that I'd disagreed with her about this latter album track. She was smiling like she'd found a worthy sparring partner.

"Lesbian music!" groaned ICP T-shirt.

"That's offensive," said Chris Walsh, who wore black nail polish.

"That *is* offensive," said Alice. "Besides, Ani, like *moi*, is bisexual, so the term lesbian music is not even accurate."

"Whatever, dyke," said ICP T-shirt.

Alice promptly flicked him off. I saw my chance at making the high school honors track fly out the window if I spent more time with these delinquents. But Alice was still focused on me. "What about Tori Amos, do you like her?"

I nodded.

"Favorite album?" she asked.

"*Boys for Pele.*"

She grinned. "Mine too."

Mr. Davis walked in with his dog and immediately, some of the Bad Kids jumped out of their seats in a rush to pet the black-and-white Border collie. Mr. Davis was bald and kind of weird, so a lot of people said mean things about him. For example, there was a persistent rumor that Mr. Davis had a dog because he was blind and this was his Seeing Eye Dog, even though it was clear he was obviously not blind—I had just watched him stroll into the classroom and check the attendance sheet. The dog's purpose was clearly to provide ease and comfort for the kids he counseled. The other mean rumor about him was that he had AIDS.

In Group, I had to introduce myself because I was new. I kept it brief.

"Hi, I'm Ellie. It wasn't my choice to be here."

Then everyone else talked about how things had gone for them since last week. Despite the tough front they put on by the school entrance, some of the kids really got into it. They talked about their messed up home lives or the drugs they'd done or some abuses they'd suffered. There were tears and shouting and Mr. Davis just calmly sat there with his dog, and as I listened to him respond to them all in a soft, soothing voice, I noticed I was the only one in the room not wearing head-to-toe black. The whole scene was tragic. The only thing that could have made me consider returning was the opportunity to see Alice (she didn't contribute much to Group either), but that did not outweigh the fact that I knew I had to do whatever I could to get out of this situation.

The next day I booked an appointment with Ms. Burke and showed up to her office with a huge smile on my face. There were two spectacular performances in this whole experience. The first was the Fiona Apple presentation itself. The second was the one I put on during my follow-up visit to Ms. Burke's office.

I told her how upset I'd been about my mom abandoning me and how the Fiona Apple presentation had really been a cry for help. I thanked her for helping me realize that. I was going to be seeking my own counseling outside of school to process my feelings, but in the meantime, it was counterproductive for me to attend Group. There was a lot of negativity in Group, which didn't feel healthy for me to be around right now.

The following week, when I walked through the school entrance, Alice stopped me. Instead of the choker, she wore a red ribbon. It made me think of that scary story where a girl has a ribbon around her neck and then when she takes the ribbon off her head falls off too.

"I see you're too good for Group and got yourself out," she said.

When I opened my mouth to object, she shook her head and said, "You're lucky. I wish I could do that too. But that's never happening for me." She reached into her bag for a pen. "Maybe we could hang out sometime. Like we used to?"

"Yeah, that'd be cool."

"We can listen to some albums." She handed me the pen and rolled up her sleeve. "Write your number."

As I wrote my number on her arm, I noticed all these red cuts, like tally marks, that had been hidden by her sleeve. I tried not to look at them, but it gave me a deeper understanding of why she wasn't going to be able to lie her way out of Group.

"I'll call you," she said, and then slid back into the Bad Kids clique.

I waited an embarrassingly long time for that call. I don't know why. Sometimes I'd decide to stay home after school, instead of going to the library to use the Internet, because I thought this might be the day Alice called. But then I realized it was just another interaction that held more meaning for me than for the other person.

High school arrived and it was a slight improvement over the tortures of middle school. I didn't see Alice at all freshman or sophomore year, so I stopped thinking about her. But now she sits right next to me in AP English. She's also in my AP US History class. And she doesn't have that Goth look anymore. Her hair is still dyed black but in a ponytail. Yesterday she wore tight dark jeans, Converse All-Stars sneakers, and a fitted t-shirt that looked like it was from the 70s. It said "Bridgeport Boys Little League." Bridgeport was the suburb next to Parkview. The t-shirt was short sleeved and I didn't see cuts on her arms anymore. Each of her hands had a black Sharpie'd X on the back.

Current Mood: curious
Current Music: Fiona Apple – "Fast As You Can"

Sunday, September 10th, 2000 | 7:39 p.m.

Um, I'm not sure what I did this weekend. I finished a book called *The Virgin Suicides*. I see a lot of you post images and collages from the movie, but for those of you who aren't familiar, it's about five hot sisters that kill themselves. That's not ruining the book. If you didn't pick that up from the title, well, you find that out on page one. I am the age of Mary, one of the sisters, but I'll never be a blonde mysterious beauty all the local boys fawn over.

I also "exercised," which means I took my CD/cassette player out into the living room and danced around. In the middle of this workout, I heard Brian's keys in the door, so I rushed to lower the volume and sit down at the kitchen table. When he walked in, it would appear as if he'd happened upon a cultured scene involving a sophisticated person quietly and maturely listening to music.

"Good afternoon," I said.

Brian gave me a suspicious look, like he knew I'd been up to something weird, but I'm sure he couldn't guess that I'd been turning the whole apartment into my own personal movie musical. He grumbled something about having to work on the weekends, grabbed his camera, and left again.

I'm not one of those smartass kids who run around calling their parents by their first names. Brian's not my dad, we're not related at all. Perhaps it would help if I provided a timeline of my major life events. There's been a lot of people coming and going.

Age 0-6: Born. Live with Mom, sometimes stay at Grandma's.
Age 6 ½: Grandma's death (stroke).
Age 7: Mom starts dating Brian.
Age 7 ¼: Mom and I leave our small apartment to live with Brian in this slightly larger apartment. The Golden Age. Everyone is happy.
Age 9 ¾: Mom no longer happy. Worst depression of hers I've ever seen. Though I didn't know to call it that then.

She was "sick" or "tired."

Age 10-16 (present): Mom leaves. Brian has been my sole legal guardian ever since.

I've never known who my father is. That's why I can't fully answer the Earl's House customers when they pry about my ethnic background. I look pretty freaking Asian like Mom, but maybe also vaguely something else. I definitely got more of my mom's side, except I didn't inherit her good looks.

"You don't have a father," she'd say, whenever I asked the question. When I was really young, I took that answer literally and later, I understood it meant, "This topic is not open for discussion."

Now that she's left, I don't see myself ever figuring his identity out. I have her last name and his name isn't on my birth certificate.

I think I'm really getting the hang of this LiveJournal thing. I like writing here and I like reading other people's entries too, even if reading about other people's weekends and fun things they've done with their friends makes me feel a little bad about myself. Or jealous, I guess. This is starting to sound pathetic, I'm going to stop now.

Current Mood: pessimistic
Current Music: P.J. Harvey – "Angelene"

Tuesday, September 12th, 2000 | 5:01 p.m.

AP US History is taught by Mrs. Ross, who is maybe sixty years old, with blondish white hair that she wears in a tight bun jammed through with a pencil. Everything about her is a little witchy and cartoonish. Like an aged Ms. Frizzle, she wears long dresses in loud clashing patterns. She started today's class by announcing that we would be forming study groups, people we'd regularly meet with outside of class to work on projects and AP exam preparation.

And then, instead of simply assigning everyone their study groups, she said, "Okay! There's twenty-four of you, that makes eight groups of three. Everybody get up—yes, that means stand up, get your butts out of those chairs—and pick those groups. And remember, you're going to be working together for the entire year, so choose people you'll work well with."

Despite her eccentric appearance, Mrs. Ross must have been popular when she was young. Only someone popular would subject her students to the humiliating process that is waiting to be chosen for a team. From kickball to science projects, I feel like I'm going to have a freaking panic attack whenever this happens.

Did I ask Alice? I thought of eighth grade, when she didn't call. No, I couldn't take another rejection. I sat back down and stared straight ahead, silently cursing Mrs. Ross and trying to see what groups were forming in my peripheral vision.

It was a real surprise when Alice walked right over, sat in the chair next to mine and asked, "Hey, do you want to be in our study group?"

Yes, yes, 100% yes.

"Yeah," I said.

"Our study group" was her and Tiffany McKee, who had traveled over with her.

Tiffany McKee's name makes her sound like a leggy blonde cheerleader, but she's actually an androgynous-looking Korean adoptee who is barely over five feet tall. She wears big t-shirts with either JNCOs or baggy khaki shorts. She also sports a very Asian bowl cut (I rocked this haircut myself from age 0 to 9). If this all sounds dorky, it is, but no one makes fun of her, because Tiff—while being a full honors track student—is undeniably cool. For one thing, she skateboards. She can often be seen holding her own with the skater boys in the parking lot after school. She's also a musical prodigy who plays the trumpet, which she carries everywhere. Our school's jazz band is considered one of the best in the county, if not the entire state. It's so competitive only upperclassmen usually make the cut. Tiff caused a minor stir when she auditioned as a freshman and made first chair, beating some seriously pissed upperclassmen for the spot. Additionally, she's got a bit of an attitude, including occasional anger issues that have flared up in class, and generally projects an air of not giving a shit about anything while being very good at everything, which is an appealing combo to everyone.

I didn't even know that Tiff and Alice were friends. But they were. And they wanted me to be in their yearlong study group.

Current Mood: hopeful
Current Music: Beck – "The New Pollution"

Thursday, September 14th, 2000 | 10:01 p.m.

Took the "Which *X-Men* Are You?" quiz and got Rogue, which was cool because she is probably my favorite of the X-Men. The results said: "You are Rogue. You have to keep people at arm's length all the time and then angst about it incessantly."

Hahhahahhahahahah.

Current Mood: amused
Current Music: Tori Amos – "Tear in Your Hand"

Sunday, September 17th, 2000 | 3:29 p.m.

I spent the morning catching up on LiveJournal posts, commenting here and there, and reading some of the larger accounts. By large, I mean ones that have many comments, and a high ratio of "friends of" to "friends." Personally, I friend everyone who friends me back. I don't want to hurt any feelings.

Brian emerged from his room with a woman I'd never seen before. She was surprised to see me sitting at the computer, or maybe surprised that there was anyone else in this apartment at all, and said, "Hiiiii" in this fake, slow voice that you'd use on an eight-year-old.

"Hey," I said.

Brian sank down in a kitchen chair and ran a hand over his narrow face. He showed little interest in this poor woman. She glanced over at him expecting some kind of explanation or introduction.

"That's my daughter," he said, waving his hand in my general direction. I shot him a look that I hoped communicated "WTF."

"Really?" she said, looking at me and back at him. We have absolutely zero physical resemblance. He's white, for starters. "Where's her mother?"

"Not in the picture anymore," he said. "She broke my heart."

I rolled my eyes and turned back to face the computer screen. At least he was telling the truth about that part. Over the years, I have occasionally heard him tell people she died in a car crash, or much less plausibly, a plane crash.

"I'm... sorry," the woman said.

They both sat there not saying anything for what felt like an interminably long time. The whole thing was so damn awkward that I considered getting up and hiding in my room until they left. Finally, she said, "Yeah, I'm going to go" and Brian said, "Okay."

She went to grab her purse from his room. When she came back, she suddenly turned to me and said, "Your dad's an asshole, you know that?" before storming out.

After a second, I burst out laughing. Brian was being a total asshole, but the whole situation was absurd.

"Sorry about that," he said. "C'mon, get off that thing. Let's go get some food."

We went to Denny's. I ordered two eggs, toast, and home fries. Brian ordered a sad bowl of oatmeal and a bottomless cup of coffee. He wore sunglasses indoors. I made a sarcastic comment about whether he thought he looked cool doing that, but despite his hungover state, he was in a relatively cheery and conversational mood.

"So, why are you on my computer all the time?"

I wasn't going to tell him about LiveJournal. I didn't think he would care enough to try and read it, but telling anyone about having any kind of diary is basically asking for them to read it at some point.

So, I chose my words carefully and said, "I'm... part of a growing online writing community."

Brian sipped his coffee. "What the hell does that mean?"

I shrugged and continued eating home fries.

"Writing what?" he asked. "Who exactly are you writing to?"

"Other girls. A few boys."

"How do you know they're who they say they are? They could be fifty-year-old men."

"They're not."

"How do you know? People can say they're whoever they

want to be on the Internet."

"Only a fellow teenage girl would be able to write the way I do."

He considered this. "Yeah, I still don't like it. Don't give out any personal information. Don't tell anyone where we live."

"I'm being careful," I said. "And you sound like you're one-hundred-years-old whenever you talk about the Internet. Don't you use computers at your job?"

"Yeah, we're converting the whole paper to Quark now. It's a real mess."

"What's Quark?"

"Publishing software that's used for newspaper design layout."

That gave me an idea. "Do you have access to a CD of Adobe Photoshop?"

"Yeah. Why?"

I'd been working hard on making graphics and digital collages as part of my personal website. I currently used a 30-day trial version of Paint Shop Pro, which I discovered could be hacked by setting the computer's clock back to the trial period's 30-day window, but I'd heard Photoshop was way better. I asked Brian if he would be able to bring me a copy of the software, so I could install it on our home computer.

"Sure," he said. "Though I don't know, maybe not if that's going to make you spend more time on there. Maybe I should be... limiting your computer time."

Whenever he alluded to doing something that resembled parental discipline, he sounded like someone reading a confusing instruction manual. I highly doubted he would enforce this, but I figured it was a good time to change the subject. "So, are you going to go on another date with that lady?"

"What lady?"

"Wow. From this morning," I said. In a whiny voice, I imitated him, "'She's my daughter. Her mom broke my heart.'"

"Don't be a smartass."

"I think you should respect women more."

"Oh, is that what you think?"

"Yeah."

"You have no idea what you're talking about. I respect women."

"Whatever."

"I respect you," he said quickly. He took off his sunglasses. "You're a young woman and I respect you. You haven't had it easy, but you're figuring it out. I was worried you'd grow up to be seriously screwed up, but..." He rapped his knuckles three times on the table. "You're turning out okay." He smiled. "A bit odd, but okay."

"Thanks?"

"How's school going?"

"Good."

"Making lots of friends?"

Sometimes I felt Brian thought I didn't have any friends, and pitied me for it, or maybe even felt annoyed by it. His assessment wasn't entirely inaccurate. Still, the idea offended me. It's not like I saw him having any friends, though he did in high school.

"I think I'm going to make two cool new friends this year," I said. "Well, one of them I was friends with before."

"Great. They're in your classes? Not on the Internet?"

The way he said "the Internet" sounded the same way you would say "imaginary."

"Yeah. They're real. Their names are Alice and Tiff. We formed a study group."

"Great. Either of them have single moms?"

"What? Ew. No—"

"Preferably emotionally damaged in some way? But I'm not

picky."

"You're being gross. And weird."

"Whatever happened to that girl whose house I'd always have to drive you to? Jen or Jennifer something? Now her mother—"

"Fuck Jenny Porter," I said. "I'm not friends with her anymore. And her mom hated you."

"I'm joking. That wasn't my finest moment. It was a difficult time."

"I know."

"She didn't need to make me feel so bad."

In seventh grade, there was a sleepover at Jenny Porter's house and Brian neglected to pick me up until 5 p.m. the next day. When he finally showed up, Jenny's mom insisted on coming outside to have a serious talk with him. You can imagine how well that went over.

"Don't feel bad," I said. "They're all a bunch of judgmental bitches."

"Bitches? What happened to respecting women?" He poured the rest of his coffee into his oatmeal, then raised two fingers to flag down the waitress for a third refill and the check. "And I was kidding about the single mom thing too, by the way." He put his sunglasses back on. "Your mother was enough for my lifetime."

Current Mood: cynical
Current Music: Cake – "I Will Survive"

Wednesday, September 20th, 2000 | 9:41 p.m.

After being assigned our first history project to work on outside of class, Alice suggested that Tiff and I come over after school. She said it would take thirty minutes to walk to her house. It still felt like summer and I knew it wouldn't for much longer. By November, or even October, winter would hit and last eternally until March/April. But today, we could still get away with wearing t-shirts.

"Do you have your license yet?" Alice asked.

"Not yet," I said. I made that "not yet" sound like I was working on it, but I didn't see the point in getting my license. Enrolling in Driver's Ed costs a lot of money and I'd never be able to save up enough Earl's House dough to buy a car. I gripped the handlebars of my bike. This would be my ride until graduation.

Tiff walked with her skateboard tucked underneath one arm and her trumpet in the other. I couldn't really see her driving either, I imagined she simply skateboarded everywhere. She still had a dorky L.L.Bean backpack, the kind everyone had in middle school, with her initials monogrammed on it. TSM. I wondered what the S stood for. It hung absurdly low on her shoulders, like she was daring adults to scold her and say she was ruining her back. Alice carried a shoulder bag with little pins on the strap. A messenger bag.

"I failed my driver's test last month," Alice said. "Total bullshit, I parallel parked fine, but apparently was too far from the curb."

"It gets everybody," Tiff said. "I can't parallel park either. It's so hard."

"I don't get it. It's not like you even need to parallel park anywhere around here."

"They should be testing whether you can pull into a three-car garage," I said. "Or the Steadmans parking lot on a Sunday."

"Right? Well, I've rescheduled for next month. Fingers

crossed."

We arrived at the Four Corners. This was it, our bustling center of town, where there stood a 7-Eleven, a Chinese restaurant, a bank, and Scott's Pizzeria on each corner respectively. Next to the bank, there was a coffeeshop called North by Northwest. Tiff wanted to get slices at Scott's. Alice said her mom would "force snacks on us," so we didn't need to do that, but Tiff insisted she was starving and ran in to grab a slice. We idled on a bench outside while she ate.

The town clock hovered above us, with Parkview's motto inscribed: *Where Life is Worth Living.* No, really. I couldn't make this shit up if I tried.

"So, how do you guys know each other?" I asked. I got the impression they were new friends. There wasn't much history in the air between them. I felt nervous asking that question, but they only laughed, happy to tell the story.

"Our dads set us up," Tiff said. "Well, my dad, her stepdad."

"My stepdad, Greg, loves to be really invested in my life, like he's my actual dad," Alice said. "He wants to control everything in general. That's why he was at the school board meeting. To complain about something he thought the whole school system should be doing his way. And you know her dad's the superintendent, right?"

I vaguely knew this. While it was hard to picture, John McKee, the Parkview School District superintendent, who looked like an older Tom Hanks, and militantly never awarded us any snow days, was Tiff's dad.

"It's so embarrassing," Tiff said.

"Greg comes to the school board town hall meeting to pick a fight with Dr. McKee about mandatory state testing and how classes teach toward the Regents—who cares," Alice said.

"So, my dad diplomatically invited him to have a longer conversation after the meeting was over. And they did. They went out for a beer. I think they talked for a long time."

"Oh, Greg couldn't stop going on and on about it. About what a great time he had hanging out with your dad. It's probably because he has no friends."

"My dad doesn't have friends either. He just acts like everyone's his friend."

"Anyway, so they come up with this brilliant idea that their daughters should hang out. My stepdad knows that Tiff's one of the best students in school, and he doesn't even hide the fact that he's hoping her good influence will rub off on me."

"And my dad acts like you're some kind of charity case. He tells me I should stop thinking about myself and my musical career all the time and help someone who might be struggling," Tiff said. "Plus, my mom loved the idea. She hates when I hang out with all guys."

"So, we get set up on what was essentially a playdate, even though we're like, fifteen, not five, and man, I was ready to hate your little nerd guts," Alice said.

"Trust me, the feeling was mutual."

"But look, now here we are."

I waited for them to say something more. They seemed to be done.

"So, you actually ended up becoming friends?"

"No," Alice said. "Not at first."

"Yeah, at first it was cold. Real cold," Tiff said.

"But then we started talking about how ridiculous our parents are and it got better from there. For once I felt there was someone who actually got me."

"Word," Tiff said.

"Sometimes I lie about hanging out with you because I don't want to give Greg the satisfaction," Alice said. She turned to me. "And now you're going to be coming over all the time. I can't stand it, Greg and Mom are going to think they're responsible for this whole new me."

I didn't say anything, but I liked the implication that we might be hanging out regularly.

I first met Alice's mom in third grade. She was still with Alice's dad back then, and they lived in a more modest house. Now, they lived in Squire Court, one of the richest neighborhoods in Parkview—each house offered its own take on a mini-mansion. Alice's house had towering front columns and a half circle driveway. As soon as we arrived, her mom rushed to greet us from the kitchen. She looked like an older version of Alice, the same saucer-big eyes, but a thinner face. Her hair was platinum blonde and she was very thin. She hugged Alice and Tiff.

"Mom," Alice said. "Do you remember Ellie? From elementary school?"

"Of course, of course!" She hugged me. I'm pretty sure she had no idea who the hell I was. I think Tiff thought so too, because I caught her stifling a laugh.

"What can I get you girls?"

"Mom, chill, we just got here." Alice gave me a half-hearted tour of her house. In the backyard, I noticed an in-ground pool and a hot tub. Then she led us to the finished basement, where there was a big-screen TV and a fortress of couches. Her bedroom was also in the basement. She said she had moved down there for more privacy.

The entire room was painted pale purple and draped in colored Christmas lights. A tulle canopy hung from the ceiling that made her room look like a secret fort. There was a lava lamp on her desk and she even had her own computer. God, what I would give to have a computer in my room! It was one of those cool iMacs too, made of translucent turquoise plastic, so you could see the insides of the monitor. At home, we had a bulky cream-colored Dell.

A few stuffed animals and Beanie babies collected dust on her shelves. The one thing our bedrooms had in common was taped up pictures from magazines on the wall. She'd made an epic collage out of Ani DiFranco pictures, a *Romeo & Juliet* movie poster, and photos of some bands that I didn't recognize—a lot of angry young men posed in different standing arrangements. There was also a wavy CD tower that rose from the floor. Before I could catch a glimpse of any CD titles, she grabbed some poster board, markers, and quickly ushered us out of her bedroom and back into the living room area.

Alice's mom came downstairs with snacks, as mentioned, and then it was time to get to work. Every study group would be presenting on a key factor that led to the American Revolution. We'd been assigned the Stamp Act. At the top of our poster, I wrote "No Taxation Without Representation" in big block capital letters and took my sweet time filling in each letter with a different color. Tiff cracked open her history textbook and outlined the Stamp Act's various injustices in neat bullet points, occasionally looking at the textbook for reference. And in the bottom right-hand corner of the poster, Alice drew a chopped-up snake. Underneath, she wrote "JOIN, or DIE."

"The Benjamin Franklin thing, nice," I said.

"It's also the logo for the hardcore band Join or Die," she said.

When we were nearly finished, Alice ran upstairs, leaving me and Tiff alone in an awkward moment of silence. Tiff and I had been on the honors track together since freshman year, but our previous interactions had been limited to tag-teaming arguments with Mr. Benson, the tenth-grade English teacher, about why the books he assigned to us thoroughly sucked, instead of discussing their symbolism or motifs or whatever he wanted us to do. Our targets included *The Pearl* by John

Steinbeck, a heavily abridged version of *Great Expectations* by Charles Dickens, and enemy #1: *The Scarlet Letter* by Nathaniel Hawthorne.

Now she sat next to me in Alice's basement and I didn't know what to say. Without Alice, there was a lull. I glanced over at her and she smiled without looking back at me.

"Um, what kind of music do you like?" I asked.

I know, I know. But it was my default question in moments like this.

"Free jazz," she said. "People you probably haven't heard of."

"What, like, Louis Armstrong?"

"No, too mainstream. More like Charles Mingus. And Albert Ayler. Ornette Coleman. Some Chet Baker."

She was right. I'd never heard of any of those people.

"Oh, don't even go there with her," Alice said, as she ran down the stairs to rejoin us in the basement. "She has the most pretentious musical taste of anyone I know."

Jazz did seem like the snobbiest musical genre. Maybe I should get into it. We finished up our poster and outlined who would say what for our presentation.

"Do you guys want to come over again tomorrow?" Alice asked, when we were done. "Not to work on anything. Just to hang."

"No can do," Tiff said. "Jazz bands auditions are after school tomorrow."

"Ugh, do you even have to audition at this point?"

"Everyone auditions every year." She raised a fist to her chest. "I must defend my title."

Alice turned to me. "What about you?"

As you might imagine, I didn't have much going on, so I said, as casually as I could, "Yeah, I can come over."

Current Mood: awake
Current Music: Ben Folds Five – "Kate"

Thursday, September 21st, 2000 | 8:27 p.m.

I went to Alice's house again after school. This time without Tiff and with no pretense of doing a school project. Things followed a similar pattern. Alice's mom said a loud hello and hugged us. We descended to the basement, trailed by Alice's mom holding a tray of snacks.

We watched music videos and *Pop-Up Video*, flipping between MTV and VH1. Alice knew the lyrics to every song. During Britney Spears' "Baby One More Time" she got up and did the choreographed dance with Britney. She hit every mark, while doing the moves in an ironic fashion, and it made me laugh. She had a good singing voice too.

Then we switched to MTV2. I hoped for a Fiona Apple video. I asked Alice if she was still into Fiona Apple and Ani DiFranco. She said yes, but that lately she was more into the local hardcore music scene. She even "sort of had a boyfriend" in one of the bands. They were playing an all-ages show tomorrow night at The Caterpillar, a music venue in the city. Did I want to go? I said I couldn't, I was scheduled at Earl's House. I was relieved to have an excuse. Hanging with Alice in her basement was manageable, but at a concert venue? With her boyfriend and other inevitably cooler friends? Terrifying.

On MTV2, "No Surprises" by Radiohead played, one of my favorite music videos. I loved its simplicity, how it's shot in one take. Thom Yorke is in a space helmet that slowly fills up with water. It looks like he might drown, he's even ready to accept drowning, but at the last second, the water drains and he lives. After gasping for air, a brief smile flickers across his face before he resumes singing. That smile makes the whole video for me. It feels like he triumphs, both over drowning and over his depression referenced in his lyrics.

We chatted and watched some more videos, but I couldn't fully concentrate. This happened to me often. I'd see a movie, or a music video, or read a book, and all I could think of was that. It was suddenly the only thing I wanted to talk about too. I remembered doing this with the old Jen/Jenny/Kendall clique, and I was certain it factored in their decision to dump me. I tried to unglue my mind from its wall of obsessions now that I was here with Alice, my first real chance at friendship that I'd had in over two years. *Don't be weird, Ellora. She doesn't want to hear you go on and on about the deep meaning of the "No Surprises" ending. Don't even think about that damn video.* Still, my engagement level in our conversation was only 50%. What truly pulled me out of this fog was when she said, as I was getting ready to go home, "Hey, I'm sorry, by the way. That I never called you. That time after you left Group."

"Oh, I totally forgot about that. No biggie."

"I wanted to, but it was a bad time for me. I didn't want to see any new people or want them to see me. Not that you were new. But you know what I mean."

"It's all good," I said. And then I took a chance and added, "I'm glad we're hanging out now."

"Yeah, me too."

Current Mood: quixotic
Current Music: Ani DiFranco – "Little Plastic Castle"

Thursday, September 21st, 2000 | 8:30 p.m.

Oh, and also, I don't think I'm going to put my Current Mood after every entry anymore. I feel many moods in a single day or even in a single moment, so how can I be expected to pick just one? Current Music, however, that's going to stay. :-)

Current Music: Ani DiFranco – "Fuel"

Tuesday, September 26th, 2000 | 6:12 p.m.

I've switched lunch tables. Previously, I sat with a group of mousy girls. None of us hung out with each other beyond the cafeteria, we simply couldn't bear eating lunch alone. Or eating lunch in the bathroom. Does anyone actually do that, or does that only happen in movies? It seems deeply unhygienic. Anyway, on Monday, I moved to sit at Alice and Tiff's table. The mousy girls noticed, I saw one of them whisper to the other, probably about my upgrade from the nerd nerds to the cool nerds. What can I say, I'm a social climber like anyone else.

At Alice and Tiff's lunch table, there are three other prominent members. Christopher, who is on honors track, and another one of the smartest kids in school. In middle school, he was often bullied, called a fag or a sissy. Then in high school, he shot up to be this six-foot-plus timeless beauty and it made him strangely untouchable. When I asked him what kind of music he liked, he answered "Shakespeare" without hesitation. It was such a pretentious answer I wasn't even offended.

Dev, another honors kid, sits across from him. He's into rap music. He and Christopher are both in Model U.N. and Debate Club together. Apparently, they always take opposite sides in Debate Club and things can get really ugly. Christopher takes the liberal view and Dev takes the conservative one because he's a Republican (ew), but then the second Debate Club is over they're friends and have been since elementary school.

The final person is Mal, who is not on honors track. She's Tiff's friend from jazz band. Mal wears a lot of clothes from Pacific Sunwear and little barrettes in her light blue hair. She likes the type of bands that go on the Warped Tour. I know this will be a controversial opinion but: pop punk is my kryptonite. I hate their whiny voices and also, why do so many of them sing about being in high school? Some of those guys are thirty-years-old, that's creepy and pathetic. Radiohead's members are in their thirties and they don't write songs about being in high school. Their existential lyrics have universal appeal for all ages.

What do you all eat for lunch? Let me know in the comments. I bring the same thing every day, I do not switch it up. I pack a peanut butter sandwich on white bread (cut diagonally not rectangularly), an apple, and pretzels. Sometimes, if I want a treat, I will buy something from the vending machine. If for some reason I am running late, I'll buy my lunch instead. This is really rolling the dice, as Parkview High School's lunches have a vast range of quality, so I usually keep the peanut butter situation in order.

Tiff's lunch is prepared for her by someone else, probably her mom. I'm basing this off her reactions to opening her lunch bag. Yesterday it was Lunchables, today it was last night's leftovers. I think it's a bit ridiculous that her mom packs her lunch still. Christopher has the school lunch, always at the mercy of the day's offerings.

Alice doesn't eat much at all. She brings a packed brown bag lunch and eats little from it. Occasionally she'll steal a single chip from Tiff or pluck a tater tot off Christopher's Styrofoam tray. I don't remember what kind of lunches Mal or Dev have.

Current Music: Radiohead – "Lucky"

Wednesday, September 27th, 2000 | 5:58 p.m.

I tried out for the school play today, *The Odd Couple* by Neil Simon. My odds aren't great, since there are only two female roles. It's pretty much a two-hander between these two roommates Felix and Oscar. One is a neurotic neat freak and the other is messy and irresponsible, so they spend the entire play bitching at each other. It's a shame Parkview High School isn't open to more non-traditional casting because I think I'd make a great Felix. I'd have gone full method, as I also have an immature roommate who drives me up the wall.

I want to be an actress. I don't think I've shared that here yet. I know that's probably a surprise, considering how freaking awkward and shy I come across in every situation, but I'm not that way on stage. If there are lines to memorize then I know what I'm doing and I can play around freely in them. It's real life where I don't know what to say.

I got into acting three years ago, when I went to the library every day after school to use the Internet. I saw a flier advertising auditions for a children's community theatre production of *Alice in Wonderland*. I tried out and ended up being cast as the Queen of Hearts and had a real good time screaming "OFF WITH HER HEAD!" a bunch.

I'm not sure I'll make it as a professional actress though, because while I've been cast in two other community theatre plays, I haven't gotten into one at my high school yet. Also, there's not that many Asian actresses in movies or television. The only major one I can think of right now is Lucy Liu on *Ally McBeal*. Getting your big break is tough for any actress, but being Asian will make it even harder for me, I think. When I see Asian people onscreen, sometimes I count how many lines they have. When they have a line, it's usually something like they're a lab technician and they're reciting data for the main character. I don't think you can make a living off of saying things like "The lab results are in, Agent Mulder" and I don't think that would be very fulfilling work either.

So yeah, I think I'm going to need a back-up plan for college in case this doesn't work out. Maybe a double major in psychology. With a degree in psychology, I'd bring a deeper level of psychological analysis to my performances, and if I audition for many things and find that there are no roles for me, then I will resign myself to my second choice of working full-time in psychology. I think I would like to help troubled and mentally ill people.

That doesn't make it any less of a bummer to think about how many roles will be off limits for me to even audition for. For example, any part in a movie where the characters are family members unless it was like, *The Joy Luck Club*. The two female roles in *The Odd Couple* are British sisters. My monologue was decent, and I did a solid British accent, but I think my chances are low compared to the other girls who tried out.

Current Music: Rasputina – "My Little Shirtwaist Fire"

Thursday, September 28th, 2000 | 9:37 p.m.

"I'm happy to have us come here for AP U.S. History projects," Alice said. We were in her basement again, working on another presentation. I think this might become a weekly thing. "But did you want to rotate whose house we go to?"

"Sure, we can go to my house sometime," Tiff said.

Alice turned to me. There was no way that was happening, so I quickly said, "I'm not allowed to have people over."

Tiff accepted this answer, but Alice said, "Really? Your mom's so chill."

"What?" I said, my heart racing.

"That birthday party you had at Ontario Park."

The summer before fourth grade, during The Golden Age, Mom and Brian had gotten season passes at the local amusement park. We went almost every Saturday. We laughed a lot on scary rides and ate sugary foods. I always got brain freeze from Dippin' Dots. One weekend, Mom suggested that I invite a couple friends to join us. Let's make it a belated birthday party, she said. A few months prior, she had spent my actual birthday sleeping in bed and she still felt guilty about that. I invited three girls to come to Ontario Park. Alice was one of them.

"She was so awesome," she continued. "You know when you're little and you see some adults that aren't like your own parents and their loser friends? People that make you think, 'oh, there are other ways to be a grown up that aren't completely terrible?'"

Tiff nodded.

"I think your mom was like that for me," Alice said.

It wasn't her fault. She didn't know. And I wasn't even that upset, I was almost curious. Curious to hear an outsider's opinion of my mom. "Why?" I asked.

"I don't know. She was younger than other moms. She dressed cool, she had a cool boyfriend. But what, is she like, super strict now?"

Usually, on the rare occasions people ask about my family, I'm able to quickly lie. It's easier, and because I've never had any behavioral problems since the Fiona Apple presentation, and few friends, no one discovers the truth. I prepared to lie again, to say, yes, she had become strict, a real strict Asian mom like Joyce Eng's, another classmate. But something about Alice and Tiff made me decide to tell the truth. Maybe I felt they wouldn't judge me, or maybe I wanted to commit to something real with them and that would involve being honest from the start.

"No, she's not super strict. She's not around at all actually. She left when I was ten. Less than a year after that party."

There was a long awkward silence, during which my heart beat so rapidly I thought I'd have a heart attack.

"Sorry," Alice said. "Sorry for saying that stuff about her being cool."

"It's okay. You didn't know."

"Wait, she just left one day and didn't come back?" Tiff asked.

"Yeah, exactly like that."

"Why?"

"Tiff," Alice said, indicating that she should change the subject, but I said, "No, it's okay."

Why. That was the question wasn't it. And I still didn't really know the answer.

"I'm not sure," I said. "She was depressed."

"Did she say goodbye?" Tiff asked.

"Tiff!" Alice said.

"No. She left a note."

"A note?!" Tiff said.

"Yeah. She called too, a week or so later. Nothing after that."

I didn't learn about the note until much later though. So I wouldn't panic, Brian had lied and told me she had gone on a vacation. When she called, I thought she was calling from that vacation. Eventually, too much time passed for that lie to be plausible, and he broke down and told me the truth.

"Wait," Alice said slowly. "Then, who takes care of you? Did you find out who your dad was?"

It surprised me how much Alice had remembered about my life.

"No," I said. "You know how you said my mom had a cool boyfriend?"

"Yeah."

"Well, he never went anywhere. I still live with him."

There was another pause while they both let this whole story settle in. But I had been right, they were not judging me or even pitying me. They were just curious.

"So, technically," Tiff said. "You're adopted."

"No. He didn't adopt me. He's my legal guardian though."

"What's the difference?" Alice asked.

There was a difference, a bunch of legal differences, the most important being that guardianship wouldn't terminate the rights of my mom, should she ever return. There was also an emotional difference. I assumed Tiff, who I believe had been adopted as a baby, viewed her adoptive parents as her parents.

But all I said was, "You know those forms that have to be 'signed by a parent or a legal guardian?' Have you ever wondered, 'damn, what poor kid doesn't have any parents and has to go the guardian route?'" I pointed two thumbs up and then towards myself.

I'd meant it as a dark joke, but it came out awkwardly and it didn't seem like either of them found it very funny.

"Okayyyy," Alice said. "Tiff, you know, on second thought, I think you live too far from school. Let's keep the study group meetings at my house."

Current Music: Fiona Apple – "Paper Bag"

Friday, September 29th, 2000 | 4:06 p.m.

I didn't get into the school play. :-(

Current Music: Radiohead – "Let Down"

Monday, October 2nd, 2000 | 3:33 p.m.

A funny thing happened this morning. I was riding my bike to school, racing past the many cars backed up at the stoplight, when one of the car doors opened and someone jumped out onto the sidewalk. I had to slam my brakes to avoid a collision. I was about to curse them out until I realized it was Tiff, skateboard in hand.

I'd always assumed she skateboarded into school. Now I understood that her mom dropped her off a couple blocks away, and she skateboarded in from there. I guess this makes sense, if she lived far from school. Still, I would have been mortified to be caught in this lie. Tiff, however, wasn't embarrassed at all. She simply winked at me and skated on ahead.

Current Music: Weezer – "Buddy Holly"

Wednesday, October 4th, 2000 | 10:04 p.m.

Apparently, there's another all-ages night at The Caterpillar that Alice's sorta-boyfriend is playing this weekend. I'm not scheduled at Earl's House so I'm going to go. Tiff and Mal are going too, which makes me feel better. It won't just be me and

Alice and cooler people. I'm still nervous about it though. For someone who supposedly loves music, I haven't been to many concerts.

In other news, we started a new book in Mr. Krasner's class—*The Grapes of Wrath* by John Steinbeck. Same guy who wrote *The Pearl*, one of the worst books ever, but he also wrote *Of Mice and Men*, which was pretty good. An early chapter of *The Grapes of Wrath* had a turtle crossing a road. That's it. That took the whole chapter. So I'm not getting my hopes up here.

Current Music: Ben Folds Five – "Philosophy"

Saturday, October 7th, 2000 | 11:55 p.m.

Tiff, Mal, and I went over to Alice's after school. At 7:00 pm, Alice's boyfriend picked us up and we headed to The Caterpillar.

"You've met Tiff," Alice said. "This is Ellie and Mal."

"Hey," Alice's boyfriend said, who didn't introduce himself, but I knew his name was Mike. Other things I knew about him: He played bass in the band The Suicidal Vigilantes. He was a senior at Bridgeport High School. He and Alice weren't "official."

The bouncer marked our hands with big X's so that no one would serve us alcohol. Alice and Mike already had X's on their hands, so he had to draw X's over those X's. Inside, it was already crowded. Mike carried his bass and went to go find his bandmates. They were going on first. The venue was filled with teens and some older people, maybe college-age, or a little older.

"Oh my God, Jon Carrington's here," Alice said.

"Everclear," I said.

Back when we were freshmen, and Jon Carrington was a senior, his band Toxic Winter performed at the school talent show. Everyone had expected them to perform one of their arty originals, but instead, to much delight, they launched into a cover of Everclear's "Father of Mine," a big song that year.

It's an autobiographical song the singer from Everclear wrote about his dad walking out on their family, but Jon sang it with an angst and pain that made the song his own. The crowd went wild, we rocked out in our auditorium seats. The energy made the teachers nervous, especially when Jon started a call and response of the chorus by screaming "MY DADDY GAVE ME A NAME" and asking the entire student body to scream back, "AND THEN HE WALKED AWAY." It culminated with him raising two middle fingers in the air and shrieking "FUCK YOU, DAD!" He was suspended almost as fast as the curtain was dropped on him and people talked about that performance for weeks.

At The Caterpillar, the four of us stared in reverence as Jon Carrington passed by.

"Legend," Tiff whispered.

"Hey, Alice," he said. He gave her a slight smile.

She blushed before turning to us and mouthing, "Oh my god." We watched him cross the room, his hips in tight jeans with a studded belt.

Later, a few drum rolls and dissonant guitar strokes signaled that the show was about to start. Everyone filed into the main area. We took a spot to the left side of the stage, where Mike was, and a few people back from the front.

"Hi," the lead singer said. "We're The Suicidal Vigilantes."

And with that, he screamed into the mic and the whole band launched into the most aggressive sound I'd ever heard. I immediately got shoved forward, because people started moshing all around me. If that's even what it was? I always thought moshing was jumping up and down. There was some of that going on with people raising their fists. But most people, especially the ones closest to the front of the stage, were simply shoving each other.

This was my worst nightmare. After I almost fell over, I ran to the back of the room, pushing past people until I escaped the fray and found a safe place to watch. Alice was swinging her arms with the best of them. Some guy pushed her and she responded by shoving him right back. Mal seemed to understand that this was the thing to do too, she wasn't as aggressive as Alice about it, but she was also wildly flailing around. I looked for Tiff. I couldn't see her at all, until she popped out from the crowd like someone had pressed an eject button. She fell to the floor with such force that she skidded across the room to my feet.

"Are you okay?" I asked. She was laughing.

"What the hell is this?" she asked. I reached my hand out, but she stayed there, cracking up, until she stood up on her own.

Despite how comatose they had looked setting up, all four boys in the band were now jumping up and down, violently throwing themselves across the stage. At one point, the lead singer looked like he was punching himself in the face, and later he deep throated the mic to end a song. There weren't even breaks for applause. A song would end, the band would stop moving, no one would clap, only for the whole thing to start up again a few seconds later.

Tiff tried to get back in the pit, but at barely over five feet, she kept being pushed out. She was falling and laughing over and over, all the while saying "this is awesome, this is awesome," until Mal finally stepped out and said she had to chill. The three of us stood by the wall as Alice continued to bounce around. The lead guitarist stage dived into the crowd while still playing and the crowd held him before throwing him back onto the stage.

Finally, it was over. Alice walked over to us with a maniacal grin. Her black hair was stuck to her forehead and eyeliner ran down her cheeks in sweaty streaks.

"So, what'd you think?"

"Why didn't you tell me it would be like that?" I asked.

Alice gave me a little pat on the shoulder and said, "You're so cute."

"Tight," Tiff said.

"They were all right," Mal said, in a snotty tone.

We went to get free water from a standing container and stood outside with half the venue to cool off. The band came outside. Now that they were off stage, they returned to their apathetic state. Mike approached Alice and I saw them walk away from the crowd and kiss.

"That was not my thing, musically," Tiff said. "But I admire their intensity. They gave 100%."

"I couldn't believe you in the pit," Mal said. "You were gonna get killed in there."

"C'mon, I was fine. It was fun."

"Look at your bruises!" she said, touching Tiff's arm. She giggled. "I saved you."

Tiff rolled her eyes but smiled at her.

"You don't think there's like, a parallel? To that kind of music and the crazy solos you do?"

"No," Tiff said. "I mean, I get what you're saying." Then she added, "But I'm better than they are."

I stood around awkwardly, with nothing to do except watch their conversation. When Alice and Mike returned, he started talking to one of his bandmates, then said to Alice, "We're going to Denny's."

"Don't you want to see the other bands?" Alice asked.

He shrugged. "You coming or not?"

"Can my friends come with us?" she asked.

"Well, I have to give them a ride home, don't I?"

While Alice went with Mike and his bandmates to grab their gear, Tiff, Mal, and I went to check out the next band. They had a similar sound to The Suicidal Vigilantes and violent moshing continued. The lead singer and the drummer had taken their shirts off, which had inspired a few other guys in the crowd to do the same.

"Time for Denny's," I said.

Our big group at Denny's took over three tables pushed together. Before going to the show, I had fantasized that maybe one of Mike's bandmates would be cute and maybe we would even hit it off, which is embarrassing to admit now, since that totally ended up not being the case. Two of his bandmates had girlfriends and the other one ignored me as much as the rest of them. Tiff and Mal and I mostly talked to each other at our own end table.

"What's with all the X's?" Tiff asked. I had wondered that too, but didn't want to be the one asking.

"They're straight edge," Mal said. "It means unlike other punk bands, they don't drink, smoke, or do drugs. How do you not know about this? Half the guys you skate with are straight edge."

"We don't talk much. All we do is skate," Tiff said. "So, you're saying I shouldn't offer them a cigarette?"

"You don't smoke."

"No, and I've never drank either. I just didn't realize there was this big political statement about it."

"We're also vegan," Alice said. I guess that explained why

most people at the table had only ordered fries, hash browns, and pieces of dry toast. Though Alice, as usual, wasn't eating much of anything.

"What about you, Ellie?" Mal asked. "You drink or do any drugs?"

"No," I said. Mal was asking in a sarcastic way, like she knew I hadn't had many opportunities to do them even if I'd wanted to. "I've smoked once before, though."

"Weed or cigarettes?"

"Cigarettes." I'd done this with the old Jen/Jenny/Kendall clique back in eighth grade. "What about you?"

"Oh yeah, everything. Drinking. Weed. Some of my mom's pills. Also, Robo."

"What is Robo?" Tiff asked.

"Robo-tripping. If you drink a bottle of Robitussin, you start hallucinating."

"Mal, what the hell?" Tiff touched her arm the same way Mal had touched her own arm bruises earlier. "Don't do stuff like that."

"I won't do it again. But I'm not going to be straight edge either. I want to be open to having fun, especially when I go to shows. Some people take straight edge too far." She jerked her head in the direction of the band. "Veganism. No coffee, no meningitis shots, no Advil."

"No Advil?" I asked.

"No Advil," Alice stressed. "And no promiscuous sex."

"We're in high school," Tiff said. "What does that even mean to you?"

"Yeah," I said. "It's not like we're adults, who go to bars, pick up women, have one-night stands, and then never call them again."

"No," Alice said, giving me a weird look. "Look, I was a little slutty the first two years of high school. And some of middle school. Fooling around with guys, girls, whoever. But not anymore. Now sex is only reserved for emotionally meaningful relationships."

I didn't ask whether being "not official" with Mike still counted as an "emotionally meaningful relationship." To be honest, whenever she had spoken about him before, he sounded like an asshole, and finally meeting him tonight didn't exactly change my mind. He didn't talk to me or Tiff or Mal much. And there was something Alice said at Denny's, her opinion on an album or something, I can't even remember what it was, all I can remember is how he muttered, "Shut up, it's not," and how it made her stop talking. Then he complained to her about driving us all home, which, well, I think if I had my license and this nice car that my parents clearly bought me, I'd be happy to drive people home who didn't.

Tiff was still hung up on the straight edge thing. "Okay, yeah," she said. "No sex with randos. Fine, I get that. But are you really not going to get a meningitis shot?"

Current Music: Everclear – "Father of Mine"

Sunday, October 8th, 2000 | 9:39 p.m.

At Earl's House tonight I was on runner, my favorite rotation. An order is placed on a tray with a number and then I find the table with that number. Rinse and repeat. No talking to anyone except for a brief "You're welcome" to the few people who say "Thank you." Ideal. I glided on the floors with grace, my mind free to float elsewhere.

"No, no, no. I told you last time, buddy, you gotta go."

I turned and saw one of the managers talking to Homeless

Guy, who had wandered in and asked a customer for money. Everyone in Parkview knows Homeless Guy because he's our only homeless person. You always see him out and about.

It was shitty that my manager asked him to leave. The McDonald's lets him hang out and nap in corner booths and even gives him free food. But most adults around here are super awful to Homeless Guy.

Current Music: Ben Folds Five – "Underground"

Tuesday, October 10th, 2000 | 10:59 p.m.

I've been so caught up in the election that sometimes I forget I don't actually get to vote next month. Mrs. Ross starts every class with updates from the Bush-Gore race. Then she inevitably rants about how she must return to teaching us towards the AP US History exam and says something like, "And noooow, back to The Gilded Age" while yawning dramatically. Sometimes she'll even bang her head in frustration against the podium, which I think is pretty inspired. I'm sorry I wrote that Mrs. Ross looked like a witch before. She still does, but now I mean witch in a cool way, because Mrs. Ross is awesome.

Compare her history teaching approach to Mr. Greenwell's last year. On the first day of class, he had us write on the board the events in our lifetime that would make the history books. We wrote things like "Columbine" or "Monica Lewinsky" only to have him cross them off one by one and say, no, none of these things would be big enough to make world history. I'd written Monica Lewinsky and I still think Bill Clinton being only one of two presidents to be impeached will make the damn history books, but honestly, the whole activity pissed me off because he'd obviously done it to make the whole class feel foolish. Sorry Mr. Greenwell, that we weren't alive during an exciting period of time like you. Please tell us again how you lived through the 1960s, when the Vietnam War was happening, and the Civil Rights movement, and everybody important was getting assassinated left and right, and how comparably, we're just a bunch of young morons living in a cushy time when nothing's happening.

Mrs. Ross doesn't condescend like that. She says there's no point in teaching us American history, if we don't also engage with the history that's being made right now, today.

This week's study group project was to make campaign videos for either Gore or Bush. We were filming it outside, because the exterior of Alice's nice house made a good background, but we were stuck on a script.

"It's hard to come up with enthusiastic things to say about Gore," I said.

"Yeah, like I feel we should make him cool somehow, and I don't know how to do that," Tiff said.

"He's not cool. He's the lesser of two evils, essentially," Alice said.

"What if we did a negative ad against Bush instead?" I suggested. "Like the examples Mrs. Ross showed us. Didn't she say those were more effective anyway?"

"Good call, then all we have to do is say 'Vote Al Gore' at the end," Tiff said.

Once we committed to the anti-Dubya direction, we got some momentum going. It's so much easier to say mean things.

Greg, Alice's stepdad, pulled in the driveway and rolled down the window of his BMW.

"Hello, hello!" he said. "What are you gals filming?"

"Campaign video for Al Gore."

"Don't you mean Al Bore?" he said and hit the accelerator

to pull into their three-car garage.

"Wow, good one," Alice said. "Mom and Greg are voting for Bush, obviously."

"My parents are too," Tiff said. "Well, my dad is. And my mom follows whatever my dad does."

"My mom said she thought he was cute," Alice said. "And I was like, really Mom? You're voting for him because he's cute? Not his campaign platform? Or the issues? She said he also has a nice family. She went on about how she loves Laura Bush and his mom, Barbara Bush. And I was like, Mom, having a nice family is not a campaign issue either!"

"Whoa, say that again," I said. "For the video."

She repeated it, and when I stopped recording, Tiff sighed and asked, "When do you think we'll turn into assholes?"

"What do you mean?" Alice asked.

"I mean were your parents always conservative Republicans?"

"I don't know, probably. I feel like Greg was an asshole from day one."

"Mine weren't. My dad used to live in Greenwich Village and protest the Vietnam War. And my mom has tons of books in her office she used to read. She wanted to write a novel when she was in college. Now she just reads beach reads, if she reads at all."

"Let's never let that happen to us," I said.

"Word," Tiff said. "What bad thing do you think we should say about Bush next?"

That night at home, I asked Brian, "Who are you voting for?"

I was on the computer, he was watching TV. He always watched the most brain-numbing television, like reality shows. This was the routine a few nights a week, ever since we got the

Internet. We looked at our preferred screens and neither of us talked to each other much. I asked the question again.

"Not voting," he said.

"What?"

"Yeah, I've never voted. I know I'm not, uh, setting a great example for you."

"Why don't you vote?"

"They're all the same."

I didn't even know what to say that, I was so annoyed. I couldn't decide whether his apathy was better or worse than Tiff and Alice's conservative parents.

"Al Gore is not the same as Dubya," I said. "One is pro-life, one is pro-choice. One is actually educated. One partied and did cocaine with his dad's money in Texas."

"Lucky guy."

"I'm serious."

"They're all politicians at the end of the day," he said. "Swayed by money and lobbyists and outside interests. They'll say one thing, then another. Ultimately, they only want to stay in power."

"What does it matter? If one's pushing for a more liberal agenda?"

"Liberal agenda? Al Gore is a moderate. And Lieberman is practically a conservative. Now Nader has some interesting things to say. I could have seen myself voting for him."

"Yeah, well, that's okay because we live in New York state. But if we lived in a swing state—"

"No, it's okay because it's a free country and I can vote for whoever I want. Or not vote at all. Which I hate to tell you, is what the majority of this country does, because they also don't care."

"I care," I said. "And I can't believe you. I want to vote so badly and you're just throwing your vote away."

"In two years, you can vote in all the elections you want. Don't get yourself worked up," he said. "Iceland."

"What?"

"That's the answer. Iceland." He pointed at the television screen. *Who Wants to Be A Millionaire?* was on. The contestant guessed Peru and lost the $60,000 he had earned so far. The show stressed me out.

"I get it, I do," he said. "I did the same thing when I was your age. Staged a demonstration against Reagan."

"Really?"

Brian was unlike other grown-ups in Parkview. Despite his other flaws, he wasn't fake. He didn't care about material things either (if the minimalist state of our apartment was any indication). Still, he lived on autopilot. I saw it in the way he came home every day and often did exactly what he was doing right now—lying on the couch, drinking a glass of whiskey and watching bad TV. I hope my adult life isn't like this. I'm not sure what I wanted it to be like. Okay, that's not actually true, I've spent a considerable amount of time fantasizing about living in New York City and attending exciting, artistic events every night with numerous friends who adore me.

"What changed?" I asked.

He thought about it. "Well, now that I'm remembering this, I don't think I was ever really into it. The whole cause. A girl I liked was though, and I wanted to impress her."

I rolled my eyes and started to draft a message to Alice, to complain about Brian's voting apathy, but she abruptly signed off.

"What is that constant door slamming noise?" he asked.

"My AIM Buddy List."

"Whatever it is, turn it off."

"When someone signs on or off, it makes the sound of a door opening or closing. I'm talking to a lot of friends right now, so—"

"Great, please turn it off. That sound gives me a heart attack."

Instead, I grabbed my headphones from my room and plugged them into the speakers, which is what I should have done in the first place.

Current Music: Radiohead – "Paranoid Android"

Thursday, October 12th, 2000 | 5:55 p.m.

Oh my god, I finished *The Grapes of Wrath* and WTF! After almost five hundred pages of Dust Bowl misery, it ends on this gross image of a starving old man suckling a young woman's breast for breast milk. Then the woman's "lips came together and smiled mysteriously." THE END. I'm not making this up. Yes, I understand that it was supposed to be religious symbolism or show the eternal selflessness of humanity or whatever, it was still the worst ending of all time.

Current Music: none

Saturday, October 14th, 2000 | 5:01 p.m.

Everyone in Mr. Krasner's class was so pissed about that whack ending of *The Grapes of Wrath*. Mr. Krasner just smiled ("mysteriously?") at us and said it was one of the Great American Novels. Usually I agree with him, but not this time. Thank you to everyone who commented on the previous post and expressed similar displeasure about *The Grapes of Wrath*.

By the way, some of your comments really make my day. I've been meaning to print them out to have with me when I'm feeling bad or if LiveJournal ever crashes. A few people have written things like, "You're one of the coolest people on my friends list" or "I added you cause you sound like me." Even comments like "hahahah, that's so funny" make me feel good. Someone anonymously wrote, "my family's kinda like yours. i live with just my grandpa. i thought i was the only one without a normal family until i read your LJ." I don't know what to say to that. It's okay, anonymous person, it's okay.

While I'm on the subject of LiveJournal friends, I want to say HAPPY BIRTHDAY SLAYER! I love reading your journal and chatting with you online. Even if we've never met, and may never meet (because you live in San Francisco, California and I live in a crappy suburb in upstate New York), you're an important person in my life.

It's funny, my offline friends are my age, but Slayer is a freshman. On LiveJournal, I talk to people as young as eighth graders, all the way up to people in graduate school writing their theses, etc. I've noticed it tends to be the older people who do more traditional art things with their journals. They take self-portraits with expensive cameras. Or they're imitating Michelle's journal, where she combines Photoshopped collages with original poetry to create this abstract expression of her daily life. Most people's entries are more like mine though. Girls just writing about their days.

Current Music: Fiona Apple – "Limp"

🔒 Sunday, October 15th, 2000 | 1:44 p.m.

There was a movie night at Alice's and the whole lunch table went. Me, Alice, Tiff, Mal, Christopher, and Dev. Mike too. We took two cars to Blockbuster and we raced all the way there. I rode with Christopher and Dev, the other four rode with Mike.

Christopher crossed a double line to accelerate ahead of Mike's car, while Dev flashed what looked like a gang symbol at them.

"Don't do that," Christopher said. "You're an embarrassment to the other occupants of this vehicle."

"Drive, bitch," Dev said. We beat Mike's car to Blockbuster.

We spent over an hour there because no one could agree on a movie. Finally, the group settled on *Fight Club*, which was a movie Mike loved and he wanted Alice to see, and I wanted to see it too.

It was really good. Edward Norton is cute, and I get the references some of you have been making on your LiveJournals now. "I am Jack's raging bile duct." "I am Jack's complete lack of surprise." The surprise twist at the end was silly, but I liked the last shot, where the narrator and Marla Singer are holding hands as the buildings explode. Mike put his arm around Alice during that part and I caught her pleased smile.

Afterwards, we analyzed specific scenes and debated their meaning. Then, during a quiet moment, Alice nudged Tiff and said, "Do it. Do it now."

"Stop," Tiff whined. "Okay." She rocked back and forth. "Yo, so, um, there's something me and Mal want to tell everybody."

Mal sat up and edged closer to her. They had been sitting next to each other for the entire movie.

"Me and Mal," Tiff said. "We're dating. We're a couple."

No one said anything until Dev broke the silence and said, "Lesbians. Niiiiiice."

He reached out to Tiff for a high five. Alice shot him an ice-cold death stare, but Tiff high-fived him.

"We've been secretly dating since the summer," Mal said.

"Yeah, so we thought you guys should know," Tiff said. "I don't expect any of you to be weird about it, but I want to make sure we're cool?"

This was mostly addressed to me, Dev, and Christopher, since Alice clearly already knew, and I assumed she had told Mike.

"It's totally cool!" I said. It's possible I overdid it with an excessively enthusiastic tone of voice and smile. Mal gave me a weird look.

"I figured," Tiff said. She turned to Christopher. "I mean, you're gay too, right?"

"Tiff," Alice yelled. "You can't just ask that."

"Sorry." Tiff put up her hands. "My bad. You don't have to say."

"It's fine," Christopher sighed. "Yes, like the greatest humans in history, I am a homosexual."

Everyone returned to talking about *Fight Club*. My mind drifted into its usual fog. When it was time to go home, I walked upstairs from the basement and saw Alice's mom and Greg cuddled together on the couch watching *You've Got Mail*. I felt smug about how we had watched a cooler movie. God, adults were so dead and boring.

Until recently, everything gay felt abstract, relegated to Ellen DeGeneres or Melissa Etheridge or artsy people who lived in New York City. Now, it's immediate. On LiveJournal, many of you talk about being gay or bi or all over the rainbow spectrum. And now one of my friends is a lesbian and presumably having lesbian sex. I wonder what the bases are for lesbian sex. I feel like I only understood what the bases were for straight sex a couple years ago and it still seems up for debate depending on who you're talking to. Third base was below the belt, but a blowjob seems like a huge jump from a hand job. Shouldn't there be a shortstop or something?

Not that I would know, I'm sixteen and I've never even kissed anybody. This is horrifying. I feel this is becoming more and more obvious in my conversations about dating with Alice and Tiff and the others. I've fallen hopelessly behind the sexual experience of my peers and it now seems impossible to catch up. Not everyone my age has had sex yet, but most people my age have at least kissed someone. And many of them back in middle school! I'm starting to think it was a huge mistake spending all those nights and weekends at the library. I would have been better off going to church. No seriously, everyone at school who talks about going to church and having "church friends" is basically bragging about having a wider dating pool. I've also fantasized about being rich and going to a sleep-away summer camp. I'm not an outdoors person and the lack of solitude would have been my personal hell, but it might have been worth enduring if I could have come back with one anecdote of a sexual escapade.

Also, please note this is my first locked, friends-only entry. Since it discusses other people's sexualities and details of their sexual lives, I'm taking an extra step to make sure it's not public or discoverable by anyone from my real life.

Current Music: Ani DiFranco – "As Is"

Monday, October 16th, 2000 | 10:53 p.m.

Another day, another walk to Alice's after school to work on the weekly AP US History project. A mid-autumn breeze rattled dead leaves over the sidewalks and streets. The wind kept blowing my hair into my face and I was constantly batting it away. As usual, I walked my bike, and Tiff held her skateboard.

"You guys want to come to my gig?" Tiff asked.

"Your gig?" Alice snorted. "You mean a school jazz band concert?"

"No, it's not at school. Mr. Flick wants us to start playing real gigs around town. The first one's at Steadmans."

"Whoa, really?" I asked.

I don't know what your town is known for, maybe a certain type of cuisine, or a landmark, or you know, culture, but I'll tell you what this town is known for: our freaking grocery store. It's called Steadmans and life here revolves around it. No seriously, everyone, myself included, is weirdly obsessed with this grocery store.

I know what you're thinking. Isn't it just a grocery store? Don't say that to anyone here because they will tackle you down to the ground, while screaming, "STEADMANS IS NOT JUST A GROCERY STORE." It's a chain that primarily exists in upstate New York, and one of the nicest, shiniest stores in the franchise is in Parkview. It's massive, things are super clean, and the produce is shiny fresh. The lighting is warm and inviting like a home. Yeah, I understand that doesn't sound like something to lose your mind over. You have to just go. Everyone goes. It's the town square. It's where the richest residents of Squire Court mingle with the poorest residents of The Pines.

Anyway, it seemed wild that Steadmans was going to be Tiff's grand stage.

"When's the concert?" I asked.

"Sunday. Not this Sunday, the next one."

"I'll come," I said.

"I might have plans with Mike that weekend," Alice said.

"Bring Mike," Tiff said. "I went to his show. He should go

to mine."

"Ugh, fine."

"You're definitely going?" Tiff asked me.

"Definitely."

"Word." She looked at Alice and grinned. "See, I told you Ellie is a better friend than you."

Alice rolled her eyes. "I'll go to your grocery store concert, okay?"

"Oh, and also," Tiff said, "everybody's parents are going to be there. Including Mal's. So that thing I told you about us. Don't bring it up. I'm probably going to act like I'm not even friends with Mal."

"I wouldn't talk about your dating life in front of your parents. Give me some credit," I said.

"Not my parents. That's another story. Mal's. Mal's dad. He's a big homophobe. I think he already suspects something, so I don't even go to her house anymore unless he's not home. We're laying low."

"You are playing with fire," Alice said. "Sneaking over there. I'm telling you."

We reached the Four Corners and turned to see Homeless Guy standing in the middle of the sidewalk.

"Oh shit," Tiff said.

"Let's just keep our heads down and walk past him," Alice whispered.

"No, no, I've always wanted to talk to him, but my parents never let me."

Grown-ups are extra awful to Homeless Guy when kids are around. They treat him like he's some terrible pedophile despite no evidence of this. But there were no adults around now. Tiff walked right up to him.

"Hey, man," she said. "How are you?"

There was a pause. Then he asked, "Are you a girl or a

boy?" He had odd, stilted speech.

"Oh my god," Alice muttered.

Tiff didn't seem phased. "Huh. What do you think?"

"You look like a Vietnamese boy. And she," he said, pointing to me, "looks like a Vietnamese girl."

"Oh my god, do you think he fought in 'Nam?" Alice said. "We should go."

"We're both Americans," Tiff said, calmly but firmly. "Like you."

There was another gust of wind that swept Tiff's bangs away from her forehead. She smiled slightly and looked like the stoic hero of an action movie.

"Got any change?" he asked her.

"Um, what about pizza? You want any pizza?" She pointed across the street at Scott's Pizzeria.

He nodded. She skated across the street and went inside. I thought she was going to buy him a slice. Instead, she came back with an entire pizza and paper plates. Yeah, we had a goddamn pizza party with Homeless Guy right there on the sidewalk. Nobody talked, we just quietly ate our pizza together. Even Alice ate half a slice because she realized the situation was so unusual.

The three of us said goodbye to him and continued our walk to Alice's house. At a certain point in the route, near Steadmans, the sidewalk ends and the road opens up to four lanes. We felt daring and walked on the shoulder of the road instead of the grass like we usually did.

"Hey, you're gonna rock that place," I said to Tiff, pointing at our famous grocery store.

"Hell yeah I am," she said.

"Get out of the road!" some guy yelled from his car. Another man rolled down his window and whistled.

"Go fuck yourself!" Alice shouted back, but with joy.

We all felt it, this invincible rush. I'd say it felt like we were in a movie, but no, it was too real. For once, I was present in my own life, I was so happy to be right where I was, walking with them. Cars honked and swerved around us. When we reached the top of the hill, I got on my bike, to enjoy free riding the decline. And Tiff did the same behind me on her skateboard screaming, "Woooooo!"

And Alice ran to catch up behind us, yelling, "You assholes!" but laughing, laughing, laughing, the whole time.

Current Music: Sleater-Kinney – "Dig Me Out"

Tuesday, October 17th, 2000 | 11:10 p.m.

Name: Ellora "Ellie"
Age: 16
Location: Suburban Hell, NY
If there are 3 wells (love, money, and creativity) and you can drink from one of them, which would you choose? Love.
Would you kill someone? Um, probably not.
Do you still have V-card? Yeah.
If yes, are you waiting until you get married to have sex? Absolutely not.
Have you ever met anyone famous? No.
Who is the famous person you'd most like to meet? Fiona Apple.
Do you keep a diary? LOL
Do you feel understood most of the time? No.
Do you think you are strong (emotionally)? Yes.
Have you ever been depressed? Yes.
In a social setting, are you more of a talker or a listener?

Listener.

If abandoned alone in the wilderness, would you survive? Nah, I'd probably die early on.

If a sexy person was pursuing you, but you knew he/she was married, would you go for it? What the hell kinda question is this??!

What do you wear to sleep? Creepy question. T-shirt and pajama shorts.

Is there a computer/laptop in your room? I WISH.

Do you wish you were someone else? Sometimes.

Do your parents care about and love you? ...

Do you think you'll be married in 10 years? I don't know, I hope so.

Do you have a significant other? No.

If so, what is your significant other's name? n/a

How long have you been together? n/a

How many people have you dated? 0

What is the sweetest thing a significant other has done for you? This survey is starting to make me feel bad.

Do you have a crush on any of your friends and if so, do you think they know? Maybe, and probably not, though I'm always paranoid about that stuff.

Do you think Britney Spears needs to put some clothes on? WTF! I don't care.

Are you against gay marriage? No. I want to see gay marriage in my lifetime.

What are your thoughts on abortion? Pro-choice.

Do you want Bush or Gore to win? AL GORE. No Dubya.

How do you feel about the death penalty? I'm not sure, maybe in extreme situations, like if the person was a serial killer of numerous people and there was zero doubt that they had done all the murders.

How much schooling have you had? I'm currently in school.

Did you enjoy school? I would not say I "enjoy" it.

What is your favorite memory? Yesterday, which I wrote about in my last entry, was pretty great. Further back, maybe some stuff with my mom. She was a hairdresser and I loved when she took me to her salon and cut my hair in her chair.

What is your least favorite memory? Brian telling me Mom was not on a vacation.

What website do you use the most? LiveJournal, hotmail, Radiohead's official site, Radiohead's unofficial sites, my personal website, my online friends' personal websites.

Do you have any online friends? Yes, a bunch.

Could you live without the Internet? I think it would be very hard at this point.

Current Music: Radiohead – "Fitter Happier"

Tuesday, October 24th, 2000 | 8:13 p.m.

Alice got her license! She wanted to celebrate by driving us all somewhere. Even though you're technically not supposed to do that. With a junior license, you should only be driving yourself, not other minors. Whatever. Me, Mike, Tiff, and Mal piled into her car.

We went to a coffeeshop in the city, a nice change from the usual North by Northwest, and then we went to Goodwill. I remember shopping at Goodwill with Mom when I was little, and I remember it being something to be ashamed about. Apparently shopping at Goodwill was cool now. I think Mom made it cool back then, she always looked good in what she bought there. Among my new friends, the most prized things to buy were vintage t-shirts, usually in children's sizes, like youth large, and occasionally the odd accessory. Retro sunglasses, silk scarves, studded belts. Alice and Mal got t-shirts, and I bought some accessories for my Halloween costume. That whole part of the trip put me in an odd mood though, being in Goodwill and thinking of my mom and her colorful patterned dresses.

The accessories I bought for my Halloween costume were a scarf and long gloves, because I am going to be Rogue for Halloween, my result of the "Which X-Men Are You?" quiz. I'm being the movie version of Rogue, played by Anna Paquin, before she gets her X-Men suit. In the movie, Rogue wears gloves because her touch is lethal. Any skin contact, actually. She absorbs the powers of other mutants, or if she touches a non-mutant, she sends them into a coma. I've gotten kind of obsessed with her, or the idea of her.

You have to keep people at arm's length all the time and then angst about it incessantly.

Current Music: Blue Clocks Green – "Hemingway"

Saturday, October 28th, 2000 | 6:44 p.m.

I had imagined Tiff's concert at Steadmans would involve the whole band gloriously marching up and down the produce aisles, but no, it consisted of the entire Parkview Jazz Band crammed into one corner of Steadmans' cafe area.

Mr. Flick, our controversial jazz band director, stood up front. Legend has it that Mr. Flick used to be a big deal musician until he knocked his girlfriend up, had to marry her, and get a real job to support the kid. This seriously derailed his musical career, so now he lives in middle-aged resentment and takes it out sadistically on the jazz band. There are epic tales of Mr. Flick making students cry. Last year, there were rumors he repeatedly whacked Jesse Stover on the head with a music binder. There have been some parental complaints, but he's tenured.

Tiff completely worships him. When Alice brought up the whole hitting Jesse Stover thing, Tiff shrugged and said, "Charles Mingus used to push players off stage if they weren't doing a good enough job. Right in the middle of a concert."

"Ugh, and what? That makes you think it's okay?" Alice asked.

At Steadmans, Mr. Flick conducted the band with precise swipes of his baton. Tiff was truly the star, as first chair she played a good amount of solos. Alice and I sat in the cafe with people's parents. Mike hadn't joined. I spotted Tiff's Tom Hanks-looking dad, her mom, and a middle school-aged boy that I presumed was her younger brother. He looked like Tiff scaled down in Photoshop and played his Game Boy the whole concert.

After a song finished, a manager at Steadmans came up to Mr. Flick and whispered something. Mr. Flick turned to the band and cleared his throat.

"Apparently," he said. "There have been some complaints. Some Steadmans customers think we're playing a little too loud for their afternoon grocery shopping experience."

He turned on his heel to stare out at the audience. "What do you think? Do you think your children have been too loud?"

Even parents were somewhat intimidated by Mr. Flick. "No?" a few murmured.

"Y'all sound great!" someone's dad shouted.

"Very good," Mr. Flick said. He turned again to the band. "But we want to be invited back, so let's make sure we don't take the Gillespie past a certain decibel."

He waved his baton and counted them in. Tiff later told

me that this song was called "A Night in Tunisia." It was an exciting song, even on the first listen. It started with the rhythm section, then the horns kicked in to play this tension-building, ominous, riff. Tiff raised her trumpet, placed what looked like the bottom of a toilet plunger over the end, and played the melody.

In every song, people took solos in the middle, improvised lines they performed in the moment. When Tiff took her solo for "A Night in Tunisia" she went absolutely balls-out avant-garde bonkers. She dropped the toilet plunger and played as loud as she could. Notes scattered all over the place, screams emitted from her trumpet. Her face went pink. I saw shoppers cover their ears and shoot dirty looks in the general direction of the band. At the end, she blew out a note that was the most ear-splitting noise I'd ever heard, and when the band jumped back into the main riff, she briefly posed with her arms out-stretched in cocky victory, trumpet still in her left hand, before picking up the plunger again with her right. She grinned and finished the song.

Alice and I immediately jumped to our feet and cheered. The grown-ups politely clapped.

"McKee!" Mr. Flick said. "What the hell did I just say?" But he was grinning wolfishly.

After the concert, Alice and I hung out with Tiff and her family.

"Great job, honey," her mom said. She gave Tiff a big hug in front of us. Tiff pretended to be embarrassed, or was embarrassed, I couldn't tell which.

Tiff's dad was still in superintendent mode and spoke to everyone in a booming formal way.

"Alice, good to see you, as always." He turned to me. "You must be Ellora. We've heard a lot of nice things about you lately."

"Dad," Tiff said.

I blushed and wondered what the nice things were. Dr. McKee shook my hand and patted Tiff on the back. "Tiff's mother and I are very proud of our little Louis Armstrong."

"I've told you before, I'm not into Louis Armstrong," she said. "He's just the only jazz musician you know."

"Very proud of you," her dad said again. "But what was going on with that solo? You've got to take it easy on your old man's ears."

Tiff's mom and dad wandered off to talk to other parents and left us with her brother.

"Your brother looks a lot like you," I said.

"No, he doesn't," she said.

"Yeah, I'm not a band nerd." This was the first thing he had said, and he didn't look up from his Gameboy. Tiff reached over and placed her hand over the screen.

"Stop," he whined. He jumped up with his Gameboy and ran away.

"Yeah, no resemblance there at all," Alice said, sarcastically.

"But we're not biologically related. You get that, right?"

"Wait, you're not?" I asked.

"He's Korean too. Isn't he?" Alice asked.

"Yeah, but he was adopted five years after me. And not from the same family or anything. Totally different time and different part of Korea."

"Oh, okay."

Tiff leaned back in her chair and smirked. "What, you think my parents got us as a package deal, or something? Two for one?"

I had also assumed they were biological siblings adopted by her parents, even if I hadn't considered the logistics. Tiff glanced over at Mal, who was sitting with her own parents in the cafe. As discussed, they pretended like they didn't know each other the whole time. I looked over at her dad and tried to imagine him being a raging homophobe. He looked like everyone else's boring dads. Same with her mom.

Alice noticed Tiff's worried look at Mal. She nudged her arm. "Hey, your solo was really sick. I'm glad I got to see it."

"Thanks."

Current Music: New Radicals – "You Get What You Give"

🔒 Tuesday, October 31st, 2000 | 8:03 p.m.

Rogue costume was a total disaster. Nobody knew who I was, much like last year's costume, Death from Neil Gaiman's *The Sandman* comics. At least that could have been explained by the fact that almost no one at school had read *The Sandman*. Most people had seen the *X-Men* movie.

It didn't matter. All day everyone looked at my outfit and asked, "What is your costume supposed to be?"

Even when I gave people a hint, even when I straight-up said I was one of the X-Men, they couldn't guess correctly.

"Storm?" Alice asked, in AP English.

"No, I'm Rogue," I said, holding up my hands. "Remember her gloves?"

Then, to make matters worse, Mr. Krasner pointed to the white streak I'd dyed into my hair and said, "Ms. Gao, you've aged five decades since yesterday."

Horrified, I went to the bathroom in between classes and washed the hair dye out and shoved the gloves in my backpack.

Current Music: Björk – "Isobel"

Thursday, November 2nd, 2000 | 6:20 p.m.

We're reading *Hamlet* in Mr. Krasner's class. To be honest, I don't think Shakespeare is something I could read on my own. I tried once, but my eyes glazed over and I knew I wasn't absorbing the lines. I needed us to go line by line through the language in class, in order to unlock it, and then it suddenly became as accessible as any modern book. That's kind of magical.

Today Mr. Krasner showed us several clips from film adaptations of *Hamlet*. One was old and starred Laurence Olivier, and the other had Mel Gibson, and the last one came out earlier this year and starred Ethan Hawke as Hamlet. Ethan Hawke did the famous "To Be or Not to Be" speech in a Blockbuster. I liked the idea that you could do one of the most famous scenes ever in somewhere as ordinary as Blockbuster, a Blockbuster that looked like the one my friends and I go to.

We all must have been a bit inspired, because next period in Mr. Tate's chemistry class, a bunch of us took out our copies of *Hamlet* and read some scenes. We discarded our safety goggles and completely neglected our lab assignments.

Christopher made a most beautiful Prince of Denmark. I bet you all thought I played Ophelia, but I was Gertrude in most of our scenes. She has more lines anyway. Some other kids played Polonius, Laertes, Claudius. We skipped around a bunch, doing only the scenes we liked the most, sometimes swapping roles. Tiff and I did the gravedigger scene together, that was fun.

Mr. Tate asked us what we were doing and we told him to go away, we were putting on a production of *Hamlet*. He's a real pushover, often intimidated by our general smartass behavior, so he did as told and went to awkwardly hover over some other kids still working.

"Frailty, thy name is Mr. Tate!" Christopher hissed after

him, which made us laugh.

I don't think Christopher has any acting aspirations. I've never seen him try out for any of the school plays, he only loves Shakespeare and that passion transcended his Hamlet to greatness. He was so good we asked him to read the "To Be or Not to Be" soliloquy for us. No one was surprised when he announced he had it memorized.

And Sir Laurence Olivier, Mel Gibson, and Ethan Hawke can all suck it, because none of them held a candle to Christopher, as he slouched over the lab sink, safety glasses still atop his forehead, and tried to decide whether living or dying was the right answer.

Current Music: Garbage – "I'm Only Happy When it Rains"

🔒 Friday November 3rd, 2000 | 9:32 p.m.

"Have you come out to your parents yet?" Alice asked Tiff at lunch. She turned to Mal. "I know you can't."

"Sort of," Tiff said. "I mean Mal's been over a lot. One time, I was like, 'Yo, let's do this.' We blatantly held hands in front of my family at dinner. I saw my mom and dad give each other a look, but they didn't say anything. They still let us hang out in my room with the door closed, which they never would have done if a guy had been over. They're so clueless."

She put her arm around Mal. They exchanged dirty glances and Mal giggled.

"My mom tried to talk to me about it later. It was sooooo awkward," Tiff said. "She came into my room and said she wanted to talk about my 'special friendship' with Mal."

"Oh god," Alice said.

"She said she was worried I was making decisions that would make my life harder and make people treat me badly."

"That's not okay," Alice said. "That's pretty much what my mom said too. In eighth grade, I told her I was bisexual and she said I was too young to make that kind of decision. What did you say?"

"I said 'Mom, it's embarrassing that you're talking to me like this, get out of my room.' She burst into tears and said, 'I just love you and I want you to be okay.' Then she ran away."

"For me, the most annoying thing is now that I'm dating Mike, she thinks it was just a phase," Alice said. "I told her it's not a phase, I'm still bisexual." She waved cookies from her lunch around the table. "Anybody want these?"

"No," I said.

Tiff and Dev both dived for them though.

"What about you?" Alice asked Christopher. "Have you come out to your family?"

Christopher sighed. "In kindergarten, I frequently reenacted my favorite episodes of *She-Ra: Princess of Power* for my mother. She knows. I do not engage with this contemporary practice of 'coming out.'"

"Well, excuuuuse me," Alice said.

He turned to Tiff. "Do you think Plato sat his parents down and came out to them?"

"Uh, sure?"

"I guarantee you he did not. He simply lived. What about Proust? You think he came out to sa chère mère after she gave him a kiss goodnight? Did Genet? Wilde? Woolf? Mr. Krasner's favorite, Allen Ginsberg? Gertrude Stein?"

"We get it," Dev said.

Christopher waved him away. "Whitman, Baldwin, Shakespeare."

"I know you know *Hamlet* better than anyone, but I don't

think Shakespeare was gay," I said.

"Up for debate," Christopher said. "Bisexual at least. His most well-known, but not best sonnet: 'Shall I compare thee to a summer's day?' Addressed to a man.

"Dickinson, hopefully. Capote. Herman Melville. Well that one's a little unclear. But he did dedicate a five-hundred-page whaling tome to 'Nathaniel Hawthorne in token of my admiration for his genius.' 'Genius.'"

"Moby Dick," Tiff yelled stupidly.

"Get off your knees, Melville," Christopher shouted.

"I don't get this. We don't live in the 1800s or ancient Greece," Alice said. "And while it's cool that all these famous writers were gay, I don't see what this has to do with the reality of our parents not accepting who we are."

"Fine," Christopher said. "If you must engage in this cringe-worthy practice, I suggest the way to talk to your parents is to point out their hypocrisy. Or if you want to put a more positive spin on it, appeal to their empathy."

"What are you talking about?" I asked.

"I'm willing to wager half our family members have had homosexual escapades or, at the very least, yearnings."

We all laughed.

"Hello, have you seen where we live?" Alice asked.

"Oh Alice, think really hard. Are there any former sorority sisters your mother talks about a little too much? Maybe she gets a real wistful look in her eye?"

"You are being ridiculous," Alice said, laughing.

But Mal looked genuinely annoyed. "Chris, be a real person. That's not how things work. Do you know how disastrous it would be if I asked my dad, 'Hey Dad, ever done any gay stuff?' He'd kick my ass. It's not going to make him accept the idea of me and Tiff."

"Too bad," Christopher said. "Because frankly, based

on the militant homophobia you've described, your father is the most likely closet case of all our parents and guardians combined."

Oh, that set everyone at the table right off.

"Did you have any gay experiences growing up?" I asked Brian.

We were in our usual locations. Me on the computer, him watching TV. Staring at screens until now. He looked shocked and hurt, which surprised me. I honestly wasn't expecting him to answer in the affirmative, I'd only wanted to say something mildly provocative. While I wondered if he was homophobic, he shook his head and laughed.

"What?" I asked.

"You have no ability to make small talk."

"I don't like small talk."

"Yeah, me neither, but you realize you have to do that? To get by?"

"Yeah. Never mind."

He muted the television and sat up. "It's like you're still eight-years-old sometimes. You won't say anything for hours and then suddenly, you bring up a random topic out of nowhere and want to talk incessantly about it. Except now, instead of demanding to know who my favorite *Star Wars* character is, you grill me on my political opinions or think it's appropriate to ask if I've had any past homosexual experiences."

"I said never mind."

"Well, since you're so curious, the answer is yes. Don't get too excited, nothing extreme. You know those skater kids I've talked about before?"

I nodded. Occasionally, he would mention his old high school skate crew, mostly as a precursor to not-so-subtly suggesting that perhaps I spend more time outdoors and befriend a crew of my own.

"Bill, the leader, he was this mean and tough guy. Drunkenly making out with him at parties was practically a rite of passage, to be part of the crew. It wasn't romantic, it was more of a dare. Bill, however, was into more serious stuff. There was this gay cruising spot. You know what that is?"

"Yeah." I felt 85% sure.

"He was going there, having sex with men more than twice his age. One night, I persuaded him to let me go with him—I know, a dumb idea, but I was doing lots of dumb and dangerous stuff when I was your age. Anyway, Bill tells me what to say to these guys parked in their cars, so I do that, and I get in a car with this man. He had to be well over thirty. We start kissing and I'm terrified. Shaking uncontrollably. The guy stops and says, 'You're cute, but I'm not sure you want to be here.' He was right. I got out of the car and before I closed the door, he said, 'Go home. Take care of yourself. It'll be okay.'"

Brian was quiet for a moment. Then he blinked and said, "Other than that, it's been plain old heterosexuality for me. And that concludes tonight's after school special." He laid back down on the couch and unmuted the television.

Holy crap, Christopher was right. I wouldn't be sharing this anecdote at lunch tomorrow, though. It was way too dark. Brian seemed to have the same realization.

"Okay, that was maybe not an appropriate story to tell you, but I wasn't sure why you were asking that question. If you're trying to tell me something about yourself, you should know I'm fine with whoever you are."

"Oh my god, I'm not coming out to you," I said. "Some of my friends are gay."

"Friends, huh. Like I said, it's all fine."

He sounded so damn smug. I changed the subject. "Are you still friends with Bill?"

"No," he said. "I didn't go home much after high school and he didn't even graduate. But I did see him once, when I went back for my sister's wedding. He was an assistant manager at the restaurant where the rehearsal dinner was. We caught up. He lived with his boyfriend in a nice part of town. It's funny, growing up I was so intimidated by him and now he was just a person with a shitty job, like everyone else. But I was glad he seemed happy. Things had looked pretty harrowing for him for a while. That was about ten years ago though, I hope he's still doing all right. I hope they all are. The kids I knew back then." I watched a sad smile surface on his face. "They got me through."

Current Music: none

🔒 Sunday, November 5th, 2000 | 10:20 p.m.

There's a new manager at Earl's House, Angie. I can't decide whether I like her or not. On one hand, when Homeless Guy came in, she didn't kick him out like the old manager. She let him quietly sit in a booth as long as he didn't bother customers.

On the other hand, she already fired someone. This guy Rob, who was about my age and goes to a neighboring high school. We had a brief five-minute meeting before we opened and she said, "I know some of you have questions about why I let Rob go. The truth is, he wasn't cutting it. He was lazy on both shifts I managed, and when I spoke to him, he talked back. That doesn't work for me. I know we all come to this job from different places, but whether you're here fifty hours a week, or this is your after-school job, I expect the same level of work. Everybody's got to pull their weight."

I was glad I wasn't on counter that night, because I sure don't pull my weight on counter. I was runner, thank god. When I ran an order to a table near where Homeless Guy was camped out, I said hello to him. He didn't seem to remember me from our pizza party.

After we closed, and I unlocked my bike from the rack to go home, I heard a voice say, "Ellora, right?"

Angie stood by the side of the building, smoking. She looked beat.

"Yeah," I said.

"That a family name? It's unique."

"No. It's the name of a girl my mom went to school with. She really liked the name, so she gave me it."

What I remembered her actually saying was that she thought it was the prettiest name she had ever heard, so she named her daughter it. My grandparents, in an attempt to assimilate, had named her the plainest American name they could find, and I think she wished her own name was more unique. That seemed like too much to share with my manager though.

"I see," she said. "Good job tonight. You really hustled on those floors."

"Thanks."

I love biking at night, the quiet of it and the way the air smells. On my ride home, I thought my name over and over, until it dissolved into meaninglessness sound in my head. In elementary school, I used to write it in cursive all over my notebooks. Ellora Gao Ellora Gao Hello My Name Is Ellora Gao.

I noticed a bunch more people have added me to their Friends list recently, so if you're just tuning in, here's my formal introduction:

Hello, my name is Ellora Gao. And my mother, the woman who named me, and later abandoned me, her name is Jane Gao.

Current Music: Bjork – "Bachelorette"

Monday, November 6th, 2000 | 4:30 p.m.

Election Day is tomorrow. The news says it's going to be close, which makes me nervous. We're having an Election Party at Alice's house to watch the results. Alice, Tiff, and I invited Mrs. Ross to it. We didn't think she would say yes, we just wanted her to know we were having an Election Party and think that was cool.

We spend a lot of time talking and gossiping about our teachers. Who we hate, who we love, and wondering what they do outside of school. Does anyone else do that or are we creepy?

"You think Mr. Krasner might be gay?" I asked.

"Why? Because his face is so beautiful?" Alice asked, sarcastically.

"He's probably not gay," Tiff said. "I ran into him at Steadmans, with his wife. She's pregnant."

"Ugh, it's so weird running into teachers in the wild," Alice said. "I remember as a little kid thinking that my teachers lived at school."

"Yeah, well, it's a nightmare running into teachers when I'm with my parents. Dad's gotta talk to everybody. He stopped and talked to Mr. Krasner and his wife for ten minutes."

"What's his wife like?" I asked.

"Nice, I guess. She wasn't that hot though, which surprised me."

"Oh my god," Alice said. "Just because you both think Mr. Krasner is so hot doesn't mean he has to have a hot wife. Have you seen how many gorgeous women are with gross guys? In real life and on TV? Hello, *King of Queens*?"

"Why do you hate Mr. Krasner so much anyway?" I asked.

"I don't hate him," she said. "I just think he tries too hard. Sure, he's hot, but he knows it and he's not as gorgeous as everyone thinks he is."

"No, he is," Tiff said. "I'm into the ladies, I think that's been well established. But if I was stranded on a desert island for ten years, and I had to get with one man in the whole world, it'd be Mr. Krasner."

"You're such a liar," Alice said. "You'd pick that sadistic tyrant you worship. Now that's a teacher I actually have a problem with. He should be fired."

"Don't talk shit about Mr. Flick," Tiff said. "He's my person."

"Your what?"

"That thing you said. About there being a person who makes you realize there are other ways to be a grown-up that aren't like your parents."

"You've got to be kidding me," Alice said. "When he's not at school, Mr. Flick probably sits around in a depressing apartment eating microwave dinners, avoiding the son he thinks ruined his big musical career. He's a divorced loser."

"Are we actually talking about Mr. Flick right now? Or your dad?"

"Um," I said.

"And he doesn't sit at home every night," Tiff added. "He gigs around town. He lives a cool life."

Alice laughed. "I've seen one of his 'gigs.' Mike and I went to get coffee at North by Northwest. He was playing to a room of three people."

Tiff shook her head. "You're being really mean right now, Alice."

"Oh, I'm being mean? You're the one who basically accused

me of having daddy issues."

Tiff shrugged in a way that said, "Well, don't you?"

"Mrs. Ross," I said, after an awkward pause. "We all like Mrs. Ross. Mrs. Ross was probably really hot, when she was young."

Alice rolled her eyes. "She's hot now. But yes, Mrs. Ross is awesome."

"Hell yeah, Mrs. Ross," Tiff said.

We agreed that she was one of our favorite teachers ever. The great thing is, I think we're her favorites too. She laughs more at our group's presentations than other people's. I know teachers aren't supposed to play favorites, but you know they do, and you know that everyone wants to be the cool teachers' favorites. Mr. Krasner has no favorites, like a true movie star, he is loved by everyone and he treats all students like equal members of his adoring public. Maybe Alice is right about him. Mrs. Ross, however, has special affection for us.

"What are you going to be doing on election night?" Alice asked her, after she politely declined the invitation to our party.

"Oh, I'll be biting my nails and watching the polls at home," she said. "With my husband and a bottle of wine. It will either be a celebratory glass, or we'll drown our sorrows if that idiot wins."

She winked at us, because teachers aren't supposed to tell the students which candidates they support.

Current Music: The Verve – "Bitter Sweet Symphony"

Wednesday, November 8th, 2000 | 1:11 p.m.

Presidential elections only happen every four years, so the

whole gang showed up to Alice's basement on Tuesday evening for the election party: Me, Alice, Tiff, Mal, Dev, Christopher. Mike was not there. Maybe the whole thing was too nerdy for him. Good.

Christopher had purchased a Dubya mask leftover from Halloween and Alice brought down a broom handle to place it on a makeshift spike.

"You liberals are so disrespectful," Dev said. "Do you see me making an Al Gore prop and hanging him in effigy?"

Alice's mom came downstairs holding a baking pan.

"Now I know we disagree on the candidates," she said. "But I wanted to make a little something for your election party."

She placed the pan on the table. It was filled with red, white, and blue cupcakes.

"Mom," shrieked Alice. Then in a lower, meaner voice, she said, "I told you to stop making me desserts."

Alice's mom stiffened and I looked around to see if anyone else had noticed this awkward moment. Tiff and Mal were making eyes at each other. Christopher was already glued to the news. Only Dev stood up and walked over to Alice's mom and placed his hand on her shoulder.

"Mrs. Sharpe," he said. "I want you to know that while I'm friends with these fools, I do not share their political delusions. I want to grow up to be like you and your husband, hard-working Americans who embrace family values. There's too many lazy people in this country looking for handouts."

The rest of us let out a loud, collective groan.

"Thank you for the cupcakes, Mrs. Sharpe." He sat back down and winked at her. "Bush/Cheney 2000."

"You're welcome, Dev." She smiled. "But it's Mrs. Lewis."

She walked back upstairs to watch the rest of the election with Alice's stepdad.

"Were you flirting with my mom?" Alice asked, but she was

amused. It wasn't the actual anger she'd shown when her mom brought down the cupcakes.

We settled in to watch the results, as polls started to close on our side of the country. We switched between the main stations, trying to find which one had the latest breaking news, who was ready to call which state. They seemed to be racing each other to do so.

We had prepared for it to be a late night but around 8 p.m., all the channels were saying Florida was going to Gore, and Florida was such a key swing state that it was enough electoral college votes to predict that Gore was going to win.

"It's over, Dev," Christopher said. "Every channel's saying it."

Dev lay face down on the floor. I laughed and patted him on the shoulder. "There, there."

We kept the channel on Peter Jennings and ABC News, where the coverage shifted to governor races in other states, and the state senate race in our own. It looked like Hillary Clinton was going to be the first female senator of New York. People hate Hillary Clinton in Republican Parkview, they call her a carpetbagger and power hungry.

Peter Jennings announced Clinton's victory and shared that the station had held a poll for viewers asking, "Do you think Hillary Clinton will run for higher office?" 84% of people had responded yes. I've been so caught up on following this year's presidential election, I haven't given it much thought myself. A female president seems cool, but kind of unlikely.

Our attention waned. We started talking about school, movies, gossip, until suddenly the news shifted. Jennings announced that they were retracting Gore's Florida win, that it was in fact still too close to call. Dev slowly sat up and everyone paid attention again.

At around 11 p.m., several newscasters announced that

Florida was now actually going to Bush and if so, considering how many of the Midwestern states also flashed red, things didn't look good. Since it was still a school night, Dev, Tiff, and Mal had to go home. Christopher and I watched a little longer before we left Alice's too.

Once I got home, I turned the TV back on. It's on now. I want to stay up watching, but if I don't go to sleep soon, I'll feel like crap at school tomorrow. Plus, I want to be alert in Mrs. Ross' class when we discuss everything.

But things are definitely looking like Bush is going to win. Fuck fuckity fuck!

Current Music: Radiohead – "Just"

Wednesday, November 8th, 2000 | 5:51 p.m.

Have you ever seen the photo of Harry Truman holding the newspaper with the incorrect "Dewey Defeats Truman" headline? I guess no one wants to make that same mistake. The newspaper was tentative about Bush's potential win this morning.

Mrs. Ross had stayed up late watching the news too.

"This is so exciting!" She slapped the podium she was so riled up. "It's Wednesday morning, the day after the election, and we still don't know who the president is. Gore was about to give a concession speech late last night, then he called Bush and changed his mind. It's all coming down to Florida."

"What do you think is going to happen?" Tiff asked.

"Too early to say," Mrs. Ross said. "Hopefully we'll see some resolution by the end of this week."

When I got home from school, I put on the television and

looked up things on the Internet. People were calling for voter recounts, talking about voter fraud. Others were saying the punch cards for voting in Florida were too confusing. There was such a waterfall of information, I couldn't parse it out.

Current Music: Rage Against the Machine – "Testify"

Friday, November 10th, 2000 | 6:51 p.m.

We still don't have a president! I don't think anything like this has ever happened in history. It's all anyone is talking about. In Mrs. Ross' class, on the news, at Earl's House, everywhere. Finally, something exciting is happening in the world.

Brian came home from work, carrying his camera and the mail. "I shot some college students today. They reminded me of you."

"What?" For an absolute split second, I thought he meant with a gun, then I realized: duh.

"We're running a story on how first-time voters are reacting to the recount," he said. "These kids are like you, caught up in the national drama."

"What's going on is really exciting. If anything, it should show you how a single vote truly does matter." I gave him a pointed look.

"No, if anything it shows what crap the electoral college is," he said. We had been having this debate in Mrs. Ross' class too. "This one kid, he said he was planning to move to Canada the moment Bush won. I told him I was very impressed. He might be putting his life on hold for weeks."

I rolled my eyes. He sorted through the mail and held up a hot pink envelope covered in girly doodles.

"Who is 'Slayer' Farmington?" he asked.

"Friend of mine." I ran to grab the envelope from him. He held it away from me.

"Do you recall the conversation we had? About not giving out personal information?"

"Uh-huh."

He frowned at the envelope. "Well, don't you think that includes giving out our home address to complete strangers? And your name, even if you use a made-up last name?"

For safety, I have used my middle name (Xuan) for Internet orders and mailings since freshman year. It doesn't really make sense to do now, since Slayer and other LiveJournal friends know my actual last name, but the extra precaution can't hurt. And I keep any entries that mention my last name friends-only.

"That's my middle name," I said. "I didn't make it up. Did you really not know that?"

"Of course I knew that."

"Yeah, right."

"Hey, I bet you don't know my middle name either."

"It's David." I reached to grab the envelope out of his hand and bring it back to the table. "And they're not strangers either."

"You've never met them. They're strangers."

I ignored him and carefully opened the envelope to avoid tearing Slayer's drawings that spiraled out to its edges. It's true, I've never met any of you, but the irony was that you know me better than Brian does, and I see him almost every day. I reminded myself I must get the mail before he does. No matter what's going on in the world, I can't forget.

"Fine," he said. "You know what? Do whatever you want. That's what you're going to do anyway." He made a noise of frustration, then left for his room.

Slayer had written me a long letter, made a mix CD, and

gifted me a tiny Rogue action figure. In the letter, she mentioned the action figure and said, "It's you. I would have known what your Halloween costume was. Fuck everyone else."

Current Music: Fiona Apple – "The Way Things Are"

🔒 Monday, November 13th, 2000 | 9:53 p.m.

There once was a time when I entertained the idea of following in the footsteps of my idol Fiona Apple and becoming a singer-songwriter. I fantasized about having fans who obsessively analyzed my lyrics and drove around the country following my tour. This dream was curbed when I realized I had no idea how to play the piano, nor any instrument, and worst of all: I can't hold a tune to save my life.

Since middle school, I've chosen choir as an elective, mostly because I didn't know what else to do. I'm starting to consider whether I should pick something else next year. It's possible my mere presence is bringing down the quality of the entire group.

I don't know an eloquent way to put this, so I'll just say it: I can't sing any of the songs, so I fake it. Yes, that's right, I lip synch every song we perform. I could try to actually sing the songs, but because my voice sounds okay at most within a range of two notes, I don't want to subject anyone to it. So, I try to overcompensate for, um, not singing, by treating choir as an acting exercise. I imagine I'm playing a character for every song we do.

"Sing with your eyes," our drippy choir director, Mrs. Carlson-Clark, always says. I sing so hard with my eyes that I've brought myself to tears during a few songs.

Our choir concert was last Thursday and we always review

the tape the following week. Mrs. Carlson-Clark declared that before we watched, she wanted to announce the student of the month. Alice shifted in her seat next to me. I think she would like to be recognized in choir. She's a good singer and recently tried out for a solo. She was mad when she didn't get it.

"When we sing, we need to sing with our whole instrument," Mrs. Carlson-Clark said. "That means more than the voice. Your whole body needs to believe these songs. Even if you sing with technical perfection, you won't move your audience if you stand up there stiff. When I watched the tape, many of you resembled a deer in headlights. You're not feeling the music." She wore this garish cape that looked like something out of *Joseph and the Amazing Technicolor Dreamcoat*. She spun around in it every time she said the words "feeling the music." "This month's student of the month is always feeling the music. I've never met another student who emotes as beautifully as she does. November's choir student of the month is Ellora Gao."

Everybody politely applauded and I nearly died. Then, to make matters worse, Mrs. Carlson-Clark played the choir tape and when the video panned to me, with my lips over enunciating every word, and my head swaying side to side as my eyes teared up imagining god knows what, she pointed to the screen and sighed, "This is what I mean, when I say sing with your eyes. Next concert I want to see fifty Elloras up there. Feeling the music."

Next to me, Alice stifled laughter, she knew all about my faking. Lily VanHoven, who sat on my other side, muttered, "what the fuck."

Mrs. Carlson Clark has an elementary school-style bulletin board that showcases the choir students of the month. She took my picture with her polaroid camera, then wrote my name at the bottom and placed it in November's gold star.

Current Music: Beastie Boys – "Body Movin'"

🔒 Tuesday, November 14th, 2000 | 3:44 p.m.

The phone rang last night and I was in a goofy mood after my absurd choir win. I answered it with a fake British accent and said, "Ellora Gao's office."

I expected it to be a solicitor. Instead, an older woman's voice asked if Brian lived here.

"Yeah, sorry, he does," I said, dropping the voice.

"Can I speak to him? It's important. I've been trying for two hours."

"Oh, weird." This was entirely my fault, I'd been online tying up the phone line. "May I ask who's calling?"

"His mother."

Brian is estranged from his family, for reasons he doesn't talk about. Actually, he doesn't talk about them much at all. Over the years, I've learned a little. He has an older sister and his parents are divorced.

He was in his room, listening to music, for once not lying on the couch drinking and watching TV. I yelled his name twice before he answered.

"It's your mom," I said, holding the phone out. The look on his face confirmed that they did not talk often. He took the phone and closed his door.

I wish I could say I'm a classy dame who minds her own business, but the truth is I'm nosy as hell. I stood outside his door trying to eavesdrop. I couldn't hear anything though. His voice was too low and it sounded like his mom was doing most of the talking. I gave up and waited to see if he would come outside after the call, at least to return the phone. He never did.

Current Music: Ben Folds Five – "Selfless, Cold, & Composed"

Thursday, November 16th, 2000 | 10:35 p.m.

They're still recounting things in Florida. I've been following for over a week now, I'm almost bored at this point.

At Earl's House tonight, I was on counter. We were short staffed, so Angie, even though she's a manager, rang up customers right next to me. It made me nervous to have her standing that close. She would have a front row seat to my screw-ups.

"I said I want the crispy chicken sandwich combo except substitute curly fries for regular fries, a cheeseburger kids' meal with the fruit cup side and cherry slushie, and a white hot dog with no pickles, extra mustard. How many times do I have to repeat that?"

I looked over at Angie, who shot me a disapproving look.

A lot of people brought in coupons too, which adds an extra discount to punch in. I knew I was being slow. And to top it all off, at the end of the night, there was another guy who, after ordering, asked me, "What are you?" The old song and dance.

"What?" I asked.

"What are you?"

"What am I?"

"Yeah, are you Korean or Chinese or what?"

When he finally went away, I looked over at Angie, hoping she hadn't heard. She had. I think she's part-Hispanic or something though, so she only shook her head, whistled, and said, "You should hear what they say to me."

Current Music: Sleater-Kinney – "#1 Must Have"

Last night we went to another all-ages show at The Caterpillar and then Alice and Mike went off on their own with his band. I hung out with Tiff and Mal at Denny's. Mal drove me home.

"Um, there's some guy sleeping in front of your building," she said.

I looked out the window, expecting to see Homeless Guy. I was alarmed to discover that it was Brian. He was sleeping on the front steps, resting against the railing for support.

"Oh, weird," I said. "Well, thanks for the ride, Mal."

"Wait," Tiff said. She turned around in her seat. "It's not safe. I'll walk you to the door."

She was doing her macho protective thing. Last week, when we were leaving school, it got gridlocked and crowded near the exit. Tiff sensed my anxiety, put her hand on my back and gently guided us out. Since then, I've thought about that touch a lot, how nice it felt. But I didn't want her involvement this time.

I opened the car door. "It'll be fine."

"We should probably call somebody to help him though, right?"

"I'll tell the legal guardian to do it," I said and jumped out.

I ran up the steps, hesitating when I passed Brian. My friend's pale faces were still watching from the car, waiting to make sure I got in safely. I knew what I had to do. I went inside and stepped away from the glass doors, to a place where I wouldn't be visible to Tiff and Mal, and counted to sixty. Then I went back out, relieved to see they had driven away.

I knelt down next to Brian and tapped him on the shoulder. He stirred without opening his eyes, so I shook him. He jumped awake and swatted my hands away.

"Jesus, it's just me," I said. "What happened?"

He looked at me like he didn't understand why I was there, then mumbled something about the door being stuck. His keys were still in his hand. The front door can be stiff, sometimes it takes multiple tries to unlock it. He must have gotten drunkenly frustrated, sat down, and fallen asleep. I wondered where he had been and whether he had driven home in his condition. I didn't want to think about it.

I hesitated. "What did your mom call about the other day?"

He ignored this and said, "I can't open the door" again, his words slurring.

I held out my hand to help him stand up. He was able to stumble walk on his own back to our apartment. He mumbled "sorry" before passing out in his room.

Current Music: none

🔒 Saturday, November 18th, 2000 | 5:05 p.m.

After several password attempts, I logged into my old email address, an embarrassing @juno.com one I had in middle school. I was searching for the archives of a mailing list I used to belong to, back when my only way to get online was to go to the library. For those of you who never did mailing lists, this is how it worked: you'd email and then wait for your message to be compiled with the others and sent to everyone in one long digest. It was sent once a week, maybe twice, if there were a lot of emails. Compared to LiveJournal, with its instant posts and comments, this is a prehistoric way to communicate, I know.

Brian can make all the sarcastic comments he wants about Mom breaking his heart, but I remember how genuinely crushed he was after she left. Not at first, he kept up good appearances for a while. It was almost a year after, once the permanence of our new reality sunk in. He'd drink and lie on our couch for hours, staring at nothing. Mom never drank, but his behavior was so similar to hers before she left that I worried he would eventually leave too. I hadn't done enough for Mom, I'd been a little kid and not known what was going on. Not anymore. Like a snake shedding its skin, I could feel my child brain molting into an adolescent brain with each passing day. No, this time, I would take action. At the beginning of 7th grade, I did some research from the public library computers and happened upon an Al-Anon mailing list.

Unlike my Fiona Apple mailing list, the Al-Anon one was entirely adults. It was ghastly stuff to read, men whose wives' addictions were running their families bankrupt or women who came home to find their drunk husbands had pissed themselves. I held off emailing the listserv because I worried I might be bothering them with my relatively small problems. I wasn't even sure if Brian was an alcoholic. When I saw alcoholic parents in movies, or read about them in books, they did monstrous things. They yelled at their children, sometimes they beat or molested them. They couldn't hold down jobs and there were bottles and trash around their house. Brian had a job and our apartment was relatively clean. And I wasn't being beaten or molested or even yelled at, I was being ignored. There weren't any movies where someone's parent said things like, "now's not a good time" if you tried to talk to them and then quietly drank themselves to sleep on the couch.

Ultimately, I decided to write. It began: "Hello, my name is Ellora and sorry I'm twelve. I think my guardian is a problem drinker. I'm looking for ideas how to help him." Then I explained my situation in a short following paragraph. When I saw my email published on the mailing list's next digest, I nearly threw up. I was certain the adult moderators would remove me for being under eighteen, or not take me seriously. Adults never took me seriously enough.

I was surprised when the reaction was the total opposite. Almost everyone in the next digest responded to me, or referred to me, writing things like, "I know many of you were deeply affected by young Ellora's email and how it stirred up your own memories as children of alcoholics." Some people emailed me directly. One woman wrote, "You are still a child and it is important that you have caretakers who make you feel cared for and safe." I didn't usually like when people called me a child, but in that email, it felt nice, comforting to read. The men were less sympathetic, they wanted to tell me what to do. "Brian's Higher Power will take care of him. You need to stop worrying about how you can help and get yourself to an Alateen meeting."

There was one woman I started a real pen pal-ship with. Her name was Hallie and she was twenty-six. She had grown up with two alcoholic parents and she currently had an alcoholic husband that she was trying to make it work with. Some people have all the bad luck. On the Al-Anon mailing list, she mentioned her husband hitting her, so in one of my emails, I suggested she go to a battered women's shelter. It was completely horrifying to reread how blunt and insensitive I had been, but she didn't get mad, she just wrote back "It's not that simple, sweetie. :-)" in her reply to that line.

But most of our emails didn't talk about drinking. She wrote about North Carolina where she lived, and the walks she enjoyed going on with her dog. I went on and on about books and movies I liked, which was also cringeworthy to reread, but I cut myself some slack and remembered that I had been lonely and twelve.

I don't remember why we stopped emailing. I think it was a combination of getting involved with other things online and hanging out with the Jen/Jenny/Kendall clique more. Also, for no reason other than the passage of time, Brian got better. He stopped staring into space for hours. He made jokes again. He didn't stop drinking, obviously, but until last night, it never returned to the level it did during my middle school years.

I started a new email to Hallie. It had been almost four years since my last reply. I wrote, "I don't know if you remember me, I used to write you from the Al-Anon list. How are you doing?" My email immediately bounced back. My first morbid thought was that something happened to her (her husband), but she probably just changed her email address, like I had. Still, I felt a small grief over the fact that I'd probably never be able to connect with her or find her again. My first Internet friend.

Current Music: none

Tuesday, November 21st, 2000 | 6:39 p.m.

Today was Decades Day. Most plebs chose the 1960s and wore tie dyed t-shirts and bandanas. A few people wore *That '70s Show*-style paisley and bellbottoms, while others sported neon accessories to represent the 80s.

Our lunch table did something particularly smartass and inspired. We hit up Goodwill over the weekend and bought oversize flannels and dowdy plaid dresses and overalls. We cut holes in them, or made existing holes in the clothes larger, and covered them with dirt. Christopher went a step further by wearing a straw hat and sticking a piece of wheat in his mouth.

"I love it!" Mr. Krasner shouted. "You all look like you stepped right out of *The Grapes of Wrath*."

But most people didn't get it. In choir, Lily VanHoven looked skeptically at my oversize flannel and asked, "What decade are you supposed to be? 90s grunge?"

"No," Alice said. "RIP Kurt Cobain, but we're the 1930s."

"We're The Great Depression," I added.

As we walked from choir to lunch, Alice asked, "What are your plans for Thanksgiving?"

"I don't know."

She looked so authentic, in her plaid dress, and her usual ponytail replaced with two black braids. Like if someone took a photo of her and converted it to sepia, it could have been an artifact from the Dust Bowl. I didn't have that malleability. I thought about acting roles again, and how, in addition to movies about families, I probably wouldn't be able to land roles in period pieces either. Only contemporary movies (where no one is related) for me, I guess.

"You should come over to my house for Thanksgiving dinner," she said.

"With your mom and Greg?" I asked. "I don't know."

"It's not just us. Mom invites half of Parkview to Thanksgiving. My aunts are there. My grandparents. Greg's relatives. Mom's friends. Some loser neighbor down the street she inevitably feels bad for."

"Is Mike going? Tiff?"

"Mike's got to be with his own family. I didn't ask her, but Tiff probably does too. I thought you wouldn't have many plans." She quickly added, "Sorry, that came out wrong."

I stared at her. I wondered if Tiff had told her about the guy passed out in front of my apartment and how weirdly nonchalant I'd acted about it. Alice might have put two and two together. She was smart like that.

Truthfully, the holidays have always been melancholy little affairs, even before Mom left. I've never had a Thanksgiving dinner with more than two other people. Me and my mom and Brian, or me and my mom and Grandma, before Grandma died. I've always longed to go to a Thanksgiving dinner like I'd seen in movies, where dozens of people laughed, and dialogue overlapped over a long, extended table. A dinner where, despite the fights and inevitable chaos, everything was resolved and wrapped up nicely after two hours.

Current Music: The Wallflowers – "One Headlight"

Thursday, November 23rd, 2000 | 11:35 p.m.

There were probably twenty people at Alice's family Thanksgiving dinner. I didn't have to be concerned about not being a member of her family, half the people there were not family. I introduced myself to everyone and forgot their names immediately. This was a bad habit of mine. Whenever someone introduces themselves, I end up focusing too hard on remembering to smile, make eye contact, shake with a strong handshake, and generally act like a normal person, that I don't retain any information they give.

Mrs. Lewis had done most of the cooking except Greg cooked the turkey. Alice passed many of the dishes without taking from them.

"No turkey?" asked a man who was either Greg's brother, or Alice's mom's brother.

"No, thanks," she said.

"No mac and cheese, either?" asked a woman who was that guy's wife.

Alice bristled. "I'm vegan."

"There's no meat in this mac and cheese," the woman said,

offended.

"Vegan, not vegetarian. That means no animal products, including dairy."

"What exactly can you eat then?" Alice's grandfather hollered.

"Nothing," her mom said. "You think this is bad? Try being the one who has to cook dinner here every night."

I felt angry that they were talking about her like this, when she clearly had a problem. Alice piled a bunch of green beans and stuffing on her plate but didn't eat it. With her fork, she angrily mashed an intricate cross-grid of lines into the stuffing and pushed vegetables around it. She looked gaunt, thinner than she did at the beginning of the year.

"Gore should concede," said the same uncle or step-uncle who had offered Alice turkey. "We don't need this to go to the Supreme Court. We need a president."

Everyone had to yell what they were saying on our side of the table, to be heard over the other end, that was debating whether *The Sopranos* portrayed negative stereotypes of Italian Americans.

"You know what we called Al Bore back in my day?" Greg shouted. "A sore loser."

"He didn't lose. He won the popular vote by half a million votes," Alice said.

"Well, he lost Florida," Greg said. "It's time he admits it."

I wanted to jump in here, but since I was a guest, I thought it would be impolite to argue.

Alice was on it though. "The punch ballots were flawed and a lot of people's votes weren't properly counted."

"Hanging chads," the uncle/step-uncle said. "Most ridiculous bullshit I've ever heard. Excuse my language."

"Can we please not talk about politics at my dinner table?" Mrs. Lewis asked.

"Yeah, why don't we talk about the family you love so much," Alice muttered under her breath. I didn't learn until later in the night what that was about.

"You know my rules. No politics or religion at the dinner table."

Alice pressed on, ignoring her. "A disproportionate number of African-American votes were not counted."

"Yeah, the blacks are always complaining about something," her grandfather said.

"That's racist. You're racist."

"Alice," shouted Mrs. Lewis.

A woman, who I think was a neighbor, piped in and said, "I find Gore so untrustworthy. So stiff. It feels like he's hiding something. He's too intellectual to be president."

I couldn't keep my mouth shut for that comment. "Wait," I said. "Are you saying you don't want a president who's smart?"

"Sorry you had to sit through that," Alice said.

Dinner was over and everyone was watching a football game. We were hiding out in her room, lying on her bed.

"It wasn't so bad," I said. "Even if your relatives are Republicans. Sorry I didn't say more in your defense, I didn't want to be a rude guest."

"It's fine. I'm just glad I had you in my corner."

"Plus, I kind of liked the chaos. It felt like a movie."

We looked up at the Christmas lights strung across her ceiling. She put a CD on, a Tori Amos one.

"My mom said something kinda fucked up," she said.

"What'd she say?"

"Last night, she was prepping some stuff for today and asked me to help. I didn't want to, but I knew it would make her happy. It was okay for a bit when we were chopping vegetables and not talking. But she was drinking wine the whole time and got a little drunk. She started asking me about Mike. I could tell she was trying to have this gossipy mother-daughter chat where we talked about boys and pretended we were close. Ugh. Then out of nowhere she says, 'When you get married, marry a man who loves you more than you love him.'

"I asked her what that was supposed to mean. She said that in every couple there's someone who loves more and there's someone who loves less, and the person who loves less has all the power. She said that Greg loves her more, but my dad loved her less. She said she wanted me to feel secure in life and do the same thing, except from the start. Marry a guy that's crazy about me, even if I thought he was only okay."

"Wow, that's depressing."

"I know right? I said, 'Mom, that is fucked up. Also, if I get married, there's a good chance it might not be to a man anyway.' She ignored that part and scolded me for swearing. It was so depressing and you know what else I got to thinking? Maybe she loves everyone a little less than we love her. She cooks this big Thanksgiving dinner like she's this amazing mom, but maybe she doesn't care about any of it. Maybe she hates it. That would actually make total sense to me."

"I'm sure she just meant that statement about her and Greg. And I don't think she's right."

"No, she's totally right," Alice said. "I can see it in every couple now. I treat Mike better than he treats me. Tiff and Mal are pretty happy, but you know that Tiff is a little more into her, even if at first glance it looks like the reverse."

"Jesus," I said. "Don't say that kind of thing. That's not what I meant. I meant that the person who loves more is not necessarily miserable and powerless."

Perhaps I was feeling defensive, because I suspect I'm always the person who loves more. Since I've never had any romantic relationships, I can only apply this idea to my friendships. While I would die if they ever read mine, sometimes I wished Alice and Tiff had LiveJournals I could spy on, so I could better understand what they're thinking. Especially Alice, maybe it would shed some light on her struggle with this eating disorder. I bet Tiff's would be funny, who knows how her weird mind sees the world. The thing was, I wasn't sure they would write about me as much I wrote about them. But my writing about them is what made them great in the first place, they were special because I saw that they were. That didn't feel powerless to me.

"Let's meet at Denny's on Sunday for our project," Alice said. We had a big end-of-term project for AP US History that could be on a topic of our choice within the Gilded Age.

"Okay," I said.

"I know we usually meet here, but I want to get out of my house."

We fell silent, listening to Tori.

"What do you think about her decision to go full rock band on this album?" I asked. "I personally love it, but there's a lot of people who think her music had more intimacy when it was just her and the piano."

Alice ignored my question and asked, "You ever think about when you were a little kid?"

"Yeah, sure."

"Remember those faerie houses we made?" she asked. "In my backyard. My old backyard, the one with the birch tree. I can't believe how much time we spent on that, collecting pebbles and arranging the twigs."

"I remember."

"Did we really think faeries were going to live in them at night?"

"I don't think so," I said. "I mean, I didn't. No offense if you thought that was real. For me it was more about designing the perfect space for hypothetical faeries to live. But I get what you mean. I can't imagine getting so lost and carried away in something like that now."

"Yeah," Alice said quietly. "Sometimes I wish I was eight again."

Current Music: Tori Amos – "Black-Dove (January)"

Friday, November 24th, 2000 | 5:30 p.m.

Slayer and I talked on the phone today. We had picked a time (4 p.m.). At 3:55 p.m., I sat and stared at the phone.

"Hello," I said, picking up after the first ring.

"Hi, is this Ellie?"

"Yeah, it's me."

"Oh wow, hi! This is brilliant. Our first time talking on the phone."

Her voice didn't sound at all like the way I'd heard it in my head. I had imagined her voice being low, sarcastic, in a register that reflected both the droll humor of her posts and the toughness of her chosen nom-de-plume. Instead, her voice was light, feminine, and she sounded... British?

I was processing this contrast in my head when I realized I wasn't speaking.

"Did you not expect me to be English?"

"No," I said. "I mean, yeah, I didn't expect you to be. Aren't you from California?"

"I live in California, but my family moved here from Essex two years ago. I don't talk about it much in my journal. Do you think I should?"

"Yeah. Being from England seems really cool."

(Slayer, I'm aware I sounded like an idiot for much of this call.)

She laughed. "The town I'm from wasn't cool. It wasn't near London. The way you write about Parkview actually reminds me of it. Only difference is older buildings."

I still didn't say anything. I wanted to listen to her voice read an audiobook.

"Where I live now is so much better," she said. "I wish you could teleport through the phone, so we could go into San Francisco tonight. You'd love it."

I'm sure I would, but considering how much simply talking to Slayer over the phone was melting my brain, I'd probably act like a total whack job if I met any of you in person. Especially those of you who post photos of yourselves. I don't think I could handle those flat JPEGs turning into live 3D human beings moving right in front of me. It would be like meeting a celebrity.

I don't have access to a digital camera, so I've never posted pictures of myself. Recently I asked Brian if I could borrow one of his cameras and he immediately responded, "Absolutely not" because I think he knew I had some Internet plans for it. If I'd told him I was planning to take photography as a high school elective, he might have been more open to the idea. I've got to be more strategic about these things. But I don't mind that you've never seen what I look like. This way you can't judge me on my appearance, only my words. And my words seem to have gotten me much more popularity than my looks ever will. I have so many "Friends of" now, I had to stop friending back everyone who friended me, sorry!

Current Music: Blur – "Coffee and TV"

Saturday, November 25th, 2000 | 11:22 p.m.

Went to Steadmans around 10 p.m. tonight with Brian. That's when he likes to grocery shop because there are no other people around. It was extra quiet after the holiday. He was in a pissy mood and I didn't think he wanted me to join. I tagged along anyway. Someone needed to make sure we got everything. As we left, Homeless Guy was outside, asking for money. Brian gave him some.

"Bless you," he said. "Bless you both."

When we were out of earshot, I asked, "What if he uses that money on drugs?"

"Then he uses it on drugs."

"It might have been a better idea to buy him food. My friends and I bought him a whole pizza once. We're right outside Steadmans for Christ's sake."

"You're too critical of people sometimes. You've got to let people do what they need to do to get by."

There was an awkward silence. We had never talked about the night he passed out in front of our apartment, so I guess the plan was to carry on like it never happened. I hadn't seen him crack open so much as a beer since.

I rambled to break the tension. "I'm not being critical, I'm concerned. Most people around here don't care. It's almost winter, where do you think he sleeps? Do you think he goes to one of the homeless shelters in the city?"

He let out a short laugh. "He's not homeless. I know you think that because of how he looks, or because he loiters around everywhere, but he lives in The Pines."

"Oh."

Homeless Guy, not actually homeless.

I felt like an asshole. I put the last of our grocery bags in the trunk, stretched my arms out to the almost empty Steadmans parking lot, spun around once, and in my flat voice, sang, "There must be more than this provincial life!"

"Okay. Please get in the car."

I knew he would not understand the Disney reference I made. I let him think I was losing my goddamn mind.

Current Music: Radiohead – "Subterranean Homesick Alien"

Sunday, November 26th, 2000 | 9:09 p.m.

I got to Denny's late. Alice and Tiff were already seated. Instead of working on our big AP US History project, they were talking about their periods.

"Speak for yourself. I think menstruation is a beautiful process," Alice said.

"Pleeeaseee," Tiff said. "Periods suck and you know it. My cramps are the worst. Plus, you're basically sitting in your own blood."

"Good evening, friends." I slid into the booth next to Tiff. "I can tell I joined the convo at a great moment."

Alice ignored me. "Who sits in their own blood? Use a tampon."

"Ellie," Tiff said. "Tell us your most embarrassing period story. The grosser the better."

"Seriously, why don't you use tampons?" Alice continued. "I know you've had Mal's fingers up your vag. That's twice the size of the most super Tampax."

"Ew?" I said.

"You're such a prude," Alice said.

"It's not sticking it up there that I'm scared of," Tiff said. "It's Toxic Shock Syndrome. That ranks as one of the worst ways to die, in my opinion."

"You're not going to die of Toxic Shock Syndrome unless you're disgusting and leave a Tampon in there for like, three days."

"Yo, literally every episode of *Law and Order: SVU* has a chick who died of Toxic Shock Syndrome, or is suspected of dying of Toxic Shock Syndrome," Tiff said, as if this provided proof of a rampant epidemic.

"You don't have to be disgusting to leave a tampon in there for three days," I said, figuring I was taking the "if you can't beat 'em, join 'em" attitude. "I haven't done that, but there have been times when I couldn't remember how long it had been and I kind of freaked out. And one time when I accidentally used two."

"You both are disgusting and unhygienic creatures," Alice said.

A waiter came over to take our order, so we curbed this conversation for a few minutes. I ordered chicken tenders, Tiff ordered a burger and fries, and Alice ordered a diet soda (ugh).

"Fine, you both think periods suck. What about erections you can't control?" Alice said.

"Okay, that's legit," Tiff said. "Like, I don't completely understand how boners work, but it kind of seems like you could have them at any time."

"They can happen at any time," she said. "Not only when you're aroused. It can be puberty, or hormones, or because your pants' fabric feels good."

"That sounds so stressful," I said.

"Also, sometimes I want to be aroused on the DL. In Mr. Tate's boring class, I'll drift off and daydream about sex. There's no way I could comfortably enjoy that experience if I knew that at any moment everyone could see my erection."

"Another legit point," Tiff said. "And I've also thought

about sex during chem."

They high-fived about this. It was a strong high-five, a real gunshot type crackle.

"There is one good thing about a boner though," I said. "You know when you like someone but you're not sure? When you agonize over whether you want to get with them or whether you just like being around their personality? There'd be none of that if I could get a boner. I'd think of the person and then look down and be like, 'yup, I guess I do like them in that way.'"

I realized that Alice and Tiff were staring at me like this was by far the most insane thing said over the entire meal.

"What," I said.

"Yo," Tiff said. "What even is your sexuality?"

I was mortified that I'd said something truly weird, but I realized I did have to give her question some serious consideration. Who did I really like? There was almost no one at school. It wasn't like the movies, where there was some boy or girl I pined for, and who (gasp!) secretly liked me too, and after a series of predictable misunderstandings, we would happily get together at prom in the end. I sometimes caught myself staring at Christopher, but I didn't want to have sex with him. I think I'd simply like to stare at him for a long time while he posed for a painting I made. (Actually, I don't know why I typed that. I have never made a painting in my entire life.) Other crushes included rock stars or actors (Thom Yorke, Edward Norton, Beck), who were unattainable, and therefore, some might say, safe. They were all male, and while my deep love for Fiona Apple could be interpreted as something beyond platonic, I think I'm being pretty honest here when I say that my love for her exists on a higher spiritual plane entirely. Like many girls in AP English, I also had a crush on Mr. Krasner, who was a slightly more attainable prospect than Thom Yorke, but no less illegal. And finally—it's time I fess up about this—sometimes I wondered if I had a crush on Tiff. She had appealing masculine swagger that gave me a rush to be around, but she also had that dumb bowl cut. The same bowl cut she was now peering out from under, waiting for my answer to her question about my sexuality. Alice was also giving me her full attention.

"Straight, I guess," I said, and they both looked at me with all the skepticism and judgment that limp answer deserved.

Current Music: Wheatus – "Teenage Dirtbag"

🔒 Thursday, November 30th, 2000 | 6:42 p.m.

Brian and I need to go to court. Something to do with his status as my guardian. He came home tonight and told me we have a mandatory appointment to see some caseworker next week. I sat at the kitchen table doing homework and watched him pace around the apartment. I asked why we had to do that, what was wrong.

"I didn't do anything wrong," he said. "I filed one of those reports last week. They want to follow up by seeing us both in person."

Brian fills out some annual update about me to a court every year. He always asks me for a copy of my report card for it.

"Follow up about what? What exactly do you write about me in there anyway?"

"Basic stuff. The school you go to. How you have no behavioral problems. Your goals. They probably just want to check up on how you're doing. There's not necessarily anything wrong."

"You have no idea what my goals are." Then I asked, "Should we be worried?" My voice sounded more nervous than I meant it to be. He stopped his anxious pacing. I looked away.

"It's going to be fine," he said. "Nothing's going to happen to you, all right? Everything will be fine."

He didn't sound like he entirely believed that himself. Still, I knew he was saying this for my sake, and I was impressed that he was stepping up to be the grown-up for once. He sat down on the couch and rubbed his eyes.

"Do you think we should do something? To study or prepare?" I asked.

"There's nothing we can prepare for. We just need to act normal when we go. Normal, normal. Like we're people who love the rules. We love the courts, we love the state, we love America."

"What does America have to do with anything?"

He ignored this. "Oh, and we should dress nice."

Current Music: Fastball – "The Way"

🔒 Sunday, December 3rd, 2000 | 11:43 p.m.

Brian didn't realize that I don't actually have "dress nice" clothes. I had a slim black dress from middle school that still fit. There were little sequins sewn in, I wore it for choir concerts, but that's not something I could wear to this appointment. Yesterday, when I hung out with Alice, Tiff, Mike, and Mal, I asked if we could go to the Goodwill.

In addition to our usual browsing of the vintage t-shirt rack, I was on the hunt for a court appointment outfit. And if I was going to buy clothes for this thing, I might as well get something I liked. Maybe a suit. There was a whole rack of geeky blazers and vests in the men's section. I imagined myself dressing like Giles from *Buffy the Vampire Slayer*.

I picked out a corduroy blazer that felt soothing to touch, matching corduroy pants, a white button-down shirt, and a grey vest. I even found a newsboy cap, but I ditched it after deciding it was way too over the top. I put the rest on over my clothes and looked in a mirror. I imagined wearing this in court and felt a wave of calm. Maybe this would be a good thing after all. Once it was over, it might be a cause for celebration. Something that would unite Brian and I better. I thought about how things used to be, when Mom was still around. I heard the sounds of us all laughing at Ontario Park, after riding some jumpy rollercoaster. Other nights we'd go to the canal. We always brought bread, so I could feed the ducks. That was fun, until this one time, when some greedy ducks got all up in my space, nipping at my feet, including these giant Canadian geese that were nearly as tall as me. "Help, help," I shouted. With a long arm, Brian took the bread and threw it as far as he could, sending the ducks away from me as they ran after it. Mom laughed and hugged me. Later, the three of us walked along the canal path together. At that age, a day lasted forever, and I loved how the sun felt on my face.

"Yo, you look good," Tiff said, interrupting my memories. "Did you see another blazer around like that? I want one."

She and Mal wandered off to browse the same men's jacket rack.

Alice laughed. "It's cool, but it's two sizes too big for you. What exactly are you wearing this for?"

"I have to dress nice for this family thing." I didn't want to tell her. She would never be in a situation where she had to defend her entire home life.

Everything did admittedly run quite large, but this wasn't the mall, there weren't smaller options. And I got it for a steal. The whole outfit cost $8.99.

Current Music: Blues Traveler – "Hook"

🔒 Tuesday, December 5th, 2000 | 5:55 p.m.

On the day of the court appointment, I went home directly after school and changed into my outfit. When Brian got home from work early, he was already wearing a button-down shirt, tie, and dress pants. He took one look at what I was wearing and said, "You've got to be kidding me."

"What? This looks great."

"You look like you're one of the pickpockets in *Oliver Twist*. That's the opposite of what we're going for. Go change."

"Into what?"

"I don't know. Whatever you were wearing yesterday. At least that looked normal."

I changed out of that amazing outfit and into the t-shirt and jeans I had on at school, and we went over to the appointment.

In the courthouse, Brian made a real show of being a well-adjusted adult. He fake-smiled a lot and flirted with the lady that checked us in. He "yes sir" and "yes ma'am"'d everyone to death and only I could see that he meant those words with scorn. When we finally met with our caseworker, the whole thing happened pretty quickly. She spoke mostly to Brian. She asked him questions about his employment, his health insurance, and confirmed that I lived at his residence. She asked if my mom had had any recent contact with us. He said no. She asked if any relatives of my mom had been in contact with us.

He said no to this also. At one point, she used the phrase "child abandonment" and I wanted to punch a wall. She was talking about me as if I wasn't sitting right there. They were both two adults talking about me like I wasn't there.

I focused on studying the ugly cream wall behind her, while wondering if it might actually be easier to imagine they were talking about somebody else, when the caseworker finally addressed me. Surprisingly, she said that the main reason we had been summoned was so she could hear from me. She asked if I was happy in my current living situation. I'm no idiot and said yes. She said that from my report card it was clear I was a top student and asked what I did in my free time. I said I read a lot of books, built websites, and hung out with friends. I fake-smiled a lot too and tried to sound as wholesome as possible. The caseworker said she was glad to see I was doing well, and that despite our unusual situation, as long as Brian was able to continue his duties and responsibilities, he would remain my guardian until I turned eighteen. So, nothing much had changed.

When we got back to the car, Brian immediately dropped the mask and returned to his miserable self. He didn't even start the car, he only stared into space. I was annoyed by that. Couldn't he act happy for once? Or at least, ask how I was feeling? I said, meanly, "Wow, it's like she signed your death sentence."

He didn't say anything, clearly not up for our usual rapport.

"I'm sure it's not too late to tell her you changed your mind. We can swing by the local orphanage and scope it out."

Brian glared at me. I knew I'd gone too far. "Stop it. Stop acting like that. You know I would never do that."

"Sorry. It was a joke."

He turned back to look at the family court building. "Christ," he said. "Why did she ask that question about whether she has any living relatives? So, they can ship you off to live with them?"

I hesitated. "Does she? She always talked about her aunties."

"Those were fake aunts. Or that's what I called them growing up."

"You didn't know each other growing up."

"No, 'Aunties' was some catch-all term for her mothers' friends when they lived in Queens. I meant my parents did a similar thing. Called their friends Aunt or Uncle to make them sound more endearing. 'We're taking you over to stay at "Uncle" Ray and "Aunt" Carolyn's.' '"Aunt" Rachel's coming over tonight.'"

"That sounds creepy if they weren't really your aunt and uncle."

"Yeah, exactly," he said. "Her fake aunts actually sounded like nice people, but they weren't her relatives. Your relatives. I'm sorry, I know that idea might be nice for you, but her parents came over here without anyone."

That I knew. Shortly before Mom was born, my grandparents emigrated, seeking a better life. Classic immigrant story, like we learned in school. Was it worth it?

Brian stared out the windshield. He said quietly, "Everyone thinks they're living the wrong life. Fantasizes about leaving it all behind. You're not supposed to actually do it. She'd say stuff like that sometimes, but I didn't take it seriously."

The expression on his face made me think of what Alice said about couples. Mom had loved Brian less than he loved her and he knew it.

"What—what kind of stuff did she say?" I wanted to know. What didn't she like enough about her life? What didn't she like enough about me?

He shook his head and started the car.

Needless to say, we did not go out to celebrate his renewed guardianship.

Current Music: none

I wish I could say that was the end of this awful episode. We went home and I tried to do my homework, but I couldn't concentrate. The whole day brought up a lot of thinking about Mom in a way that I hadn't in a long time. I didn't feel angry at her, or like I missed her, or anything you might have expected. I only felt confused, almost to the point where I felt nauseous. Not in my stomach, but in my head. A wave of nausea in the head. I laid down in bed and felt very sorry for myself. I looked out the window and watched it get dark outside in real time.

My room is narrow, with a sliver of a closet. It fits only a twin bed and a few plastic drawers. There's not space for a desk, so I always sit at the kitchen table for serious study or homework. I've never minded my room's size, at night it feels like I'm tucking myself into a cozy cocoon. The wall over my bed has a magazine collage of musical heroes that I had recently encircled in white Christmas lights, an interior decorating move I blatantly stole from Alice. I also have a tall stack of cassette tapes aligned against the wall, a collection I've been building since age ten by checking out favorite CDs from the library and copying them onto blank tapes. Track lists are carefully written on the cassettes' blank white inserts. Basically, I was illegally downloading music years before MP3s. If Metallica's offended by Napster, well, they should have seen my bootlegging enterprise back in eighth grade. Usually, I took pride in my secret music library, but not tonight. Tonight, I saw those bootlegs and felt like a bootleg kid, unloved and undeserving of the real thing. I kicked the whole tower and the tapes slid to the floor, without making even a satisfying noise.

I opened the door to my room and glanced down the hallway. Brian was thinking about her too. He laid on the couch with the TV blaring. I could see a glass of whiskey on the coffee table, which made me feel worse. An old grudge arose in me:

A year after she left, I snuck into their room to look for the clothes she had left behind and it was all gone. Her clothes, make-up, drawing supplies, photos he'd taken of her—he had thrown everything out. At that point, there was still hope she might be coming back. Now it seems she never will, but I should have been the one to decide what to do with her things. He had no right.

Current Music: none

Wednesday, December 13th, 2000 | 10:09 p.m.

I've been feeling like crap lately and instead of giving me a break, the world continues to beat me down with more bad news. Al Gore conceded! It's not like I didn't know this was coming, but I was still holding out. Dubya's going to be president. :((

Current Music: Radiohead – "The National Anthem"

Thursday, December 14th, 2000 | 4:57 p.m.

I walked to school instead of riding my bike, playing "The National Anthem" over and over on my discman. No one mess with me today, I thought, as I power strode into Parkview High School. Since Mrs. Ross' class is the first class of the day, my friends and I have taken to gathering in a hallway nook across from her room. It's nice to meet up with them in the morning and it allows us time to get a little homework copying circle going. If someone hasn't done the homework for any class, someone else will offer to let them copy their homework, and you know that person will pay it forward eventually.

When I arrived, Tiff, Alice, Mal, Christopher, and Dev were already sitting in the nook. I removed my headphones and joined them. Except for Dev, everyone looked as miserable as me.

"BUSH II, BABY!!!" he shouted.

Mrs. Ross sure wasn't hiding her bias either. She wore her usual eccentric accessories, but today's outfit was all-black lace. Clearly, this was a signal that she was mourning American democracy.

At the top of class, she said, "Well, it sure has been a long month and a half. I don't think even the Republicans will feel like celebrating."

Dev let out a whoop whoop to let her know he was still feeling the party spirit.

"They'll need your optimism, Dev," she said. "He'll be taking office and half the country doesn't feel he legitimately won the presidency. And that's only the beginning of his struggles. Our economy is slowing, the dot-com bubble too. American industry itself is changing. In the past few years, major employers in this city had a record number of layoffs. Some of your own parents were affected.

"Bush is also relatively inexperienced in foreign policy. Let's review the international items we've been discussing all year. In Iraq, Bush may have to take actions against Saddam Hussein and decide whether to withdraw our presence in the Balkans. He'll also set the tone for U.S. relations with the new Russian president Vladimir Putin..."

She went on and on. Look, I don't want people to die or be hurt, I just want Bush II to fail and be known as the worst president ever.

Current Music: Radiohead – "Idioteque"

This week everyone had mandatory appointments with the guidance counselor to discuss their future college and career plans. Thinking about applying to colleges next year stresses me out. I will need to take out student loans and apply for financial aid and I'm unsure how you do all that.

The high school guidance counselor Mr. Stewart wore a rotating set of argyle sweater vests. I imagined him opening his closet every morning, scanning the row of sweater vests, and feeling real pleased with himself as he selected the day's look. As a guidance counselor, I wondered if he had access to a deep folder of each student's history, and I feared he might bring up my middle school Fiona Apple incident. Instead, it seemed like he simply had a standard script of questions and a printed copy of our grades.

"So..." he said, looking down at his papers. "Ellora. I see you have an excellent GPA and great grades across the board." I got weird déjà vu, remembering the court caseworker saying almost the same thing. "I'm sure you've been thinking about college. Have you given some thought about which schools you'll apply to and potential majors?"

"I want to major in acting/theatre," I said. "I heard NYU was one of the best colleges to do that. But I'm also thinking, I don't know, maybe I should have some kind of back-up plan? There aren't many Asian actresses out there."

He frowned. "It's important to keep a positive attitude,

Ellora. I just saw *Charlie's Angels*. Did you see that?"

Last month, my friends and I had indeed seen *Charlie's Angels*. I was not sure why Mr. Stewart had.

"I'm sure the actress in that movie wouldn't have gotten her role if she'd had your attitude."

"Lucy Liu," I said.

"Ah, yes. But you're right about the arts being a competitive field with no guarantee of stable employment. Let's hear more about this back-up plan."

"Psychology. A double major in psychology and acting."

"Psychology was my major! I'm biased, but I do love hearing when students are interested in pursuing a career in counseling."

There is no way I want my career to resemble yours, I thought. I diplomatically phrased this as, "Well, I'd be more interested in the field of abnormal psychology. People who have mental disorders and emotional problems."

"I see."

"I'd like to help people who are suffering from those things," I added. "I'm interested in doing high-level research at a major university."

I rambled on about running "clinical trials" and "observational studies" on patients. It was something I'd heard on a television show.

"These are very noble goals," he said. "Well, let's make sure you're set up to have many options. Do you do any extracurriculars here? Any clubs?"

"I've tried out for the plays, but I haven't gotten in." It felt so pathetic when I said it out loud.

"There are other extracurricular activities that provide opportunities for performance and public speaking. Have you considered Model U.N. or Debate Club? To be competitive for colleges, you need to have more than good grades."

"Well, I have a job. That takes up a lot of my time. I work at Earl's House."

"Excellent, we should include that." He made a note in my folder. "There's a story I heard recently, Ellora. A parent asked the Stanford dean of admissions whether their child should spend the summer doing a fancy internship at a law firm, volunteering in Africa, or going to NASA space camp. Guess what the Dean said."

"I don't know."

"He said, 'He should spend the summer pumping gas.'" Mr. Stewart burst into a fit of nebbish laughter. "The point of that story is that sometimes what colleges are looking for is a strong work ethic and perseverance. Real world experience over privileged experience." He added, "But you do need to be doing something. They don't want to hear you've been playing video games every day."

I wondered if spending hours on the Internet was analogous to playing video games. Sometimes it did feel a bit like a game.

Mr. Stewart reached into a large box next to him and pulled out the *Fiske Guide to Colleges 2001*. The whole box was filled with identical copies.

"Hot off the presses," he said. "Why don't you take a look and browse your options. You'll want to make a list of safety, match, and reach schools."

I thanked him for the book. I've been reading it tonight and while it's nice to imagine what my life might be like in two years, it's made the process even more overwhelming. The cost, the low acceptance rates. Seeing those numbers right in front of me was a total reality check. I briefly considered how, to be an actress, you don't even need a college degree (though it helps to have some professional training).

Mom didn't get to go to college, because Grandpa got stomach cancer, and she had to help Grandma take care of him. I know she wished she went to art school. I imagined her graduating from Rhode Island School of Design (34% acceptance rate) or Cooper Union (8% acceptance rate, lower even than Harvard, because it has free tuition), instead of getting pregnant. She had me at age twenty-one. That's only five years older than I am now.

Current Music: Radiohead – "How to Disappear Completely"

Wednesday, December 20th, 2000 | 5:01 p.m.

At lunch today, people were all aflutter about holiday break. Mal was going on some trip with her family, so she and Tiff were extra-PDA-y. I couldn't help but think sheesh, she's going to be gone for two weeks. That's nothing. Alice has been moody the past couple days and I'm not sure why. When I asked, she said she was fine. I watched her sit across from me in an oversize sweater and complain about being cold. It took some self-control not to scream back that she was cold because she didn't ever eat anything and had no body fat.

Maybe Brian was right, I'm too critical of people sometimes. I don't mean to be, I want to help Alice. I searched "how to help a friend with anorexia" online the other week and it said you should set aside a quiet time to talk with your friend, rehearse what you say, be gentle but firm, and use "I" statements not accusatory "you" ones. Maybe there will be a time to do this over winter break, if we're hanging out alone. I see it going down like a Lifetime movie, where I place my hand on top of hers and say, "Alice, there's something I really want to talk to you about." Cue the cheesy music.

But if I'm honest, even if the opportunity arises, I don't

think I have the nerve. In the moment, I'd screw something up, I'd be awkward. The worst part is when I imagine her actual reaction, which wouldn't be movie-of-the-week tears and hugs. It would be the venom she directed at her mom when she brought down those Election Day cupcakes, except it would be directed at me.

"Fight! Fight! Fight!"

Everyone in the cafeteria turned to look. Usually when a fight breaks out, it's two guys or a group of guys. This time it was two girls, which provoked more enthusiastic cheering than usual. One wore a black latex trench coat. The other had a black tank top, plaid skirt, and studded choker. Goths. Some of Alice's old clique, maybe.

"What do you reckon their squabble is about?" Christopher asked.

Tank top swung a blow that knocked off trench coat's glasses, and it made trench coat so mad she started clawing at the other girl's eyes.

"Daaaamn," Tiff and Dev said, almost in unison.

Both girls fell onto their cafeteria table now, scratching at each other's eyes and screaming. A big Goth guy next to them looked like he was doing jumping jacks until I realized he was waving down the security guards for help. They rushed over from the other side of the cafeteria. Cheers and shouting continued.

Security guards finally broke the two girls up and started dragging them off to the principal's office. Tank top wrestled away ready to lunge at trench coat again, but the security guard grabbed her before she had the chance. Then they all disappeared out the double doors. A cafeteria monitor grabbed a megaphone and demanded we calm down.

"The excitement is over," she said. "Everybody sit down, the excitement is over."

I do love when a good school fight breaks out. There's something buried deep within me that worries I secretly like violence or have the capacity to be violent. Don't read that the wrong way, I'm not going to pull a Columbine on my school. Nothing like that. But sometimes I feel this rage that needs to be let out. I think about how good it might feel to take it out on another person, to make them feel bad. Sorry, I sound psychotic. I'm not saying I'd ever do anything like this, or think it's justified, only that it seems easier to understand the mentality of people who do.

Current Music: Beck – "Devil's Haircut"

Monday, December 25th, 2000 | 11:09 p.m.

Christmas could have been worse. Brian moped around all day. I told him he was really Ebenezer Scrooge-ing it up and he didn't say anything. I added that maybe he'd be more grateful for what he had if he was visited by the ghosts of Christmas past and he said, "Yeah, no thanks."

"Wow, dark," I said.

When dinnertime rolled around, I think he felt bad for being so miserly because we went over to Golden Apple, the local Chinese restaurant. It's the only restaurant open on Christmas, so it was a hopping scene. All the misfit families of Parkview were there.

It was crowded, but it wasn't loud. Most tables sat together in sad little bubbles of loneliness and we weren't an exception. We didn't even say anything to each other until the server set out the sauces and utensils. They brought only one set of chopsticks. For me.

"You're really getting special treatment around here," he said.

I felt weirdly furious, towards him and also the servers. I looked around and noticed I was the only other Asian person in the restaurant besides the people working. I didn't want them to do anything to point out I was like them. Then I felt maybe that was an awful thing to think, it was like I thought I was better than the people who worked at Golden Apple. And maybe if I'm being honest... that was what I thought? Shit, I was a shitty person. And also racist against other Asians or even against myself or something?

"I know how to use chopsticks too," Brian said. He looked around for the waiter. "I'm going to ask for some."

"Oh my god, don't," I said. "Please, don't say anything." Please don't do anything to make me stand out. Or to make us stand out, more than we already do.

He stopped and grinned at my obvious embarrassment. When the food arrived, he made this big show of struggling with his fork, which admittedly did make me laugh a little.

Later, he said, "I have something for you. A gift of sorts." He reached into his coat pocket and pulled out a photograph.

It was a picture of me at the aquarium, age four, standing in front of Mom and Grandma. I don't know who took the photo, not Brian, this was pre-Brian. A stranger probably. Neither Mom nor Grandma are smiling in the photo. I'm not even looking at the camera, I'm staring like a wide-eyed Muppet at something in the aquarium that you can't see in the frame. No one has their arms around each other either, the only touch connecting us is Mom's hand that rests on the top of my head.

"This must have survived the purge," I said, hoping he would finally apologize for (or at least admit to) throwing out her stuff behind my back.

"I found it under the fridge when I was cleaning."

I held the photo in front of me. I'd always felt disappointed that I never looked much like my mom. I don't have her soft beauty, her oval face. Now I looked at Grandma and recognized my own square jaw. Mom had arty bangs back then and she wore a red dress with matching red lipstick. The dress had unfortunate 80s shoulder pads, but a striking print of white flowers.

"She looks pretty," I said.

"Yeah," he said. "Put it in your bag."

I ignored him and kept the picture on the table with me for the rest of the meal. There were two other Chinese people in the restaurant now.

After dinner, Brian and I were both in better spirits. We walked around one of the developments near the apartment complex to check out how people had decorated for Christmas.

"Let's see who kept it tasteful and minimalist, and who has gone completely overboard." He clapped his hands together like we were off to watch a great sport.

Even though he thinks it looks tacky, I think if I ever have my own home I'm going to go all out. Colored lights covering every inch of the house, blinking in different rhythms. Multiple inflatables and little dramatic Biblical scenes spread over the lawn. Really drill up the electric bill for my family in the month of December, oh yeah. But then again, I'm also not going to live in the suburbs when I'm an adult, so I don't think I'll even have a home to do this with. I'm just speaking hypothetically.

Merry Christmas, everyone. I hope you had a good one.

Current Music: Vince Guaraldi Trio – "Christmas Time is Here" (Instrumental)

Saturday, December 30th, 2000 | 3:44 p.m.

I hadn't seen Alice and Tiff or anybody the entire break. I assumed they were busy with their families. I picked up a couple more shifts at Earl's House for extra dough and spent too much time online. I feared my friends had forgotten me, until this morning Alice finally called.

"How was your Christmas?" she asked.

"Good," I said quickly. "How was yours?"

"Terrible. It was totally Thanksgiving, Part II."

"They must be really happy about Bush."

"Yeah, they're overjoyed."

There was a brief silence.

"You want to come over for New Year's Eve?" she asked. "We can have a New Year's party. Go in the hot tub."

"Yeah, that sounds good. Who else is going?"

"Just you and Tiff. I didn't invite anyone else."

"What about Mike?" I asked. I couldn't imagine she didn't want to kiss him at midnight.

There was a longer silence this time and I knew I shouldn't have asked that. Finally, Alice said, "We broke up."

"I'm sorry. Do you... want to tell me what happened?"

"I was the one who broke up with him. Mike sucks. You were right."

"I never said Mike—"

"I could tell you never liked him. It's fine, you were right. I'll tell you what happened later. Maybe. Let's just have a good time tomorrow."

"Okay," I said.

I looked forward to seeing her tomorrow, ringing in the New Year with her and Tiff. 2001 felt so anticlimactic, compared to last year's New Year's being the new millennium. Remember everyone freaking out about Y2K? Yeah, I knew that was going to be total bullshit. Last NYE, I was home by myself and I blasted the song listed below over and over. I danced around the kitchen, watched the ball drop on TV, and when the clock rolled over to midnight I knew a few two thousand zero zeroes had no chance of stopping the Internet.

Current Music: Prince – "1999"

Monday, January 1st, 2001 | 2:44 p.m.

Top Holiday Movies/TV Specials

1. *Home Alone*
2. *A Charlie Brown Christmas*
3. *How the Grinch Stole Christmas (animated version)*
4. *The Muppet Christmas Carol*
5.—100. All other Holiday movies ever made

101. *It's a Wonderful Life*

When I got to Alice's house, she was in the basement watching *It's a Wonderful Life*.

"I hate this movie," I announced.

"You hate a lot of movies," Alice said.

"I'm picky about my taste."

Seriously though, *It's a Wonderful Life* sucks. It's a real favorite around these parts because Bedford Falls is rumored to be a fictionalized Seneca Falls, a town about an hour away. But I've always hated it. I hate how slow it is, and how the party doesn't really get started until Jimmy Stewart considers offing himself and that angel shows up, and how it takes Jimmy

Stewart fucking forever to grasp that he's entered an alternative reality where he doesn't exist, and then when he finally does and returns to the real world he's so goddamn grateful for what he has, even though he's spent the entire movie dissatisfied with his life, and honestly, I think the whole thing is a subliminal message telling you to settle as a grown-up for complacency and mediocrity.

"There should be a movie called *It's a Wonderful Life*, except the title is ironic, where when the angel shows him the alternate reality, everyone's lives are actually better because he doesn't exist and nothing's changed because he's never had any impact on anything," I said.

"Sounds emo," Alice said.

I started mapping out the plot to this, and how it would obviously end with him choosing to off himself anyway, and then the angel wouldn't get his wings, since he'd failed at his one and only job. And then of course, the natural progression was to apply this scenario to my own life. In a world where I didn't exist Mom wouldn't have been a mom, which obviously would have been her preference, and she could have pursued what she wanted to pursue, and never done something horrible like abandon that same child because that child wouldn't exist. Brian and my mom would have still dated, and whether they would have stayed together is unclear, but if they had broken up, they could have simply broken up and gone their merry ways, like any other couple, instead of Brian being unable to let go because he still had to see the daughter she left behind every day. He would be free to live his mess of a life, and drink all he wanted, and not have to awkwardly explain why he had some teenage girl living with him who was not his daughter. Or maybe, he'd be less of a mess, because he wouldn't have the added stress of supporting said person who was not his kid.

And Alice and Tiff would still be friends, because they were friends before I became friends with them, and they would have picked some other third person to be in their study group. I'd see the three of them hanging out, and I would realize how utterly replaceable I was, and could always be. And Alice would still be starving herself, because in reality I was a mediocre friend who had done nothing to help her. And Tiff would still be her same extraordinary self, because she didn't really need anybody. She was destined for greatness, and soon I wouldn't even be a blip on her radar.

"Helloooo," Alice said. "Are you there?"

"Yeah, sorry." I tried to pull my head out of this spiral of self-loathing.

"We don't have to watch this if you hate it so much. Let's go in the hot tub. Did you bring your bathing suit?"

I had. We changed and got in the hot tub. Or, more accurately, we ran in screaming because we were wearing bathing suits in thirty-degree weather.

Mrs. Lewis pulled open the deck's sliding door and shouted, "Please don't jump into the hot tub!"

"Mom! Shut up and bring us champagne!"

Champagne? I guess in addition to breaking up with Mike, Alice wasn't straight edge anymore. I wanted to know what happened between her and Mike, but I figured she'd tell me when she was ready. Maybe it was for the best we weren't talking about it now though, because I couldn't pull myself out of the *It's a Wonderful Life*-induced funk. I only half engaged with whatever she was talking about.

"You're really quiet tonight," she said.

"Sorry."

"Are you still pissed that you had to watch ten minutes of a movie you think sucks?"

"No. It just got me thinking about stuff. Sorry."

"What kind of stuff?"

I shrugged. "I don't know. How I don't make much impact on people myself, I guess."

Alice leaned back in the hot tub and closed her eyes. She looked amazing in the bikini she was wearing, like a model. I looked at the stars and thought: Ellora, be a normal person who talks about normal things. Alice had issues, but she talked about normal things. Yet it was her who brought the conversation back to the movie.

She said, "If you were Jimmy Stewart and some creepy angel took you around town to spy on me, I promise you, you would see how different my life was."

"Yeah, right. You'd be doing exactly the same things and mostly hanging with the same people, and you know it."

"Okay, sure. Like, maybe externally you wouldn't see anything different about me. But internally, I'd be different. Which wouldn't make a good movie. Well, maybe it could be a low-budget indie movie."

"Okay," I said, still not buying it.

"All the things I love about every day, like when we were at Denny's being gross about tampons, or that day we ran down the hill, that's with you," she said. "That's the stuff that makes life. Not the big dramatic changes. And when dramatic things do happen, it's enough to know... you're there. Like, around."

Alice looked away, and off into the darkness of her own backyard. I couldn't read her facial expression. I thought about what to say next.

This was interrupted by Tiff's arrival. Already in her swimsuit, she opened the sliding door, and said, "Holy shit!" at how cold it was, and practically canon-balled into the hot tub.

"What's going on?" she asked, once she'd fully submerged herself almost to her neck.

Alice snapped back from the darkness and said, "Can you tell Ellie that if she died our lives would be forever devastated?"

"Okay, that's not even what happens in *It's a Wonderful Life*, nor was it what I was talking about," I said, but Alice waved me away in a way that meant "shush."

"Jeez, of course," said Tiff. And then she said simply, "Love you, Ells."

Alice's mom came out with glasses of champagne for us, deeply in Cool Mom-mode. We cheered and started talking about other things. I'm not going to go into detail about what, because it was basically mean things about our classmates in AP US History and you'd probably judge the crap out of me if I wrote out the catty things we said. But safe to say, we had a good laugh. And then, would you believe, almost cinematically, snow started falling. I loved to see all the snow falling on my friends' hair.

Alice's mom came back to top off our glasses.

"Girls, it's officially 2001!" she said, a little too loudly. "Did you know that technically January 1st, 2001 is the first day of the new millennium? Greg and I just heard that on TV. Everyone thinks it was last year, but in fact, the first day of 2001 is really when—"

"Mom, you're an alcoholic, stop pushing your wicked ways on us," Alice said. She rolled her eyes but tipped her glass to receive her mom's generous pour.

"Cheers, yo!" Tiff said. "Happy New Year!"

"Happy New Year," I said.

"Happy New Year, my great friends," Alice said, and then she turned to me. "It's a wonderful life, bitch."

And indeed, in moments, it is.

Current Music: Semisonic – "Closing Time"

2001

Sunday, January 7th, 2001 | 11:00 p.m.

"Oh my god, you're going to get murdered," Alice said.

Christopher had shared that he was going to meet some guy he met on the Internet. We were in Blockbuster, arguing over what to rent, as usual. I turned to face the New Releases shelf, so no one could see how giddy my face looked. The idea that one of my real life friends also had a secret life on the Internet was thrilling.

"Where'd you meet him?" I asked, as casually as possible.

"On a Harry Potter message board," he said quietly.

The idea of Shakespeare-snob Christopher on a Harry Potter message board cracked me up and I admired his honesty. I would've made something up.

"Harry Potter message board? Seriously, dude?" Dev said.

"Who cares what site you met him on, where are you going to meet up?" Alice asked.

"We're meeting in a public place, it's safe," said Christopher. "Westport Mall. He lives in Syracuse, he's driving from there."

"A mall is exactly where a pedophile would tell you to meet," Alice said.

"He's not a pedophile, he's just a fellow gay nerd boy. I've seen what he looks like. He sent me a photo."

"Stock photo," coughed Dev.

"No," Christopher said. "He has a webcam. I had him take pictures of himself doing things to prove it was really him."

"Kinky," Tiff said.

"No." He blushed. "I didn't mean it like that. It was things like 'hold up a sign you wrote that says, 'Hi Christopher.'" I know what I'm doing, all right?"

"All I'm saying is be careful," Alice said.

"So, do you guys have cybersex or what's the deal?" asked Tiff.

"Cybersex?" Alice laughed. "I can't believe you just said that."

"This one time, Tiff and I were bored in this chat room and we started typing the craziest things to everybody," Mal said.

"Oh man, we wrote some sick shit," Tiff said. She giggled. "My house is probably permanently watched by the FBI now."

"But people loved it!" said Mal. "Like, they were typing 'oooooo i'm so horny baby.'"

"Well, no surprise, people are messed up," Alice said.

As always, it took us forever to decide on a movie. We settled on *Buffalo '66*, a cool indie movie that took place in Buffalo, the city next to ours. The filmmaker (Vincent Gallo) really captured upstate New York. Maybe not the hypocrisy and suburban ennui of Parkview, but the grimness overall. How hopeless the winters look. The constant variations on shades of grey. There's one part where the main character (also Vincent Gallo) crosses a multi-lane highway and it feels like the bleakest thing in the world. Mainstream movies always look a little too bright.

After the movie, Christopher gave me a ride home. I was excited about the chance to talk to him about his Harry Potter message board alone.

"Christopher." I put my hand on his shoulder. "I too, have 'Internet friends.'"

I don't know why I said it like that. I guess I wanted to give the revelation some drama.

"You do?" He sounded only mildly interested. "Have you ever met up with them?"

"No, they live too far away. My closest friend lives in California. Another lives in Texas and another in Nova Scotia."

"I don't understand why everyone had to be so judgmental," he said. "I know what I'm doing. With Dan. That's his name. It's easy for them to laugh when they're in relationships. Tiff and Mal. Alice and—wait, did Alice and Mike break up?"

"Yeah, I'm not sure what happened."

"Well, I'm sure she'll have no trouble finding someone else. It's not like that for me. There's nowhere to meet people."

I thought about how arrogant Christopher had acted during his "many famous writers were gay and maybe your parents are a little gay too" monologue. But now, when it came to his real life, and the prospect of a real guy he might date, he sounded so insecure. Even his speech was different, he dropped that fancy, intellectual way he had of talking.

"I don't meet people either," I said. "I mean, in any romantic sense. Either online or in real life."

"Yeah, but there's not even choices for me at school. Who would I possibly date, Spencer Lyons?"

(Spencer Lyons has won choir student of the month a record-breaking five times. I know a good portion of the *Rent* soundtrack because he's always singing it in the hallway. Obviously, he and Christopher would be a poor match for each other.)

"I hope college will be different," he said.

"Have you looked at Sarah Lawrence College?" I suggested. "*The Fiske Guide to Colleges* said that Sarah Lawrence has a high percentage of gay men."

"Ellie," he said. The snark was back in his voice. "I am not going to Sarah Lawrence. That would barely be a safety school for me."

Current Music: The Avalanches – "Frontier Psychiatrist"

Sunday, January 7th, 2001 | 12:21 p.m.

I understood how Christopher felt. Besides feeling hopelessly behind the sexual experience of my peers, I also felt like I was running out of time to have a great high school romance. I'll admit it, I want the things I've seen in the movies. Two straws sharing an ice cream sundae together at Denny's. Holding hands together in the hallways. A mix CD made for someone that's more than a friend. I already know the songs I'd put on it ("True Love Waits" by Radiohead, "I Know" by Fiona Apple, etc. etc.). And better yet, I'd finally understand those songs. Sometimes I listen to my favorite songs about love and feel I'm experiencing them like an actor. I'm only imagining what it might be like, those feelings aren't really mine.

Current Music: Aimee Mann – "One"

Friday, January 12th, 2001 | 4:00 p.m.

GOOD NEWS GOOD NEWS. I got into the spring school play! I didn't tell you I was auditioning, because I was certain that this would result in another failure, like the last five school plays I've tried out for.

It's an ensemble romantic comedy called *Those City Girls!*

set in the 1950s. It takes place in a NYC sales agency, and the plot concerns various work antics and romances. No one is related to each other, so I did have a better feeling about this one.

AhHhJskLjoijIJ92hhhh I can't believe it! What a rush to finally see my name on the posted cast list. I'm not playing Meg Miller, the protagonist whose move to the big city (and subsequent rising career and turbulent love life) the story revolves around, but I am playing one of the secretaries in the office. It's a character named Franny, and if she has a name, she must be a real character, with some actual lines.

Current Music: Sheryl Crow – "A Change Would Do You Good"

🔒 Wednesday, January 17, 2001 | 6:15 p.m.

The first rehearsal of *Those City Girls!* started out fine and dandy. We did introductions and a full read-through. It confirmed that my character, Franny, was a strong supporting role, and I had a significant number of lines—all good things. Then we reached the last few pages. As I mentioned, it's an office romantic comedy and the characters pair off in the end. Franny is a shy lonely secretary who thinks no one notices her and she will die an old maid. In the end, her stuttering friend Will from the mailroom (somewhat predictably) confesses his feelings, and she admits she has always been fond of him too. And then: *They share a kiss.* Yes, that's the exact stage direction written in the script.

I know that if I become a professional actress, I will have to kiss other actors and probably engage in full on simulated sex scenes with strangers. That's not the issue here. The issue is that I didn't want My First Kiss to be such an unromantic situation. It's supposed to be something special. I envisioned the inevitable moment future college friends, dates, grandchildren asked, "So, who was your first kiss?" and me replying, "Jay Arflin, my knucklehead scene partner in this vaguely sexist school play I was cast in."

Ms. Millhauser, the theatre director, said we shouldn't worry about the kisses, she knows they are awkward (three different couples kiss over the entire play) and we wouldn't have to actually lock lips until dress rehearsal. Jay looked as relieved as me. I immediately thought, "I must kiss someone before April 14th, the date listed on our schedule as the tentative* dress rehearsal." But let's be real, that's not going to happen. Maybe it's cruel and perfect. My first kiss will be on stage. OH, THE SACRIFICES I MAKE FOR MY ART.

Current Music: Ben Folds Five – "One Angry Dwarf and 200 Solemn Faces"

🔒 Saturday, January 20th, 2001 | 9:55 p.m.

I didn't get out of bed until 5 p.m. today. I've done that a couple times in my life. There have been days when everything seems flat, and without school or work or anything that required me to get up, I simply didn't. Immobilized, I stayed in bed, where things I remembered being excited about only yesterday seemed impossible to enjoy ever again. Finally, in late afternoon, hunger my only motivator, I got up to fix myself a peanut butter sandwich, still in my pajamas.

Brian was lying on the couch watching television. He

jumped. "Christ, I didn't know you were home. Are you sick or something?"

"No."

"No?"

"I just didn't feel like getting up."

He was watching a recap of today's inauguration. Bush is officially president for four years, which feels gross and forever. So much could happen in four years.

Four years ago, I was in seventh grade and I had a very different social life and friend group.

Four years before that I was in third grade and I had a very different home life and family.

Four years before that I was four.

Four years (and some change) before that I was a zygote.

"What do you mean you didn't feel like getting up?" asked Brian.

"I don't know."

"How long have you felt this way?"

"Just today. What's the big deal? You act depressed all the time. You're acting depressed right now."

"That's different."

I finished making my sandwich and started to walk back to my room, but Brian said, "Your mother, before she left. I don't think you understood what was going on. I think you thought she was sick—physically sick."

That's because you told me that, I wanted to say. Instead, I said, "I get that she was depressed. Now."

"Stop saying depressed, it was more than depressed. She hallucinated things."

"Hallucinated?"

"Yeah, she used to say she saw glowing light around your head, my head. Or that there was a glass wall between her and the rest of the world."

"Isn't that like, schizophrenia?" The idea of Mom being schizophrenic seemed way more terrifying than her suffering from major depression, which is what I had always assumed.

"Not necessarily. She knew they were hallucinations, or irrational thoughts. You can have symptoms like that with bipolar disorder, borderline personality disorder, other disorders. I did some reading."

"Well, I've never hallucinated anything." And if I did, I thought, it certainly wouldn't be a halo around your head.

"Good, but it's genetic. I read that too. I'm not saying it to scare you. I'm saying that if you continue to act like this, you're going to a doctor."

No way was I going to a doctor or therapist. I imagined how it would go, like a movie. I'd sit there and pout and say sarcastic things to some adult who thought they could understand me.

"Did Mom go to a doctor?" I asked.

"No."

"Why not?"

He didn't say anything. As unbelievable as it sounds, we had never before talked so directly about her mental illness, or whatever it was. Brian had no problem throwing around bitter remarks about her being "crazy" or "a lot to handle" but now that we were talking about it in a real way, every word sounded like it took him extreme effort.

"Why not?" I asked again.

"I brought it up, suggested maybe she needed to talk to someone. She didn't want to. Apparently, her mother told her not to complain about her 'moods' growing up. It was frustrating to hear her say things like that when she was clearly struggling. We had a fight. Why was she still being obedient to her parents, when they weren't even alive anymore? She said that I didn't understand, that I was being disrespectful to them and stereotyping her at the same time."

I opened my mouth to say something. I didn't even know what I wanted to say. Not that I got a chance.

"We're done talking about this," he said. He pulled a blanket off the back of the couch and covered his entire self with it, including his face. When he spoke again, it was muffled. "You usually have such a good head on your shoulders, but if there's [inaudible] you don't feel like getting up again, you're going to a doctor. That's how this whole [inaudible] started, her not wanting to get out of bed. I'm not going through this with you."

Back in my room, I pulled out the photo that Brian gave me, the one with me and Mom and Grandma. I tried to imagine Grandma telling a teenage Mom not to complain about depression or saying that therapy wasn't for people like them. They had always had a complex relationship and it carried into Mom's adulthood. I think Grandma disapproved of her being unmarried with a child, but she still took care of me a lot when I was little. When Mom had to go to work, or wanted time to herself, she would drop me off at Grandma's house, the same house she herself had grown up in when they moved to Parkview from Queens. I hated going there. The wallpaper in her house had a clustered pattern that filled me with dread. I remember thinking mean thoughts every time I went: Grandma's house was boring, Grandma was boring, why hasn't Mom picked me up yet. She spent a lot of time staring out the window, saying floaty things in a mix of Mandarin and English.

"You need to speak English to her," I remember Mom saying. And later, to me, "Your grandmother's English used to be so much better. She was almost fluent. She's really regressed since your grandfather died."

That anecdote maybe paints Mom in a cruel light, so I

want to make sure to tell you that she could also be kind to Grandma. If my grandmother spent too much time staring out the window, Mom would take her hand in hers and gently say, "How about some fresh air, Ma? Let's go on a walk." That memory also uncomfortably reminds me of myself. A few years later, when Mom would decide to spend a whole day lying in bed, I would curl up next to her. Her long hair, which she usually wore up, looked like a bottle of black ink spilled on the white pillows. "Mom, I made you a 'Get Well Soon' card because Brian says you're feeling sick. I wanted to put it in the mail, so you would open the mail and be surprised, but he said it would be silly to mail things to ourselves and to give it to you now instead."

I thumbed the glossy surface of the aquarium photograph. Grandma died before she was sixty, yet she behaved like a much older lady. I wondered why. Had the loss of my grandfather and the hardships of immigrant life worn her down? Or had she also suffered from some mental affliction? Maybe a combination of both.

I didn't need Brian to tell me that mental illness was genetic, it's already something I've read about myself and I don't like the idea. It's like how in school we sometimes debate between fate and free will. I am my own person and I don't want to accept some inevitability that I will become Mom or Grandma. For starters, I would never be the type of person who abandons the people I love, no matter how overwhelming my mind gets.

I pledge today that no matter how bad I feel I will get out of bed and get dressed and do at least one thing every day, even if that one thing is only going online. I am writing this publicly in my LiveJournal to hold myself accountable.

Current Music: Fiona Apple – "Get Gone"

"I want you all to know that I was sent the email. But I didn't look," Dev said, at lunch.

"Dev, no one emailed you that photo," Christopher said. "And if they had, I'm 100% certain you would have rushed to open the attachment."

A scandal had developed around school and it involved Kendall, she of my former Jenny/Jen/Kendall clique. Apparently, she'd been seeing Ian Marks and sent him an email with an attached topless photo. It was just for Ian, but he forwarded the email to a couple of his friends and they sent it to their friends and now most of the guys in the junior class have seen this photo of Kendall.

"Man, she's a dumbass," Tiff said.

"Don't say that," said Alice. She smacked Tiff in the arm.

"Since when do you care about Kendall Barton? She's kind of a bitch," Mal said.

"I don't care if she's a bitch, there's nothing funny about this. It could ruin her life. Ian may have ruined her life."

Since their eighth grade dumping of me, I'd spent a not insignificant amount of time hoping that bad things would come upon Jenny/Jen/Kendall. Nothing like, seriously bad. I wasn't hoping for their deaths or anything demented like that. I mostly envisioned scenarios where they would be humiliated or ostracized from their peers, and forced to feel a gnawing loneliness, one even greater than the one I felt.

I hadn't engaged in any of those fantasies lately, maybe because my own loneliness had been significantly chipped away by Alice and Tiff and the rest of them. And I didn't feel like rejoicing now that Kendall's humiliation had arrived. Sure, I wasn't crying a river either, but I was surprised at how much I didn't care. Also, Alice was right, what Ian did was awful.

I wondered if Kendall's other popular friends would stand by her. A strange transformation had happened to the popular kids in the last couple years. They've gotten weirdly religious. I don't know who started it but they're all going to Young Life and putting that stupid Jesus fish thing on their cars and backpacks and binders. It seems like a weird choice for the popular kids and I'm not sure whether they actually believe in Jesus or whether Jesus is simply trendy now or what the deal is. At last year's student assembly, Jenny Porter announced that she was waiting for marriage to have sex and I'm pretty sure that was as bullshit as when Britney Spears said it. But somehow, I suspected those hypocrites would not take kindly to Kendall's passed around topless photo.

Current Music: P.J. Harvey – "Big Exit"

🔒 Sunday, January 28th, 2001 | 9:13 p.m.

Tiff got her license. I was surprised, I thought she'd live in a world of skateboard utopia and her mom furtively driving her to school forever. I guess everyone's pursuing this driver's license business except for me. She picked me up and drove me to Alice's house for our AP US History study session. It was too brutally cold to bike or walk. Walking from my apartment door to her car was torture enough.

We ran to Alice's door, and Tiff was about to ring the bell, until we heard yelling inside. It was Alice's mom.

"You gave her a fifty-dollar bill? That's your plan? Bribe her to eat dinner like she's some kind of child? We spend a fortune on groceries and now we get the honor of paying her to eat it too?"

"Mom, shut up!" That was Alice's voice. "Both of you, shut up!"

"And you thought you could do this behind my back? I can just imagine what you said to her. Oh, I can hear it! 'You've been upsetting your mother. Here's $50, please eat dinner so she shuts up.'"

"I did not say it like that." Greg's voice now. "I told her that we were both concerned about her. She looks sick."

Tiff and I looked at each other. We both knew we shouldn't be listening to this, but we couldn't walk away.

"This is what you do. You think you can make problems go away by throwing money at them. Instead of talking to me, or anyone."

"I don't know how to talk about this with her," Greg shouted. "Or with you. I don't get this. I don't get this not eating. Eating is one of the joys of life."

"That's because you're clueless. About everything."

"Mom, you're being a huge bitch right now."

There was a long silence. I thought Alice's mom might slap her, like in the movies. Instead, I heard her start crying.

"Do you know that if you keep doing this, you might never be able to have children?" she finally said.

"Good, I don't want kids. I don't want to screw them up like you."

More crying from Alice's mom. "Fine, then. Do you know that you could stop your own heart? That's how Karen Carpenter died. I couldn't stop thinking about that last night. I went downstairs to put my hand on your heart, to make sure it was still beating."

"You snuck into my room while I was sleeping?"

Alice sounded angry, but my own heart felt something hearing Alice's mom saying that. It was the first time I didn't see her as a ridiculous person.

Tiff made a noise of frustration and ran back to her car, either because she couldn't handle hearing their argument anymore, or she couldn't stand out in the cold any longer, or both. I ran after her. We jumped back in the car and she cranked the heat to full blast.

We sat in silence for a few seconds before Tiff said, "Well, at least her parents know."

"At least *you* know."

"What's that supposed to mean?"

"I thought nobody noticed but me."

"Ellie, everybody knows."

"Then why do you and Dev always take her food at lunch?"

"To end the awkward situation, duh. And it's not like she's going to eat those cookies if I don't take them. She'll throw them in the trash, why let them go to waste?"

"We need to do something," I said.

"What could we do that her parents aren't?"

"I don't know. Clearly, they don't have a handle on it."

"No shit. But what are we going to do different?"

"Maybe we need to... stage an intervention or something."

I imagined my Lifetime movie scenario, and how maybe it would be easier to do if friends were involved. Tiff looked at me skeptically. "We've just got to be her friend and if she wants to open up to us, she can."

"That's not enough," I said. "If something bad happens to her, we're going to hate ourselves knowing that we could have done something to help and we sat around instead. I don't want to be like that."

Tiff shook her head. "If we try to talk to her, she's only going to get mad and push us away. It's not going to make her change."

After a few minutes passed, we started a loud fake conversation as we approached the front door again and rang the bell.

Alice answered right away and gave no indication that she had been in a huge fight with her mom and Greg. The only sign that anything was off at all was the fact that Alice's mom didn't bombard us upon arrival with her usual big hugs and snack offers. We went down to the basement and ran through some practice AP questions. Tiff and Alice acted like everything was normal. I had a hard time readjusting and didn't understand how they could.

Alice shadowboxed the Bush mask that was still there from the election party. "Have you heard what people at school have been saying about Lucky's?"

"Yeah, some of the seniors in jazz band were talking about it," Tiff said. "How they got in."

"It's only on Tuesdays, I think. Or slower nights when nobody gives a shit. On weekends they card."

I didn't care about this topic of conversation. I wanted to scream, "Hello?! Why is everyone walking around completely fucked up but acting like everything is fine?"

"Do you guys want to try to go?" Alice asked.

"Whoa! Straight edge Alice is calling. She wants to know what happened to you," Tiff said.

Yeah, Alice, I thought, tell us about it. Why don't you tell us what's going on, or what happened between you and Mike, or why you have no interest in going to The Caterpillar anymore.

"That whole phase was dumb," Alice said.

"So, you thinking this Tuesday? What time?"

"It's got to be after nine, maybe closer to ten. That's what people have been saying. Enough people need to be in the bar already, so you don't stand out too much."

"No can do. My parents won't let me stay out that late on a Tuesday."

"Okay," Alice said. "Probably best if it's just me and Ellie anyway."

I hadn't said I was interested in going, but whatever. It was one thing to drink champagne in Alice's hot tub or a Smirnoff Ice in her basement, but it was a whole other thing to engage in illegal underage drinking in a public high-risk scenario where we could get caught.

"Hey, what's that supposed to mean?" Tiff asked.

"I want you to come with us, but..." Alice gestured to Tiff, in her bowl cut and usual baggy clothes. "Sometimes you look like you're twelve."

"Yo, I do not look like I'm twelve. I'm seventeen, that's older than both of you. Fuck you!"

Alice was right, in a bar where we'd hypothetically have to be passing for twenty-one, Tiff wouldn't stand a chance.

"I can't go this Tuesday anyway," I said quickly. "I've got to work."

That was a lie, I was not scheduled that night at Earl's House. But hey, what was one more lie on top of all the lying we'd already done today. As always, if you can't beat 'em, join 'em.

"Bummer," Alice said. "Well, another Tuesday then."

"Sure," I said.

Current Music: Björk – "Hunter"

🔒 Friday, February 02, 2001 | 10:15 pm

Tiff, Mal, Alice, Christopher, Dev, and I were at Denny's. We'd had a school assembly earlier in the day and a student talent act always opens. Usually it's someone performing a song, but the surprise performer this month had been Dev, with a Republican standup comedy routine. Many of the (conservative) teachers loved it, but most of the students thought it was straight-up bizarre that this 16-year-old was cracking Newt Gingrich jokes. Some jocks boo'd and Dev responded with a quick comeback about how he sure hoped they were getting athletic scholarships, because even daddy's alumni status wasn't going to be enough to get their weak GPAs into college. While his humor wasn't to my taste, I had to admit that Dev had presence up there. His delivery was spot-on, it was easy to imagine him on television.

"I can't believe I've been slumming it with you in Debate Club," Dev said to Christopher. "I'm going to start a comedy club, I've already talked to Tollz about it."

Tollz was Mr. Tolley, the school vice-president, who approved any new clubs.

"You'd leave Debate Club to pursue comedy?" Christopher asked. He said the word "comedy" with disgust.

"I'm not leaving Debate Club, Harry Potter. I'm going to be the founder of Comedy Club, while still being in Debate Club. And since I'll be sharpening my verbal skills in both clubs, I am going to destroy you in every debate."

"Nonsense."

"I'm down for comedy club if your meetings don't conflict with jazz band," Tiff said.

"Hell yes," said Dev. "Dev Khatri, President of Comedy Club, just signed his first member—Tiff McKee, my good homey and vice-prez."

They high-fived. Maybe I'd join them in Comedy Club, I heard a lot of actresses get their start in comedy troupes in Chicago and NYC. They have to improv though, which scares me. I need a script, I can't think on my feet.

"I'm in too," I said. "Maybe."

"Bam," Dev said. "This club is heating up. Ellora Gao, Comedy Club's Secretary of State and Head of National

Defense."

Denny's was hopping. I looked over at a table next to ours. A young Asian woman sat in a booth with her daughter. The mom was pretty. There was something about them sitting silently together and the way the daughter ate her fish sticks, taking the smallest of bites, that made me think of what Alice had said: "Sometimes I wish I was eight again." This girl was younger than eight, maybe five or six.

I noticed Tiff looking at them too. I watched her watching them and she immediately caught me staring. She winked and returned to joking with Dev about their plans for Comedy Club. Tiff winks at people all the time, I've seen her do it and it's so devastatingly flirty. I know, winking is flirty and suggestive when anyone does it, but she does it with such cockiness, such confidence. Has she ever been bad at anything in her entire life? Whenever I made her laugh, I made a mental note to remember the moment, so that I could replay it later in my mind. There was no better feeling than when you held her attention.

When I looked back at the Asian woman and her daughter, an Asian man sat across from them. He must have been in the bathroom. He said something and it made his daughter laugh. She less resembled my younger self now, so I returned to my friends.

Later, Alice gave me a ride home.

"Do you really think Dev is going to start that club for comedy?" she asked. "And if he does, are you going to join? In addition to doing the plays?"

"Maybe. Plus, getting into one play doesn't mean I'll get into the play next year."

"It usually does. Maybe I'll try out next year."

"Yeah, you should do that," I said, but I could hear the hesitation in my voice.

"Nah, it's your thing already. I wish I had a thing."

I felt guilty that she articulated what I had been thinking. "Why don't you try out for show choir next year? You have a great singing voice."

"But I can't dance," she said. "And show choir is just...." She made a face and did sarcastic jazz hands. We both laughed.

"Yeah, show choir is too much," I said.

We launched into a scornful rendition of "Favorite Son," the show choir's signature piece from the musical *Follies*. The choir sings the song while sitting in a long row of chairs and the "choreography" is a ton of jazz hands and coordinated slapping of each other's thighs. Alice and I flailed around and slapped each other on the thigh repeatedly until we were both nearly crying of laughter.

"You've got to stop, or I'll run us off the road."

"Okay, okay," I said, but not before I got one last slap of her knee in.

We laughed again, until we reached my apartment. She idled in front of the building and without any transition she asked, "Can I tell you why I broke up with Mike?"

"Yeah, sure." I knew not to sound too eager.

She didn't speak for a long time. "Mike, he would—if we were hanging out and fooling around and I wasn't into it, or even outright said no, he'd say the meanest things."

I didn't know what to say in response. "What? What kind of things?"

"Like how I was a slut for not wanting to give him a blow-job when he knew how many guys I'd blown since I was a freshman. Or he'd compare me to other girls and how they looked and how they would definitely have sex with him. He'd say stuff like that and not leave me alone until I gave in."

"He did?"

"So, I'd lie there and do whatever he wanted, but he was so mean after. One time we had sex in the basement and after he finished, he said, 'See. I told you. You liked it' and he left. Like walked upstairs and left my house."

Her voice broke and I couldn't stand the silence. "He said that?"

"Yes. Why do you keep asking stuff like it's a question? You don't believe me?"

"No, I believe you. I believe you!" I said. "I'm sorry. I never liked him, but I didn't realize he was so bad."

"Well, he was. You barely knew him."

"I know. But I mean, like, people in general. It's hard to imagine people doing such horrible things."

"Then you're really naive." There was a mean edge to her voice.

Stop talking, I warned myself, knowing that I'd keep saying the wrong thing as I kept trying to correct myself and I'd make it worse. I needed to stop time and sit down and carefully consider the right thing to say.

Instead, I blurted out, "Did something like this happen to you when you were little?"

"What?" Alice said. "No. I mean I'm pretty sure my uncle's been staring at my boobs since I was thirteen, but he's never tried to touch me or anything. Why? Did something happen to you?"

"No," I said. "But in fifth grade, the legal guardian thought something had, when we were at the park with one of my friends and her dad. He saw her dad put his hand on my shoulder and went totally ballistic on him. I've never seen him that angry."

"But nothing actually happened to you?"

"No, he was just acting crazy. It was right after my mom left."

"That must be hard," Alice said. "The stuff with your mom. I don't know why you don't ever talk about it. But I also don't understand why you'd decide that now was the right time to tell me something random from years ago that didn't even happen to you when I'm trying to tell you about something that did happen to me. That happened repeatedly. And only stopped a month ago."

"I'm sorry."

"Stop saying you're sorry."

"I don't know what you want me to say. I feel bad for you."

"I don't want you to feel bad for me. I just needed to tell you. And I needed you to listen, not ramble on about something unrelated."

I couldn't help but say it, because otherwise I was going to cry. "I'm sorry."

"I'll talk to you later."

"Alice. Please don't be mad at me." I knew this was not the right thing to say either.

"I'm not mad. Just go."

There was nothing to do but utter a meek "bye" and get out of her car. I really screwed up. I can't say the right thing when people are hurting. I can't stop thinking about them after, but in the moment, I don't know how to act fast enough and I can't read people and I say self-centered things. One time I even said a very mean thing. I'm going to go lie down and think and maybe I'll write more later.

Current Music: none

🔒 Saturday, February 3rd, 2001 | 3:14 p.m.

Before packing two suitcases, getting in her car, and driving away, my mom wrote Brian a brief note and left it on the kitchen table. It said she was tired of her life and wanted a break from it. She needed to figure things out alone. After discovering the letter, Brian lied and told me Mom had gone on a vacation and that she would be back soon.

A week later, when she called to check in, I asked her how her vacation was going and she said, "Vacation? Oh, it's fine." Her voice was flat, faraway, but that was how she had sounded for months. She asked if Brian was taking good care of me and I said yes. We'd ordered pizza from three different places and held a contest to decide which slice was best. We'd gone to see *Ace Ventura: Pet Detective* and I hope she didn't mind that it was rated PG-13. As always, I tried to say things that would cheer her up. This was the last time I ever spoke to her.

I've imagined many times how this call could have gone differently. If I'd known she was not actually on a vacation, I would have demanded to know where she was and begged her to come home. Instead, I thought things were okay, so I acted okay, even when Brian took the phone back and spoke to her alone in their room where I couldn't hear.

I also feel guilty about how I acted those first couple weeks. She had been so barely present, that it was almost a relief to have her physically gone. I kept doing well in school and in my free time I went over to friends' houses or enjoyed being by myself. Brian and I got out of the apartment as much as possible. We'd idle at the park or the movies or the library or restaurants. Time was a thing to waste until she returned home.

At the library, in the children's section, I curled up in a beanbag chair with a book. Brian grabbed a book from the adult's section and sat in another beanbag chair. Only kids are supposed to sit in those, I said. Says who, he replied.

Within minutes, he fell asleep with a book on his chest and when I was bored of reading, I woke him up. He apologized and said he hadn't been sleeping well. I asked if that was because Mom had been on vacation too long and he said yeah. I asked when she was coming back and he said "soon" in a lost way that made me too nervous to ask anything more.

Another day, at the park playground, Brian said I should go play and went to go lie in the grass by himself. He hadn't even brought a book, he only stared up at the trees. I was getting too old for the playground, but I still liked to swing a lot, pretend I was flying. I ran into a new friend there, Naomi Abbott, a redhead from my class whom I'd later form the Jen/Jenny/Kendall clique with in middle school. Naomi was there with her dad. Naomi and I started to do this thing where we'd swing as high as we could and then jump and try to land on two feet. Mr. Abbott saw this, shouted, and immediately waved us over. He told us to stop jumping, that was extremely dangerous. He put his hands on our shoulders to make sure we understood. I'd instigated the swing jumping and I was so worried that I was going to get us both in trouble, that I didn't even notice Brian had walked over. He told Naomi's dad to stop touching me. Mr. Abbott wasn't mad, he apologized, said there was a misunderstanding. Brian didn't let it go, he said there was no misunderstanding and called him a fucking creep. Mr. Abbott said don't swear in front of my daughter and Brian replied, I'm fine swearing in front of your daughter so she knows who you are. Naomi was upset now too. Who is that, she asked me. I said, he's kinda my stepdad. Brian continued to rail at her poor father, it was like he'd been waiting to finally yell at someone. It was scary to hear his voice sound so different from its usual burnt monotone. Mr. Abbott said, you need to calm down or I'm going to get someone to call the police. Two other younger kids were there with their moms and they were all staring. Naomi started crying, but I didn't. Let's go, I said to Brian. Let's go home. I pulled at his sleeve and he actually listened to me.

Once we got in the car, I said wow thank you for completely embarrassing me in front of my friend, and why would you think that about her dad. That wasn't some stranger danger that was her dad. He said you don't understand. I can't watch out for you all the time, he shouted, so stop being stupid. Being called stupid hurt, but I knew how to be meaner. I said I want my mom. When was my mom coming back. That shut Brian up, so I decided to really twist the knife and said, I'm glad she dumped you, you freak. She's going to come back to get me and you're going to die alone.

Brian didn't say anything to that. We returned to the apartment and as soon as he parked, he immediately got out and leaned against the car for support. He looked like he was going to be sick and I thought it was because of the hateful thing I'd said. I'm sorry, I said. I'm sorry I didn't mean that. He said it wasn't my fault, that wasn't why. He kept taking these short and quick breaths, like he was struggling to get air. I asked if he was going to throw up and he said he was fine in the most panicky not-fine voice ever.

We went inside, and he locked himself in his room. I waited in the living room, on the couch. It felt like hours but maybe it was only a few minutes. When Brian finally returned, he was holding a piece of paper. He had calmed down.

"You're not stupid, all right? I'm sorry I said that. I'm the stupid one."

I nodded.

"Also, I'm sorry about what happened back there. I thought that man wanted to hurt you."

"He didn't."

"I know, I overreacted." I heard an edge of irritation in his voice again. Then he sat down in a chair across from me, looked me in the eye, and said, "Your mom is not on a vacation. She was never on a vacation. But I think you already know that."

"Where is she?"

"I don't know. She's having a hard time and wanted to go be somewhere by herself."

He handed me the piece of paper. It was her note. I instantly recognized her scratchy handwriting, its mix of cursive and print. The tall loopy l's in Ellora. *Please take care of Ellora while I figure things out.* Why was my name only in one sentence of this short paragraph? Why wasn't it at the top? I wanted the note to be addressed to me, not him.

"When is she coming back?"

"I don't know. I really don't know what's going on with her anymore."

I folded the note in half and then did it again and again until it was only a tiny square in my hand. "I want to be where she is."

"I know. I miss her too," he said. "But we'll get through this until she comes back. Deal?"

Deal. We shook hands, which was absurd considering how awful the day had been, yet the formalness of the gesture made us both laugh. And well, I guess you know the rest of the story.

In fifth grade, I didn't understand why Brian flipped out on Naomi's dad. I think I do now. I think someone must have hurt him when he was a kid and seeing Naomi's dad put his hands on my shoulders stirred this horrible memory and he had some kind of panic attack. Maybe the person even looked like Naomi's dad. I don't know, I get really upset thinking about it.

I wish I could go back in time and save the kid version of Brian from this person, whoever it was. I know that sounds ridiculous, maybe even childish, but I'm flooded with rage when I think about people harming my family and friends.

Mike's face flashed in my mind. He was not an adult and I was not afraid of confronting some guy one year older than me. He was sitting there at Bridgeport High School waiting for me to take my revenge.

I couldn't sleep. An hour ago, I had heard Brian go to bed, so when I went out into the living room, I didn't turn on any other lights, only the computer. I sat in the dark and let the blue glow of the screen reflect on my face. I signed on and saw that Alice was online, with an Away Message up. I messaged her.

lostchildOKC: Hi

She immediately put her Away Message down.

XJoinOrDieX: hey
lostchildOKC: Okay. I know you don't want me to say sorry, so I won't say that, but I didn't react the way a good friend should have tonight. I want you to know that I'm here for you always.
XJoinOrDieX: ok, thank u
lostchildOKC: I care about you so much. You are one of the most important people in the world to me.
lostchildOKC: Also, I want to hit Mike with a baseball bat.
lostchildOKC: Okay, not really, but I do want to go to Bridgeport High School. Maybe a bunch of us can go over there and threaten him.
XJoinOrDieX: i don't know if ur being serious but if u are, please don't
lostchildOKC: Why?
XJoinOrDieX: because u would make things worse

Instantly, I understood that the possibility of me taking down Mike was as unlikely as my time machine revenge fantasy. Sure, I could wait for him outside his school and shout at him, but he wouldn't get expelled, or get in any kind of trouble actually, and it would only upset Alice more, which was the last thing I wanted.

XJoinOrDieX: i know what i told u was upsetting but u can't go around acting like a psycho saying you want to beat people with baseball bats

lostchildOKC: I just want to help you.

XJoinOrDieX: u already did

lostchildOKC: I didn't do anything.

lostchildOKC: And now I feel bad. It's like your comforting me and I should be comforting you.

XJoinOrDieX: well what i told you was heavy stuff and it would be a lot for anyone to hear

XJoinOrDieX: especially u

lostchildOKC: What's that supposed to mean?

XJoinOrDieX: don't take this the wrong way but ur kinda innocent

lostchildOKC: I'm not that innocent.

XJoinOrDieX: okayyy britney spears

lostchildOKC: hahaha

XJoinOrDieX: lol

XJoinOrDieX: i just wanted to tell someone was all. i didn't want u to be somebody u aren't

lostchildOKC: Are you going to be okay?

XJoinOrDieX: no

XJoinOrDieX: yeah i'll be fine

XJoinOrDieX: also i didn't tell u this part but i got to dump him. he wasn't expecting that because he thought i'd always have bad self-esteem or whatever. he didn't see that coming at all. that felt good.

lostchildOKC: Good.

XJoinOrDieX: u wanna know why u helped even if u think u didn't

lostchildOKC: Yeah.

XJoinOrDieX: if I wasn't friends with u and tiff i wouldn't have been able to do that

XJoinOrDieX: it's like what i said on new years

XJoinOrDieX: it was enough that u were around

XJoinOrDieX: i knew i'd still have u guys when we broke up

XJoinOrDieX: i wouldn't be alone

XJoinOrDieX: and i like hanging out with u more anyway

"I wouldn't be alone." No Alice, you wouldn't. I finally knew the right thing to say.

lostchildOKC: Do you want to hang out tomorrow?

XJoinOrDieX: yes :]

We said goodnight and signed off shortly after that. Anyway, I know this was a lot to read. Especially since I know (from reading my Friends page) that some of you have been raped or molested or felt as helpless as I did hearing about those things happening to your friends or family. But maybe if people share their stories on here and other people read them, and believe them, that's something.

I don't know what else to say. I hope you all are okay and taking care of yourselves. Good night, <3 Ellora.

Current Music: none

Thursday, February 8th, 2001 | 7:41 p.m.

I wandered the nearly empty hallways during a weird half-hour of downtime between when school ends and play rehearsal starts. A few kids lingered around for after-school activities. I peeked into classrooms to briefly spy on teachers who hadn't yet gone home. They hovered over their desks grading papers.

I walked to the nook outside Mrs. Ross' room, figuring I'd sit there and read before rehearsal, but Kendall Barton was sitting there in her Varsity soccer uniform, quietly crying. We made eye contact for a split second, and I kept right on walking. When I was almost at the stairs, I stopped and debated what to do. People at school were still talking about the topless pic she sent to Ian Marks.

I didn't want to get involved. I mean, for one, fuck Kendall. I didn't owe her to be nice. Also, maybe it was one of those things where it would be better if we both pretended it didn't happen. Sometimes I want to break down and cry, and if I did, I certainly wouldn't want anyone to see, or call more attention to it. But Kendall, from what I could remember, wasn't like that. I remembered all the (frankly trivial) things she got upset about in middle school: some boy that didn't like her, a fight with her mom and dad, and how she always wanted me and Jen/Jenny/Naomi to listen. I don't think she's the type of person that likes to spend lots of time alone.

I reluctantly walked backwards (I literally walked backwards) to the nook where Kendall was sitting.

"Hey," I said.

She didn't say anything. I could see in her eyes that I wasn't on the top of the list of people she wanted to see right now.

I dropped my backpack and sat down next to her in the nook. I didn't say anything to make her feel better or give her a hug or anything like that. I simply sat next to her and listened to her sniffle.

After a few minutes, she said, "Bye, I've got to go to practice" and stood up and left. Whatever. I wasn't even really thinking about her. I was thinking about Alice and how strange it was that I handled things better with Kendall than I did my own best friend. All by shutting up for once.

Current Music: Radiohead – "Meeting in the Aisle"

Tuesday, February 13th, 2001 | 6:05 p.m.

I haven't written in over a week because LiveJournal was down. Twice! Usually this happens for a few hours, but last week, as many of you know, it was down for a full two days. I was lost, lost, lost without an outlet to express myself. What do you people expect me to do, write only for myself? Hahahahahaha.

Current Music: Björk – "The Modern Things"

🔒 Wednesday, February 21, 2001 | 4:33 pm

Last night Alice and I finally went to Lucky's, the bar that doesn't card. I could only say I worked on Tuesdays for so long.

We met at her house, so she could do makeup that would make me look older. I sat in her room, her perfect room. She lined up her makeup on her desk. Foundations and lip glosses and mascaras and eye shadows.

"Don't overdo it," I said. "I want to go for a more natural look."

"Is that supposed to be a dig at me?" she asked. She looked back and forth between the makeup and my face, deciding how she could work with this material.

"No, your makeup looks good, but it wouldn't look right on me. All that eyeliner and stuff."

"Let's just try some things out. If you don't like it, we can take it off."

"Okay." I pointed to a severe metal object that looked like a tiny torture device. "What the hell is that?"

"That's an eyelash curler, nerd."

Alice picked up one foundation, shook her head, set it down, selected another one. She opened it, grabbed a brush and started painting away at my face.

"You're so tense, I can tell by the way you're sitting. Didn't your mom ever show you this stuff?" She paused and then quickly added, "Like, before."

"No, I never really asked."

"God, I loved her style. And hair."

"Yeah, well, that was her job."

Mom became a hairdresser because Grandma had been a hairdresser. She hung around the salon Grandma worked at in Queens and at age fourteen, shortly after they moved to Parkview, she started working with her at the new salon. It was her after-school job, her Earl's House, and at the end of high school, when her father got cancer, it became her full-time job. They needed to bring in more money, especially since her dad could no longer work. After a few years, she was so skilled that she got better jobs than Grandma ever did. Before she left, she worked at the fanciest salon in Rockdale, the city's wealthiest suburb.

"Maybe it's not my place to ask," Alice said. "But how is your mom missing?"

"What do you mean?" I asked.

"Like, when my parents got divorced, my dad totally dropped off the face of the earth, but it wasn't like I didn't know where he lived."

"Well, it's not like that."

"Doesn't she have any relatives you could call? See if they heard from her?"

"No," I said. "My grandma died when I was six. And my grandpa died a year before I was born. She missed him a lot. I think losing him was one of her reasons for keeping me."

"Keeping, as in—"

"As in not aborting."

"Wow, you went there." Alice pulled back from brushing the foundation on my face and looked at me. "C'mon, you don't really think that."

"Okay, she never outright said that, but I think she was in a bad mental place after he died. So, when she got pregnant with me, even though it was a one-night stand or something, she thought it was a sign to snap out of it. She said that to me once. 'You were a sign.' Like, now that her father was gone, she needed to bring someone new into her family."

"Whoa, like reincarnation? Was your mom Buddhist?"

"What? No." I rolled my eyes. "She meant it more symbolically. Anyway, I'm still pro-choice and I don't have any other relatives."

Alice leaned back again to examine her work. "I think this color is too light on you. What do you think?"

She held up a mirror and yup, it looked like I was trying to play a sick person in a play.

"This is the darkest shade I have. I actually don't use it, because it doesn't work for me. Maybe I can try blending it in more?"

"I think I should just take it off. I don't like the way it feels on my skin." Alice handed me some makeup removing wipes and I started rubbing my face with them. "It's not like my mom is missing and can never be found," I said. "I'm sure if I had the money to hire a private detective, I could track her down."

"What about the legal guardian? Couldn't he do that?"

"I can barely get him to sign forms from school. He's not going to hire a private detective. And he wouldn't want to. Sometimes, when I mention her, his face is like, 'How dare you bring up the woman who completely ruined my life.'"

I wasn't being fully honest. Even if Brian wanted to, I didn't want to search for her. I was afraid of what I might find. Maybe she lived in some sad state of squalor. Or worse—maybe she was thriving, successful, better off without me. What if she had a new family? Every potential outcome filled me with dread. Meanwhile, Brian and I remained in the same apartment where we all had once happily lived. If she wanted to come back and see us, she could easily. She didn't.

"Close your eyes," Alice said. She started brushing eyeshadow on my lids. "That's ridiculous. He should get it together. I can't stand it when grown-ups don't act like grown-ups."

"Yeah, that's what I used to think too, but—"

"Stop flinching or I'm going to mess this up."

"Sorry! It just feels so weird. Should we be doing eyeshadow? I said natural, remember?"

"I'm keeping it natural. It's brown. Anyway, what were you saying?"

"I used to think that too, about the legal guardian. That he should grow up. I mean, I still do. But lately I've realized that maybe he went through some horrible things. I'm trying to be more understanding."

"So what? I don't think I'm going to have kids, but I am not going to be like that when I'm older. I am going to have it completely together by the time I'm... twenty-six or something."

I was glad I had to keep my eyes closed while Alice penciled eyeliner, because otherwise I would have looked extremely skeptical. How did she see herself when she was twenty-six?

Wearing a business suit, eating three square meals a day, no depression?

"Yeah, but don't you ever think about your mom and dad or Greg as kids? And how they might have been going through some of the same stuff we are? Maybe even worse?"

"Sure, I think about that stuff, because Mom reminds me all the time. She loves to bring up how hard it was for her growing up compared to me. 'You're so spoiled. I grew up sharing a bedroom with my two sisters.'"

"That's not exactly what I meant." I sighed. "Other people's suffering is so loud."

"God, you're so emo. Look, sometimes I need my mom to be my mom and love me and not bring me into her adult problems. And I think you deserve the same. Open your eyes." We looked at each other. "Okay, that's good. Do you want to do your own mascara? I'd do it for you, but it's hard to do on another person."

"What's the point? I barely have any eyelashes."

"Fine then, you're done. Take a look."

She handed me the mirror. She'd done a variation of the same eye makeup she wore, but on my eyes it didn't look right. I didn't have those big doe eyes of hers with lids that eyeshadow and thick winged eyeliner would rest well on. I had a tiny eyelid crease where all the makeup she had put on me was now crammed. And then I felt weird thinking that. It was like how I had felt in that Chinese restaurant on Christmas.

"You're right, I wish my mom had shown me how she did her makeup," I said.

"Wow, you're welcome." She grabbed a lip gloss from her desk. "Maybe this will cheer you up. And quiet the screams of everyone's suffering."

It was a glittering pink lip gloss and Alice knew that anything sparkly pulls me in like a tractor beam.

"Nice," I said. I put it on.

"Keep it if you want. It looks good on you. Let's go."

I put it in my pocket and wished we weren't going. Why couldn't we spend the night in her room talking instead? I'd even let her do more of my makeup.

We were silent on the car ride into the city. Suddenly she said, "Oh my god, I just had the best idea."

"What?"

"You should look up your mom on the Internet."

Oh, Alice. Sometimes, in a role reversal, she was the innocent one.

"Uh, yeah. I already did that once or twice."

As soon as we entered Lucky's, I was certain we were going to get caught. I also realized I'd never ordered from a bar before and didn't know what to say. Should I get a beer? If so, what kind of beer? I tried to look for a sign that might be a menu, but there wasn't one, there was only the tap handles and I couldn't see what their names were and if I stumbled on a name, surely it would give me away. I thought of the whiskey Brian drank, but I figured someone who looked like me ordering whiskey would also stand out. Thinking of Brian's drinking depressed me, it was one of the reasons I didn't want to come here in the first place. I stood there half panicking and half frowning and when the bartender walked over, Alice took one look at me and said, "Two rum and Diet Cokes." He served us them without question.

Alice didn't look nervous at all. She handed me my drink and looked around the bar, said she was on the lookout for "cute people to flirt with." I dreaded her leaving me standing alone, but she didn't find anyone to her liking. There weren't many people in the place, which made me more anxious.

"Wow, it's dead tonight," she said, as if she was a regular.

After such a build-up, the whole experience was completely anticlimactic. We had our rum and cokes in this nearly empty bar, got bored, and went home.

Current Music: U.N.K.L.E – "Rabbit in your Headlights" (feat. Thom Yorke)

🔒 **Monday, February 26th, 2001 | 11:32 p.m.**

There won't be much to report this week because it's winter break and most of my friends are on the expensive school trip to France. Alice watched snobby French films in anticipation, while Tiff and Mal were mostly thrilled about how the trip's minimal adult supervision meant a whole week to fool around the City of Love. Meanwhile, I was stuck in Parkview. I'd like to go to Europe, but I'd really like to go to New York City. I've never gone anywhere. Okay, in third grade, Mom and Brian and I did go on a day trip to Niagara Falls, one of the seven wonders of the world. Honestly, I was not that impressed. You can only look at a big waterfall for so long.

I was surprised when Christopher instant messaged me asking if I wanted to come over for dinner. Considering all the European writers he worships, I assumed he was on the trip too.

I'd never been to his house. I figured he lived in a place like Alice's, so imagine my surprise when he picked me up and we approached The Pines. And yes, suddenly, everything about Christopher made a lot more sense. Of course he wasn't going on the France trip. I tried to focus my face on betraying no reaction to us pulling up to The Pines.

I'm ashamed to admit that I assumed everyone who lived in The Pines lived in pure squalor, or sterile prison cells. In reality, Christopher's apartment looked more inviting than mine. There were homey decorations, a lot of knick-knacks. Porcelain baby angel figurines lined up on shelves, things like that. I saw the boxy HP computer where Christopher posted on Harry Potter message boards and chatted to Dan.

Dev showed up for dinner too. It was clear he'd been over before. Christopher and his mom were sweet together. He would feign annoyance while calling her Mother ("Stop insisting Ellie have a third helping of casserole, Mother!"), but it was a big act. She insisted I call her Susan and she called me "honey" a lot, which I liked. Am I such a glutton for a mother figure?

On the way home, Christopher detoured and pulled into an empty parking lot. He handed me a thin black cigarette.

"This is a clove," he said. "Don't inhale."

"Your mom's really nice," I said. "Tell her thanks for dinner again."

"She liked you." He held his own clove like he was posing for a photograph. "I wanted to host while Tiff and Alice were away. So they wouldn't be offended by their lack of invitation."

"Why wouldn't you invite them?"

"I don't know, sometimes I don't relate to them at all."

"Who do you relate to?" I was fishing here, because I knew what the answer would be.

"You."

And still, I couldn't help but ruin the moment with sarcasm. "Why? Because we're both not rich?"

"No," he sighed. "Dig a little deeper."

We smoked our cloves in silence.

"How did it go with Dan?" I asked. "Did you meet up at the mall?"

"Indeed, we did. It was fine."

"Just fine?"

"We had a fun evening. We went to Game Stop and the arcade. We got Orange Julius. It was all very date-like. But we didn't have chemistry."

"So, nothing happened?"

He waved his hand in the air. "We made out, or whatever, in his car."

What base was "whatever?" I figured it was too nosy a question to ask.

"We're going to stay friends, though. We talked about it online when we both got home," he said.

"I still can't believe you met someone from the Internet," I said, starry-eyed. I blew clove smoke and imagined Christopher bringing home an Internet boy to meet his mom.

"Maybe it's not my place to ask," I said, aware that I was imitating Alice's own preemptive words to me. "But is your dad still in the picture?"

Christopher waved his hand around again. "Somewhat."

"They're divorced?"

"No, he's incarcerated."

"What?"

"He's in prison, Ellie."

I let that bombshell land. Christopher's dad was in jail? For what? I wanted to ask, but he didn't offer that information, and again, I felt I couldn't pry anymore. We changed the subject and then he drove me home.

Current Music: Sheryl Crow – "Sweet Rosalyn"

🔒 Thursday, March 1st, 2001 | 11:37 p.m.

"Are you planning on going to Steadmans any time soon?" I asked. "There's nothing to eat around here."

For most of the winter, Brian had doubled down on his post-work routine of drinking on the couch and turning the TV up to a blurry volume. Tonight was no different. I opened an empty cupboard and slammed it shut.

"Did you hear what I said?" He avoided eye contact and kept staring at the television. "Are you okay?"

Without speaking, he reached into his back pocket and placed his wallet on the coffee table. I looked at it and then back at him.

"Seriously?"

"Yeah, go get whatever you want."

His voice sounded flat, faraway. On *Survivor*, one of the contestants had passed out and fallen into the campfire. He ran screaming into the water, to ease the pain from third-degree burns on his hands.

"I can't watch this." I took forty dollars from his wallet and threw it back at him.

I walked to Steadmans just to get out of the apartment. I thought of wanting to be the type of person who was understanding of people's problems and then I thought of Alice saying that adults' problems should not be our problems. Unreliability was Brian's most reliable quality, but this food situation was next level. If he couldn't get it together enough to buy groceries, was he going to remember to pay rent? The electricity bill? Would he stop going to his job? I could feel my shoulders tense up as I stomped home with the groceries. Heavy plastic bags wore down my wrists as I blew cold angry breaths into the air.

Current Music: Radiohead – "Climbing Up the Walls"

Saturday, March 10th, 2001 | 1:13 p.m.

I was on counter at Earl's House. I was tired and people's voices were loud and the lights were loud. No one asked me where I was from, no one asked me anything. They only yelled because I was slow or I didn't understand their order. I fantasized about faking fainting to get out of my shift.

Angie took orders at the register next to mine and I could see her look over every time I asked customers to repeat themselves.

"The combo meal," a man said, his wife and three kids in tow. Even his children were staring at me like I was an idiot.

I needed to get more sleep. It was possibly my fault that I was sleep-deprived, because I often stayed up too late on the Internet, but wasn't it also the world's fault? School began at 7:30 a.m., which was an unnatural start time for my body, and then I had a long strenuous day of AP classes, and then sometimes play rehearsal, and then sometimes this job, and everything involved talking to people, which was so draining. I imagined lying down in a large open field for hours, with no sensory stimulation except the occasional cool breeze.

"We want the combo meal," the man shouted. "It's not $9.99, it's $8.99. I was just in here last week."

"That's what it's saying," I said weakly.

"Are you trying to tell me the price changed in a week?"

I wanted to scream or say, "Fuck you." I was able to stop myself, but not without making a weird agonized "AhHhHHhh" noise of frustration. The man stared at me like I was a freak.

"Ellora!" Angie said. "Take a five. And wait for me by the back room."

As I walked away, I saw her calmly take over for me.

"I'm so sorry about that, sir," she said, her voice like butter.

"Combo meal, right?"

I waited by the break room. I was surely getting let go. I had a 4.0 GPA at school. Why couldn't I do this simple job? This job where I felt superior to everybody because I had that perfect GPA, which made me feel like an asshole, but I guess the joke was on me because I was about to be fired. I was a failure, I was a failure. I'd be fired from every job, I wouldn't be able to cut it in the real world. I wouldn't be able to support myself as a waitress while I went on auditions and waited for my big break. I squeezed my face together over and over in a repetitive cringing motion until I saw Angie arrive in the back room. She did not look happy.

Be professional, I thought. Charm her, think "how to win friends and influence people and keep this job." Instead, I immediately blurted out, "Please don't fire me," before she even said anything. "I need to keep this job. I need to make sure I have money for emergencies."

A sympathetic look flashed across her face, before she resumed frowning.

"I'm not firing you," she said. "This is a warning. I try to put you on runner or dishwasher as much as I can, but on Friday nights, I need counter people. I know you're... shy and it isn't easy for you. And I know half of our customers are creeps or assholes, but this is the job you signed up for. You've got to pull it together."

I nodded. "I will, I will. Thank you. I can go back now."

Angie stopped me before I could return to my register. "No. Take the rest of the night off. I'll still clock you out at ten, but this means you've got to bring your A-game next time."

Current Music: Hole – "Celebrity Skin"

It was one of those freakish days in mid-March when the temperature shot up to sixty-two degrees. It had been below freezing the day before. Everyone rolled into school wearing khaki cargo shorts and t-shirts.

After school, I biked home and rode a few laps around one of the suburban developments. I felt happy and in my body, momentarily freed from the clutter in my head. I wish I'd stayed outside longer, because if I had, I wouldn't have been home to answer the phone. It was Angie, saying that a dishwasher had called in sick. Was I available to come in and do dishes for two hours during the rush? She would pay me time and a half. I knew I couldn't say no.

I had finished changing into my uniform when our door buzzer rang. I hesitated. Nobody ever rang our buzzer. We never had visitors.

"Hello?"

"Ellie?" a voice said.

"Yeah."

"It's Tiff. Can you let me in?"

I hadn't recognized her voice. It sounded strangled, garbled. I buzzed her in, worried about her seeing my small apartment, until I opened the door and realized my apartment would be the last of her concerns. Tiff was crying, really ugly crying. I'd never seen her shed so much as a tear before. As usual, she carried her trumpet and her skateboard, and she immediately dropped them both on the floor. I noticed a bloody gash on her upper cheek below her eye.

"He caught us," she said. "Mal's dad."

She was sobbing so hard it took her a few tries to tell me the story, but essentially: she'd gone over to Mal's house after jazz band and they'd been fooling around on the couch. Her parents were usually at work, but Mal's dad had stayed home that day for some reason. He walked downstairs and saw them.

"Did he do that to your eye?" I asked.

"No, not really."

"No or not really?"

"Not intentionally. That's how I got away. He started yelling and grabbed me and said you're not going to turn my daughter into someone like you. I kicked him and pulled away as hard as I could. When he let go, I fell against the coffee table. He was shocked and actually said, 'I'm sorry.' How fucked up is that? But it gave me time to grab my things and run away."

Tiff burst into tears again. "She should have run with me, I just left her there." She hit my door, repeatedly saying, "I suck, I suck," until I shouted "Tiff, stop!" and she backed away, paced around my living room for a few seconds, before heading for the door again. "I've got to go back and get her."

I blocked her path. "You cannot go back there."

She nodded and sat down on the couch and cried some more. "I just want to go home. But my mom will ask what happened. I can't deal with that."

"Then stay here for now. We'll figure things out," I said.

Tiff sniffled and pointed at my Earl's House t-shirt and baseball cap. "Aren't you going to work?"

"Shit!" I looked at the clock. "I can't call out."

If I didn't show up, I would surely be fired. I considered calling back and saying an emergency had come up and I wouldn't be able to cover after all. Somehow, I didn't think that would be acceptable either.

"Go to work. I don't want you to get in trouble."

"I'll be back in three hours at the most," I said. "Stay here. Watch TV. Do not go back to Mal's."

"Okay," she said.

"Oh, and if the legal guardian comes home, tell him you're

my friend and I got called in to work. He'll probably want to nap on that couch, so hang out in my room until I get back. He won't care that you're here."

"Okay."

"We'll figure things out. I promise, it'll be okay."

I gave her a hug and she half-hugged me back before I biked to work. The whole time there I fretted over whether I did the right thing. Should I have said screw my job and the inevitable consequences and stayed for Tiff? I attacked the dishes with steel sponges and ran the water as hot as I could tolerate. Angie ducked in once and nodded approvingly.

As soon as my shift ended, I jumped on my bike. While it was probably only due to the proximity of my place to Mal's, I was excited that Tiff had run to me in a time of crisis. I felt ashamed thinking that, but it didn't stop me from fantasizing about ways to cheer her up when I returned home. I imagined her sitting on my bed and making her laugh and flushed with shame again.

When I turned into the apartment parking lot, I was struck by the sight of Tiff standing under one of the streetlights, perfectly lit. She leaned on the post, her arms crossed. She didn't see me, she was watching Brian skateboard around on her board. He moved with surprising speed and even though it was dark, I could see a lightness in his face that I had not seen in a long time. After gaining momentum, he did a kickflip down the apartment building's front stairs. Tiff looked impressed and she never looked impressed. He passed the board back to her.

I braked to a stop a few feet away. "Um, hi."

"Ellie!" Tiff said. She said my name like we were two people being reunited after months apart, not someone I'd seen sobbing three hours ago.

Brian raised his hand in greeting and then, without a word, went inside.

Tiff and I faced each other, her board under her arm. I held the handlebars of my bike. I waited for her to say something about Mal and her dad. Instead, she said, "You didn't have to lie, you know."

"What?"

"That time Mal and I dropped you off. He was the guy passed out."

With everything that had happened, I had completely forgotten about that.

"Yeah, sorry."

"It's cool. He's cool. Was it weird to see us bro-ing out?"

"No. Actually yeah, it was weird. How'd that happen?"

"I was watching TV when he came in. I told him what you told me to say. That I was your friend and I was waiting for you to come back from work. I could tell he was trying not to look at my eye or notice that I'd been crying. I was going to go hang out in your room, but he asked me about my board. We started talking about skating and then we came out here." She shrugged. "How was work?"

"It was whatever," I said. "Tiff."

"Yeah?"

"Nothing."

We briefly went inside so she could call her parents and then we sat in the parking lot waiting for them to pick her up. I couldn't believe she was pretending like what happened didn't happen, so I asked, "What are you going to tell your parents about your eye?"

"Tell them it happened skating. They'll buy it."

For a second, I saw a flash on her face of the mess she'd been before, then she shifted her posture, and her cool reserve returned.

"You'll see Mal in school tomorrow, you guys can talk," I said. "I'm sure everything will be okay."

"Yeah."

We talked about nothing after that, but when her mom and dad pulled up, she gave me a strong hug.

Back in the apartment, Brian read a book on the couch. He wasn't drinking and the TV was off. He wore reading glasses that I'd never seen him wear before. Without looking up, he asked, "Is your friend going to be all right?"

"Yeah, I think so. Thank you."

He nodded. I grabbed a book from my room and sat at the kitchen table to read too. It made me think of when I was small and we'd go to the library together and read in those beanbag chairs.

After about a half hour, he announced he was going to bed early. "I'm beat, that was the most exercise I've done in years." He looked like he wanted to say something else, but all he said was, "Goodnight, Ellora. Don't stay up on the computer all night."

As soon as he closed the door to his room, I jumped on the computer and signed online. I looked for Tiff or Mal or Alice on AIM but none of them were online. I plugged my headphones into the computer and turned on the song written below. I thought it would make me feel hopeful about the world. I'd listen and marvel in wonder about the feelings everyone keeps hidden, maybe for survival. I surprised myself by bursting into tears about the same thing instead.

Current Music: Smashing Pumpkins – "Tonight Tonight"

Monday March 19th, 2001 | 4:00 p.m.

Tiff and Mal broke up. Obviously because of her dad. Friday

morning, the day after the incident, they looked solemn and cuddled together more than usual in the nook before school. But by lunch, I saw Tiff whisper something in Mal's ear and they both laughed. What an intimate gesture. So, I thought everything would be fine, but today, when I got to the nook, Christopher and Alice were sitting with Tiff, who had her head in her hands. Mal had called on Sunday night, and calmly, coldly, without any explanation, told her they were done.

Current Music: Fiona Apple – "Carrion"

🔒 **Wednesday March 21st, 2001** | 6:58 p.m.

Between classes, I spotted Mal's blue hair with barrette clips and elbowed my way past people to catch up with her. I hated seeing Tiff so miserable, and I knew why they had broken up, and I still felt useless from last week when everything had happened in the first place.

"Mal, I don't know how to say this, but—you shouldn't care what your dad thinks," I said. "You and Tiff are great together. You can get through this. We'll be there for you."

She stopped walking and shot me the meanest look. "You don't know me, you don't know my life."

"I—I didn't mean to sound like I did. I just wanted you to know—"

"God, shut up," she groaned. "Everyone knows who you used to hang out with."

"What?"

"Stop acting like you're so alternative and pro-gay rights. If you hadn't done that sad presentation about wanting to kill yourself, you'd still be following Jenny Porter around."

Jenny's clique had dumped me before the Fiona Apple presentation, not after. Mal had it all wrong, but I was shocked into silence by her cruelty. How did she even know about that presentation? She hadn't been in that class, or in Group. Did everyone in school see me this way?

Mal wasn't done. "You know, the best thing about breaking up with Tiff is not having to spend time with her friends anymore. You're all so pretentious."

"We're your friends too," I said.

"No, you're not. You look down on me, because I've never heard of some dead writer or because I'm not in your AP US History study group writing annoying skits about Andrew Jackson. God, get a life. You're so pretentious," she said again. "And you're hypocrites. Take Christopher, with his fancy way of talking, and acting like he waltzed out of Ancient Greece. Everyone knows his mom's white trash and his dad's in jail for meth. And Alice, lecturing everybody on riot grrrl feminism. How feminist is anorexia?"

"That's fucked up. It's fucked up you're saying this stuff."

"You know I'm right," she said. "Because you, Ellie, you are the biggest poseur of them all."

Have you heard of this French term "l'esprit de l'escalier?" I learned about it in the last book I read (which was by a living writer, not a dead one, thank you very much). Basically, it's when you come up with a great comeback long after the moment has passed. I've since thought of many comebacks to say to Mal, but in the moment, she'd sliced a clean incision into my deepest insecurities, so I could only stand there speechless, with my guts spilled out on the floor.

Current Music: Tori Amos – "Waitress"

Friday March 23rd, 2001 | 7:02 p.m.

Tiff's heartbreak continues, it's reaching epic levels. Her usual goofy, shit-eating grin has been replaced by a brooding mope. At lunch, she chugged a half-gallon of milk.

"Aren't you lactose intolerant?" Dev asked.

There has been an empty space at our lunch table until today. Kendall Barton, of all people, brought her lunch and sat with us, in the spot between Tiff and Alice, where Mal used to sit. Right across from me. I avoided eye contact. We had not interacted since that day I sat with her crying in the nook. Dev's eyes bugged out the second she sat down and I knew he was trying to not look at her boobs. Tiff barely noticed anything different. She spent lunch staring at the back of Mal's head, where she sat with another clique now, pop-punk stoners. Christopher was at a loss for how to speak to a new person.

It was Alice, of course, who swiftly turned to Kendall and started talking with her, about something that had happened in gym class. She acted like Kendall sat with us every day.

Current Music: Sublime – "Santeria"

Wednesday March 28th, 2001 | 10:02 p.m.

At Alice's house we worked on a presentation about the expansion of the railroads during the Gilded Age. Tiff was not pulling her weight. She looked seconds away from crying at any moment and ran a marker over the same spot on our poster again and again.

"Okay, stop, this presentation can wait," Alice said. "You know Mrs. Ross is going to give us an A anyway. It hurts to see you like this. Talk."

Tiff capped the marker and didn't say anything for a while. Finally, she said, "It's just hard seeing her. I can mostly avoid her, since we're not in the same classes, but there's still jazz band. I have to sit in the same room with her and breathe the same air as her and we're going to have gigs every other weekend together for the rest of the year and next year too."

"Sorry, Tiff," I said.

"I guess I better get used to it. When Hannah and Rob broke up earlier this year, there was some drama, and Mr. Flick gave the jazz band this lecture about dating your band members. He said, 'You want to be a real working musician? Then prepare to shit where you eat, because when you practice eighty hours a week, those are the only people you see. You think a few hours of jazz band is hard? Boo-hoo, try going on tour with your ex-old lady. That's twenty-four hours a day you spend together. On the bus, on stage, or back at the hotel, where you have the pleasure of hearing her and her new fella, who is also in the band, in the next room—"

"This story sounds completely inappropriate," Alice said. "I really don't want to hear about Mr. Flick. I'll be back." She ran upstairs.

"Did he really say 'prepare to shit where you eat?'" I asked.

Alice returned holding a pint of ice cream, a spoon, and a stack of *Cosmopolitan* magazines. She jumped on the couch, tossed ice cream and spoon to Tiff and opened the top magazine to a random page.

She cleared her throat. "'16 Surprising Ways to Please Your Man. Number 1: Make two fists around his shaft and twist them in opposite directions as fast as you can.'"

Tiff ate ice cream and moped some more, but I caught her stifling a laugh when Alice read, "'Take his penis between your open palms and, using your hands like ping pong paddles, very lightly bat it back and forth.'"

"No way. It does not say that!" Tiff tossed the ice cream to me and grabbed the magazine from Alice. She read, "'Get a glazed donut and stick it around his you-know-what. Nibble around the donut while stopping to take a few licks from the real treat every now and then.'" She dropped the magazine in her lap. "Wow, straight people are really weird."

"I'm only half-straight," Alice said. "And I will never put a donut around a guy's dick."

"No dick donuts," I confirmed.

We read some more absurd *Cosmo* sex tips to each other, trying to top each other by finding the grossest and weirdest suggestions.

"Well, well, well, it's good to see you finally crack a smile again," Alice said to Tiff. "I'll admit, this brilliant operation was not completely selfless. My birthday's on Saturday and it would be a real bummer if you moped through the whole thing, because I have something nice planned for us."

"I'm not going to ruin your birthday," Tiff said. "What's the plan?"

"I thought about having a party, but I decided we could go to Serenity Salon and have like, a spa day. We'll get massages and our hair done."

"Like a makeover?" Tiff made a disgusted face.

"Don't worry, they're not going to do anything girly to you. You can freshen up your bowl cut." She tousled Tiff's hair. "It's just a relaxing thing to do. They pamper you. My mom's paying for everything, I already asked. I go there with her every month and this time I wanted to go with my two best friends. Treat them." She turned to me. "That okay with you? Saturday, 2 p.m. You're not working?"

I shook my head and tried to make my expression neutral. Serenity Salon was the salon where my mom used to work.

Lately, there were flinty reminders of her everywhere.

Current Music: Fiona Apple – "A Mistake"

🔒 Saturday, March 31st, 2001 | 12:56 p.m.

A short history of hairstyles in my apartment:

Mom had long black hair that she often wore in an elegant updo, a feminine twist of knots piled on her head. Sometimes she'd do this just to go to Steadmans. I once tried to do this look for a seventh grade dance, but I couldn't get it to stay. I think you need hairspray and a lot of pins.

Shortly after we moved into the apartment that we live in now, Mom and Brian bleached each other's hair blonde. Remember: this was the early 90s, grunge was in. They screamed and laughed at each other in the bathroom because the bleach chemicals burned. I felt left out and asked if I could dye my hair too. Mom said no, it would damage my hair. Well, then why do you get to do it, I asked. Maybe it was one of those things grown-ups did—like smoking—that was bad for you but perfectly allowed for them. I kept pestering, until she finally relented and bleached a single section of my hair, no thicker than a crayon. I showed it to people at school, who were less impressed. Half the girls were natural blondes. And the current hair trend was wrapping your hair in spiral friendship bracelets, a rainbow staircase of embroidery thread.

Mom soon dyed her hair back to its natural black, but Brian kept some variant of his longish bleached hair for a long time. He let the roots grow out. I was glad when he cut it, he looked mildly demented. Now he keeps his hair its natural dark brown and brutally short. Close to the scalp.

As for me, I have slightly-above-shoulder-length black hair in a shade one notch lighter than Mom's. When it gets too long, I simply put it in a ponytail and chop part of the ponytail off. No one has cut my hair professionally since Mom.

One of my happiest memories is when she'd take me to her salon, as opposed to simply cutting my hair in the apartment. I'd sit in her chair and she'd treat me like I was one of her clients, an important one. I wasn't getting anything special, just regular maintenance on my Asian bowl cut, much like the one Tiff still has. But I loved the way she looked at me, the feeling of her lasered attention, like I was a challenging puzzle to be solved. My favorite part though, was when she'd wash my hair before the cut itself. I'd lean back into the bowl, and she'd massage my scalp with shampoo, followed by gentle detangler. She'd wrap my head and neck in a warm towel.

This is going to sound a little weird, but sometimes at night I massage my head like that with my own hands. I'm not pretending it's her or anything, it's just a reassuring touch, the way other people hug themselves or touch their faces.

Current Music: Fiona Apple – "Love Ridden"

Saturday, March 31st, 2001 | 9:33 p.m.

"Today, I am as old as ABBA's 'Dancing Queen,'" Alice said.

We were in the car, on the way to the salon. Alice's mom drove. "So, what kind of styles are you girls getting?" she asked.

Tiff shrugged. She was still feeling down. "Just a trim, probably."

"I'm mostly looking forward to getting my hair professionally washed," I said. "Will they wash our hair over those porcelain bowls?"

"Yeah, they always do that," Alice said.

"You should chat with your stylist about what's right for you," chirped Mrs. Lewis. "They might have some ideas on what will look best for your face shape."

"I'm going to get a bob," Alice said. "Like Louise Brooks."

Louise Brooks was a beautiful silent film star with a 1920s flapper haircut. She was glamorous, bisexual, and spent her last days living as a tragic recluse in our city. Alice idolizes her.

"Tiff," said Mrs. Lewis. Her eyes flashed in the rearview mirror. "I heard you went through a hard break-up recently. You know what they say. 'You gotta wash that—"

"Mom," Alice warned.

She put her hands up briefly before placing them back on the steering wheel. "All I'm saying is that a haircut is sometimes the pick-me-up you need after a heartbreak."

"Yeah, cool, thanks for taking us, Mrs. Lewis," Tiff said, forcing a smile. "It's really cool of you."

The salon didn't look at all like how I remembered. My memory might have been inaccurate, or more likely, they remodeled since the early 90s. They washed our hair in porcelain bowls, and that part was as great as I remembered. In the chair, the hairstylist asked what I was looking to do today. I asked if I could dye my hair blonde.

She laughed. "With your dark hair, we'd need to triple process it. You'd be here all day long."

"Oh."

"How about some red highlights?"

I didn't really want that, but I said yes.

"And a nice trim," she said. "You've got quite a lot of split ends, hon."

She went to work. Apparently, you needed to make small talk with the hairdresser while she cuts your hair. I saw Alice's mom do this and Tiff, who can talk to anybody.

"How long have you worked here?" I blurted out.

"Oh!" she said. I realized that was a nosy question, or maybe I'd asked it in a rude way. "Almost two years."

There wasn't a chance she would have known Mom then. "Did you ever hear of a Jane working here? Seven years ago? Asian? She's a relative of mine."

"Hmm, doesn't ring a bell. But that's quite a while ago. No one's been here that long. We have different owners now."

I fell quiet and tried to think of other ideas of what to talk about. Perhaps I should have brought some questions in advance. She made the chitchat going forward.

"You in high school, hon?"

"Yeah, I'm a junior."

"What do you plan to do after you graduate?"

"I want to be an actress."

"Oh!" she said again. She sounded surprised and I tried not to read too much into it. Was she surprised that someone like me wanted to be an actress? Or was she already skeptical at my chances?

"I'm in the school play," I added.

"That's great!"

I gave up on the small talk after that and watched her paint strips of my hair and press them in tin foil. Then I had to go sit under a light. Alice was doing the same. She had touched up the roots on her dyed black hair. And her Louise Brooks bob looked perfect. It was right for her face shape, but everything was right for her face.

The trim felt nice, but my highlights looked stupid. They were very red and didn't look natural. I made a good show of liking them though, I didn't want to seem ungrateful.

It was Tiff who had the greatest transformation. Her stylist had been younger, with a matte face full of makeup, a rockabilly bouffant wrapped in a red bandana, and tattoos peeking out from under rolled-up sleeves.

She'd given Tiff a buzz cut. Her bowl cut was gone and she no longer looked like a little kid. She looked like a badass.

"Sick," Tiff said. She ran her hand over her head.

Her stylist laughed. She unhooked the cape from around Tiff's neck. "Helloooo, heartbreaker. Let me grab a mirror, so you can take a look at the back."

Tiff stood up and examined her new appearance in the mirror. She smiled in a way that I'd seen her smile at Mal before, but this time, she was looking that way at herself.

Current Music: Beastie Boys – "Intergalactic"

Monday, April 2nd, 2001 | 5:06 p.m.

"My mom hates my haircut," Tiff announced at lunch. "She started crying when she saw it. She said, 'I don't know why you'd choose to do that to yourself.'"

"What'd your dad say?" Alice asked.

"He said I looked like I was about to enroll in the military."

"Did you tell him that you wouldn't be allowed in the military?"

"Uh, no Alice, somehow it didn't feel like the right time to remind him I'm a big homo."

"'Don't ask, don't tell.' What crap," piped in Dev.

"Wait, you're pro-gays joining the military?" Alice asked.

"Of course I am!" Dev said. "That crap was started by your

big, bad, liberal blowjob daddy Bill Clinton. Everybody should have the right to enlist. Gay, straight, bisexual—as long as you want to serve our beautiful country, be loud and proud."

"You are the weirdest Republican ever," Alice said.

"Don't let the parental units grind you down," Dev said to Tiff. "You look fly, my friend."

Christopher stared at me, like he was trying to figure something out. "Did you also... alter your appearance?"

"I got highlights," I said.

"Ah, yes. The stripes."

"Shut up. I know it doesn't look good."

You've got to give my friends credit for keeping it real. No one argued me with me to make me feel better. Dev slapped me on the shoulder as consolation. Only Kendall, who was now sitting with us every day at lunch, said quietly, "You look fine, Ellie."

Current Music: Ben Folds Five – "Best Imitation of Myself"

Friday, April 6th, 2001 | 7:57 p.m.

Well, it finally happened. I'm nearly seventeen and I've just had my first kiss. It was dress rehearsal week and we did the kiss for real. At this rate, I'm on track for losing my virginity around age thirty.

I've embraced the idea of the play being my first kiss. Sure, some of you had super romantic first kisses with the loves of your lives, but I know that for an equal amount of you, it was slobbery and nothing special. Is that really any better than your first kiss being a stage kiss?

There was so much excitement leading up to dress rehearsal

week that I didn't have much time to be nervous about the kiss anyway. We got fitted for our costumes. While the dowdy long skirt and cardigan of a 1950s secretary would never be something I'd wear in my real life, there was still a magic to embodying a character, even if that character was Franny Smith, who ate solitary dinners with her cat and believed the solution to all her problems would be a man. And the lights, oh the lights and the stage crew made it real. Right now, there was only Ms. Millhauser sitting out there giving us notes, but next week, there'd be a full auditorium. My friends would be there, cheering me on.

I exited stage left, telling the other office girls I was looking forward to another Friday night with my cat, while hanging my head, as per the stage direction. Backstage, I remained in character and sat alone. I concentrated on my own deep, existential emptiness and tried to apply those feelings to Franny's more surface-level lack of self-esteem and old-fashioned attitudes about dating.

Jay Arflin strolled backstage, the scene partner I'd lock lips with in approximately five scenes.

"Hey, we've got a big scene coming up," he said.

"Yeah. No more fake air-kissing. The real McCoy."

God, this forced joking was awkward, life was so awkward. Jay added, "I had to tell Erin about it. I didn't want her to be surprised when she came to see me in the play. Erin is my girlfriend."

"I know."

Jay talked about his girlfriend constantly. He did it so much that at first I thought she was his beard (he was a theatre kid, after all), until I realized he was simply insecure and wanted everyone to know he was getting laid.

"She was pissed. And I told her, that's what's in the script? I didn't write this stupid play."

"This play is total sexist crap," I said.

"Yeah. And then she asked, 'Who's playing Franny? The girl you kiss.' I told her it was you and then she was like, 'Okay, fine.'"

What the hell was that supposed to mean?

"Yeah, I got it," I said. "We're all professionals here."

When the time came for the kiss, I was still so shocked by how rude Jay had been that I was thrown off by the well-acted look of adoration on his face.

"'Franny,'" he said. "'I'm sorry—Miss. Smith. Or, may I call you Franny? I must confess I've always been quite fond of you.'"

"'Oh, Will, I've always been fond of you too,'" I said.

I closed my eyes and he pressed his lips to mine. We basically pushed our faces together, that was it. We both had chapped lips. I wrapped my arms around his neck, like the blocking we practiced. And three seconds later, bent my knee to raise one leg in the air, another part of the blocking. This was supposed to be a comic moment, where mousy Franny Smith imitated her favorite romantic movie heroines. We split apart.

"'And now I'm very, very fond of you,'" I said. The lights dimmed, end of scene.

When the lights came back up, Ms. Millhauser gave us some notes. "I know the first run through of the kiss is awkward," she said. "But Ellora, you looked terrified. Remember, Franny likes this guy! She secretly liked him the entire play. Girl, loosen up a bit!"

I swear to god, my humiliation never ends.

Current Music: Ben Folds Five – "Satan is My Master"

Tuesday, April 10th, 2001 | 11:30 p.m.

Tonight, around 5 p.m., I signed on AIM. Alice was online.

> **lostchildOKC:** Hello
> **XJoinOrDieX:** hey
> **lostchildOKC:** Do you want to do something tonight?
> **XJoinOrDieX:** sure, what are u thinking
> **XJoinOrDieX:** o god, i see that yr typing a lot

I wasn't typing a lot, I was typing and hesitating and then backspacing and typing again.

> **lostchildOKC:** I don't know how to say this, but it's my birthday?
> **XJoinOrDieX:** what?!
> **XJoinOrDieX:** wtf
> **XJoinOrDieX:** why didn't u say anything at school today
> **lostchildOKC:** *shrug*
> **XJoinOrDieX:** it was just my birthday and u heard me talk about that for days
> **XJoinOrDieX:** what do u want to do?
> **XJoinOrDieX:** tiff says whatever we do invite the legal guardian
> **XJoinOrDieX:** tiff's here btw
> **XJoinOrDieX:** she can't stop talking about how he's tony hawk or something. she's obsessed she
> **XJoinOrDieX:** I AM NOT OBSESSED
> **XJoinOrDieX:** THIS IS TIFF

They were hanging out without me? Sure, I hung out with Alice without Tiff, but I couldn't believe they were doing this on my birthday of all days, except that was irrational, because they hadn't known it was my birthday. I considered signing off in a fury. They'd hear the door slam sound effect and think "what the hell, where did she go." I'd be hiding in my bed under the covers feeling sorry for myself.

> **XJoinOrDieX:** happy birthday ellie!
>
> **XJoinOrDieX:** let's partysklf
>
> **XJoinOrDieX:** wifjeilwfl:;
>
> **XJoinOrDieX:** this is alice again, i knocked tiff off the computer
>
> **XJoinOrDieX:** i knocked her out cold
>
> **XJoinOrDieX:** she's lying unconscious right now
>
> **lostchildOKC:** haha
>
> **XJoinOrDieX:** so what are we doing birthday girl
>
> **lostchildOKC:** I don't know. What do you guys think?
>
> **XJoinOrDieX:** oh my god it's yr birthday. u get to pick!
>
> **lostchildOKC:** Maybe go to Steadmans? Do the cookie cake writing thing?
>
> **XJoinOrDieX:** okayyyy sounds good
>
> **XJoinOrDieX:** tiff and i will get u in 20 minutes

It took nearly an hour, but finally Alice and Tiff picked me up and we headed to Steadmans. The cookie cake writing thing was this recurring gag we had with the bakery department, where we tried to get them to write something offensive on a cookie cake. They won't print something outright offensive, no swear words, so the game is to get them to either print a) something offensive that they don't realize is offensive or b) something potentially offensive that we can defend our right to print by claiming innocent intent.

Around Christmas, we got a cookie cake with "God NOT Jesus" printed. The man taking our order frowned, but reluctantly agreed when we explained our reasoning. God didn't get enough credit on Christmas, we insisted. It was all about Jesus, Jesus, Jesus, and wasn't God truly the Big Kahuna? Dev ordered a cake that said "Skeet skeet skeet skeet" on it, which is rap music slang for ejaculate, so bless the unassuming lady who essentially wrote "Cum cum cum cum" in nice cursive on that cookie cake.

I wanted my birthday cake to be a tribute to Fiona Apple. I thought of asking the baker to print the full 90-word title of her masterpiece *When the Pawn...* but that wouldn't have been secretly offensive. Then I had a stroke of genius. Fiona, as many of you know, made a brilliant speech when she won an MTV Music Video Award. She talked about how false celebrities were and how you should not imitate your life around them. She notoriously said, "This world is bullshit." I went to Altavista BabelFish and translated the phrase into Mandarin.

There was a teenage boy, not much older than me, working at the bakery. He squinted at a piece of paper, where I'd written these characters:

这个世界是狗屁

"I don't get paid enough to write in other languages," he grumbled.

"All you have to do is copy the lines. It's easy," I said.

"It's her birthday, man," Tiff said.

"What does it say?" he asked.

"It says happy birthday, obviously," Alice said. "In Chinese."

Thirty minutes later I held my "This world is bullshit" birthday cookie cake. We ate it right there in the parking lot, sitting on the hood of Alice's car. She had a few bites. Steadmans shoppers gave us dirty looks like we were a bunch of loitering delinquents. We glowered right back. This world is such bullshit. 这个世界是狗屁. Best birthday ever.

Current Music: Fiona Apple – "Criminal"

Sunday, April 15th, 2001 | 1:01 p.m.

For weeks, I had been having these terrible stress dreams where I forget my lines on opening night, or I find myself in an entirely different play. None of this happened. Every night I remembered all my lines perfectly, and said them the way I wanted to, and the audience even laughed at my character's cheesy jokes. And I loosened up about the damn kiss after that dress rehearsal's mortifying run-through. I think when I have my second kiss, aka my first kiss outside the framework of a fictional world, it'll probably follow the same path. Initially, I'll be awkward as hell, then I'll get more practice and be able to bring some real romance. And I could make this look good, like I did on stage, I'm not an undateable alien. Someone even whistled from the audience during the kiss scene. Pretty sure it was Tiff.

The whole lunch table came out to see me on Thursday, opening night. Alice brought flowers. A sweet gesture, though I hate flowers. I get stressed out thinking about how they're already on their way to dying.

On closing night of the play, the whole cast went out to Denny's to celebrate. It was a nice change to be hanging out with some new people and I don't think I was too awkward. We shared the same passion and I felt a special bond with them over that. Over and over, I thought: this is what I want to be doing for the rest of my life, and I'm certain it was reflected in the goofy grin I had on my face the entire weekend.

Current Music: Weezer – "Holiday"

🔒 Saturday, April 21st, 2001 | 11:50 p.m.

Alice and I returned to Lucky's. This time, we took a risk and went on a Friday night instead of a Tuesday, and the place was packed. I was able to order a rum and coke on my own, without panicking. Despite the large crowd, much to my relief, Alice wasn't interested in finding anyone to flirt with. Instead, we grabbed our rum and cokes and sat in a two-seater by ourselves, chatting under an antique lamp with a red bulb that emitted sleazy light. We stopped talking only to get a second drink.

"Do you think we'll stay friends after high school?" she asked.

"Yeah, we have to," I said.

"That's what I think too. But Greg said I was being silly, that you don't stay friends with your friends from high school. And Mom's only friends are other moms in Parkview, people I don't think she even likes."

"Well, we're not like them. Plus, they didn't have AIM and email growing up. It'll be easier for us to stay in touch."

On our third rum and coke, two guys approached us. I was annoyed to be interrupted, and assumed they were here for Alice, until I realized that one of the guys was talking to me, not her, and even more unbelievably, I was flirting back. My tipsy self was charming, a word I never used to describe myself. I felt a strange warm heat in my face, an odd sensation which usually would have caused me to panic, but I was too busy chatting. Alcohol did not have to be a tool to self-medicate your misery, it could be fun! My self-consciousness was shed, my worries were over, I could talk easily to strangers in a way like never before, I could be the life of the party.

Alice was cackling. I didn't know about what. She touched my shoulder and laughed a lot and I swear to god at one point I thought she was going to kiss me.

"I'll buy you a drink," one of the guys said. I noticed they were college age, possibly older.

"I can get my own drink," Alice said.

"C'mon, don't be rude. What do you want?" He touched her waist and she elbowed him, hard.

"Get your hands off me."

"Hey," the guy said, raising his hands. Alice took a step towards him as warning and accidentally bumped into me, and since my balance is already iffy when sober, I fell backwards. Alice reached to help and I took her down with me. She laughed again. I started to think things weren't funny anymore, but everything around me blurred and split. I was a little kid again, when I didn't know how to act and I simply copied what other people did, so I laughed too. Probably too loud. My laugh has always been weird and suddenly I was very aware of this.

Another guy, who had been working behind the bar, helped us up. Then he frowned.

"You girls," he said, and he stressed the word "girls" as a warning, "are calling way too much attention to yourselves."

I looked around and noticed a few others in the bar were staring at our little scene.

"It's time for you to go."

"Buddy, I got half a drink to finish," Alice said, still laughing.

"Out. Now," he said.

We took the hint and left. As we approached Alice's car, I said, "Stop. You can't drive."

"I'm fiiiiine," she said, in a sing-songy voice.

"You're not fine," I said. Now, when I felt that heat in my cheeks, without any social distractions, I couldn't stop touching my face. "You can't drink and drive."

"'You can't drink and drive,'" mocked Alice.

My heart raced and my body felt inflamed. I couldn't shake the feeling that I was trapped in my own itchy skin, my own shell. Something was suffocating me, I couldn't breathe, but maybe it was because I wasn't remembering to breathe.

"Ellie." Her voice turned from cruel to concerned. "Are you okay? You're like, breaking out into a rash."

"I don't know. I feel weird. Can you please just call your mom and have her pick us up? Can't you see that if you drive you could get us killed?"

I could see that I was getting through to her even if it meant acting like a whiny baby. She sighed and pulled out the cell phone from her purse that was to be used "only for emergencies" and called home.

A half hour later, we both sat awkwardly in the backseat of Mrs. Lewis' SUV. Alice tried to make up some lie about how she'd had a migraine and couldn't drive, but her mom saw right through it.

"You're drunk," she said. "You're both drunk."

"We're not drunk."

"Don't lie to my face, Alice. I know it's hard for you to believe, but I was a teenager once too."

Mrs. Lewis started crying. Her cheery facade was gone, she was the frustrated woman I'd heard behind the door when Tiff and I eavesdropped on that cold day in January.

"I give you everything," she sobbed. "I take you and your friends out on your birthday. I let you stay out late. I've made so many sacrifices for you. And this is how you repay me? You sneak into a bar. I thought with your new friends, things were getting better. But no, you drag her right into this with you."

"I'm just as responsible here, Mrs. Lewis," I said. "I told Alice to call you. If it wasn't for me—" Alice smacked me in the arm and I stopped talking.

I might as well not have even been there anyway. The energy was between mother and daughter. "You're grounded," Mrs. Lewis said. "You're not going anywhere for a month."

Current Music: P.J. Harvey – "Down by the Water"

🔒 Saturday, April 28th, 2001 | 01:06 p.m.

It was a dull week, my mind felt flattish. Under Alice's curfew, friends could still come over, so Friday night was spent at her place. She complained, but I didn't see what was all that different, it was always her house we hung out at anyway. Tiff brought over a movie, and I didn't notice anything strange between Alice and Tiff. The movie was called *Chungking Express*, directed by a Hong Kong filmmaker named Wong Kar-wai. It was the first movie I'd ever seen where the whole cast was Asian, without it having to be a period piece or involve martial arts. Maybe this was where I could act, I thought, but two seconds later I remembered my ability to speak Asian languages didn't go beyond plugging a few phrases into Altavista BabelFish. The international cinema market wouldn't be a possibility for me either.

After the movie, Tiff headed home, saying she had to do something early in the morning with her family and Christopher left too. I stuck around. I should not have stuck around.

Alice smiled. "I'm going to tell you a secret."

"Okay."

"Tiff and I have started dating."

"What?"

I only half-processed what she was saying as she rambled on. "Or we're friends with benefits. I don't know what we are yet. I invited her over to hang out last week and something felt different. It just happened. Maybe we've always liked each other."

I considered how they acted on my birthday and tried to remember whether I'd noticed anything different about their behavior. People were always deceiving me.

"I always thought she had a little crush on me, but I've only seen her differently since that new haircut."

I wanted to slap her.

Alice didn't notice my anger, she was smiling to herself. "I did not expect her to be so dominant."

"Ewww, I don't want to hear this."

She turned to look at me. "What? You're not happy for us?"

"No," I said. "No, I'm not."

"Why are you such a prude?"

"I'm not a prude! Stop saying that about me. I just don't want to hear about my two friends going down on each other, I think that's a perfectly reasonable request!"

There was nothing more cutting than being at the receiving end of Alice's cold stare, and now, a cruel smile. "What, are you jealous?"

"No, I'm not jealous," I said. "It just—it changes the dynamic of our group. Our friend group, between me and you and her. I'm going to be some left out third wheel now."

"You're not going to be the third wheel. Get a grip."

"Are you doing this to get back at me?"

"Why would I be doing this to get back at you?"

"Because you're pissed off that I made you call your mom to take us home from Lucky's and it got you grounded."

"You are really self-centered if you think this is about you."

"I didn't want to go to Lucky's in the first place, by the way. I don't know what you're planning on doing with your life, but I'm not messing mine up. I can't risk having some kind of criminal record. I can't afford to make the same mistakes you can."

"Lower your fucking voice," she hissed. "Mom and Greg are right upstairs. And why didn't you say that before? I wouldn't have made you do anything you didn't want to do. I thought you wanted to go."

She had a point. The only objections had been in my head. I had acted like I had wanted to go along with it, because I didn't want her disapproval or rejection, which was in full force now. She continued, "You never say what you really want, you always go along with everybody else. It doesn't matter what it is. It could be the movie we're renting at Blockbuster or your own birthday. You almost made me pick your birthday activity for you."

I barely heard her. People would keep abandoning me, either for each other or because of some flaw of mine. Life was people leaving, and in the moment, the only way to stop them was by saying the meanest shit possible.

"Tiff's clearly on the rebound. She's only ever dated Mal. Don't you think there's a difference of experience between you two? Are you even bisexual? Or is that something you say for attention? Like everything else."

Alice laughed a high-pitched shriek. "For attention? Fuck you. The first person I ever did anything with was a girl, but you didn't know that, did you?"

"No—"

"No, because you don't know everything about me. You just think you do. Her name was Maria Markham, and it was awesome. It was one of the few times I actually felt good about myself. God, fuck you. Why can't you admit you're jealous instead of being such a bitch? Instead of slut-shaming me? I've seen how you stared at Tiff. Mal saw it too. That's partially why she hated you."

I panicked. "She hated you too. She called you a hypocrite anorexic. And it's about time someone said that to your face. You have an eating disorder and we all know. So, stop offering your lunch to everyone and stop complaining about being cold."

She stepped toward me with her hands in fists and I thought, finally, let's do this. Let's really have it out, Alice. This has been a year in the making. Longer probably, it's been brewing since we were troubled youth in Group. We were always a heartbeat away from being goth fuckups, no matter how good our grades got, or how many extracurricular clubs we joined. So let's fight like the delinquents we truly are and it won't be like the bitch fight we saw in the cafeteria where they clawed at each other's glasses. Let's punch the crap out of each other. *Fight Club*-style.

But instead of punching me, she released her palms and made a flicking motion. "Get out. Leave my house."

"I don't have my bike," I said. It was nearly 10 p.m. and the temperature had dropped. It would be an hour's walk back to my apartment.

"Too bad. Go."

I tried not to cry, I didn't want to cry in front of her. This was it, our friendship was really over. As I trudged up the stairs from the basement, Alice couldn't resist getting in the last word:

"And learn to drive. Everyone's sick of you mooching rides."

Current Music: Tori Amos – "Cornflake Girl"

🔒 Sunday, April 29th, 2001 | 5:36 p.m.

An AIM Convo with Slayer:

lostchildOKC: My two best friends are dating each other.
SlayerLux88: hahahaha
lostchildOKC: hahahaha?!
lostchildOKC: It's not funny?
SlayerLux88: Aw, c'mon. It's a bit of a laugh
SlayerLux88: It's like some big lesbian soap opera
lostchildOKC: :-(
lostchildOKC: Did you even read my post?
SlayerLux88: Of course, I'm trying to cheer you up. That fight sounded awful
lostchildOKC: I said some mean things.
SlayerLux88: Yeah you did, but we've all been that person. Everyone has their ugly bits etc
lostchildOKC: Yeah.
lostchildOKC: Sometimes I feel you and other LiveJournalers are the only ones who know the real me.
SlayerLux88: I feel that way too
lostchildOKC: Every day I'm exhausted, trying to present my best self to the world, somebody people might like, but here I can keep it real. It's where I can write my ugliest thoughts and know I won't be judged. Or I can talk about feeling depressed, and it's not like doing that in real life, where that brings down the party. It's the opposite, people love it and comment that they feel the same way.
SlayerLux88: And hearing that makes your own depression more tolerable
lostchildOKC: Yes yes totally.
lostchildOKC: I wish the real world was more like LiveJournal.

SlayerLux88: Well, let's not get carried away now

lostchildOKC: What, you don't?

SlayerLux88: Ogoddd no, that would be way too much

SlayerLux88: You don't want people emoting at level 100 all the time

SlayerLux88: I do wish you and I could hang out in real life though

lostchildOKC: Me too. :(

lostchildOKC: What if Monday is like eighth grade for me all over again? Friendless.

SlayerLux88: So many people have friended you on LiveJournal, haha

SlayerLux88: You almost have as many friends as me :P

lostchildOKC: That's not the same and you know it.

SlayerLux88: Still trying to cheer you up. You have a growing and dedicated fanbase

lostchildOKC: The other day, I was thinking about when I was little, like really little, first grade. I barely talked. I remember how I wanted to talk to other kids. Make friends. Except I couldn't make it happen, I couldn't get myself to talk as quickly as I was having thoughts. So I never spoke. And I was thinking recently how far I've come from that, and feeling proud, but now I think I haven't made much progress at all.

SlayerLux88: I'm worried about you. Can I call you tomorrow?

lostchildOKC: Yeah. I mean I'll be home. Where else would I be?

SlayerLux88: Gtg now. Mum's calling me for dinner. I'll call you tomorrow. Late afternoon your time. Xx

SlayerLux88 has signed off

lostchildOKC: <3

Current Music: Blur – "You're So Great"

🔒 **Monday, April 30th, 2001** | **12:52 p.m.**

Slayer called and while she couldn't make me feel much better, it was kind of her to reach out. I know she's helped others too, when things have gotten bad. When Michelle was hospitalized, Slayer talked to her every day and kept her closest LiveJournal friends updated.

I didn't want to go back to school tomorrow and see Alice, Tiff, everybody. I laid in bed so filled with dread I was unable to sleep. It wasn't quite like my usual depressions and anxiety spells. This time, I actually had something to be miserable about.

Around midnight, after tossing and turning and trying to sleep, I went out into the living room and opened a cabinet where I knew Brian kept a bottle of whiskey. He'd gone to bed an hour before. I poured myself a small glass. It tasted like cleaning fluid, absolute shit. Halfway through, I felt that same heat in my face that I experienced at Lucky's and nearly freaked out. Instead, I powered through and finished the rest and eventually, my panic calmed. The heat transformed into a slow warmth. My anxieties dulled and I got the result I wanted—I cared less, I cared about everythingless.

I'm finally sleepee, goingto bed now;.

Current Music: none

🔒 Monday, April 30th, 2001 | 5:36 p.m.

Today was as bad as I expected. I got to school right before the bell rang, so I wouldn't have to see everyone gathered in the nook before Mrs. Ross' class. I looked at Alice. Maybe, just maybe, if I pretended Friday night never happened, it would go away. The cold death stare she returned told me that I wouldn't be pretending anything away. I looked over at Tiff. She avoided eye contact, but I could tell from her nervous leg tapping that she was aware of the situation. This chill continued into Mr. Krasner's class. I couldn't concentrate on anything he said.

When lunch rolled around, I briefly considered eating alone, or returning to the mousy girls I sat with freshman and sophomore years, but I braved sitting down with my overachieving friends and across from Alice. She refused to talk to me the entire lunch period or even look at me, turning her body to face Tiff. I tried to strike up a conversation with Christopher about something, anything, as he arched his eyebrow. He knew something had gone down. Dev didn't notice anything different. He clearly has a crush on Kendall, who was now part of our group. It was agony, the longest forty minutes I'd ever experienced. How would I survive doing this for the rest of the year? I went home and cried and cried.

Current Music: none

Wednesday, May 2nd, 2001 | 7:30 p.m.

Brian's doing better. He has been doing less drinking and television watching and he's not in that weird mental fugue state anymore. Thank god. The last thing I needed, on top of everything else, was the continued stress of worrying whether he was going to neglect to buy groceries or pay a utility bill.

He's even socializing. I saw him at North by Northwest tonight, possibly on some kind of date. Our study group obviously didn't meet this week, or more likely, Alice and Tiff met up without me and fooled around to their hearts' content. I biked to the coffeeshop to console myself with a sugary drink, an iced mocha, the more sugary the better. Halfway through my ride, I briefly stopped to take off my light jacket and tie it around my waist. I looked up at the bright sky. The winter was finally over in Parkview, it only took until early May. There was something spiteful about a sunny day when I was in a lousy mood, it only emphasized how out of step I was with the rest of the world.

Inside North by Northwest, Brian chatted with a blonde woman. Going on a coffee date at 5:30 p.m. was a wholesome change for him. His eyes widened when he saw me ordering at the counter, but neither of us said hi to each other. I grabbed my drink to-go, quickly turning to flash him a thumbs-up before rushing out the door.

Outside, Homeless Guy, or maybe I shouldn't call him that anymore, was asking for change. He was back again too, now that the seasons were cycling through once more. I gave him my coffee change.

Current Music: No Doubt – "Simple Kind of Life"

Friday, May 4th, 2001 | 7:22 p.m.

Alice sat down next to me in AP US History and spat, "It's over, by the way. That thing between us."

Next to her, Tiff looked shifty and said, "Yeah. Got too weird."

"I'm sure you're glad," Alice added.

This didn't, however, mean she was speaking to me again. At lunch, she was as icy as ever.

Later, Tiff messaged me on AIM. She had been the one to call things off, which was the opposite of what I would have expected.

TritoneTiff: better to end things now
TritoneTiff: before they got really weird
TritoneTiff: i didn't think it was a big deal
TritoneTiff: but alice is mad @ me
lostchildOKC: Welcome to the club.
TritoneTiff: yeah i don't like how she's treating you
TritoneTiff: it's not cool
lostchildOKC: Thanks.
TritoneTiff: i think she and i just need a week or two to be chill
TritoneTiff: then things will be back to normal

I couldn't understand this mentality. If I ever date anyone at school, I'm certain I would need to avoid them until graduation if we broke up. And that was if it was a random person, I can't imagine how I'd feel if it was a close friend I cared for outside of the romance.

TritoneTiff: she'll get over her beef with you too
lostchildOKC: I'm not so sure about that.
TritoneTiff: she will
TritoneTiff: you were right
TritoneTiff: our friend group has a special thing going
TritoneTiff: no need to add drama to that

TritoneTiff: or whatever you said to her

Alice was online, idle. Some sad Ani lyrics monopolized her Away Message. A little on the nose, I thought.

lostchildOKC: I've got to go to work.
TritoneTiff: cool ttyl
TritoneTiff: make that $$$
lostchildOKC: Talk to you later.

I put up my own Away Message while I changed into my uniform. Before signing off completely, I saw Tiff had sent me one last message.

TritoneTiff: want to come over tomorrow?

Current Music: Air – "Playground Love"

Sunday, May 6th, 2001 | 2:01 p.m.

Tiff and I had never hung out alone, at least not for an entire evening. I worried about what I was going to wear as if it was a date. I selected jeans and a Goodwill t-shirt she had complimented, then I found a green army jacket of Brian's in the coat closet and figured he wouldn't miss it for an evening. On me it was oversize, but in a way that looked cool. I sensed Tiff would approve, a prediction that was confirmed when she picked me up, nodded, and said, "Sick jacket."

"Thanks."

She put a CD on. Chaotic jazz as usual. I jumped, and she changed it to a mellow, brooding track. I asked what it was.

"Charles Mingus."

"I think that guy inspired a Radiohead song. One of my favorites. 'The National Anthem.'"

"He's the best. I'll burn you a copy when we get to my house."

Tiff lived fifteen minutes away, in a rural area of Parkview. As we drove, I watched the landscape change from suburban shittiness into farm country. A long driveway secluded her house from the road and the nearest neighbor was so far away she could practice trumpet in the backyard. It might not be that way much longer. New housing developments were sprouting up and the houses were even more cookie-cutter than the ones in Parkview proper.

"Let's take a detour, you've got to see this ugly shit," Tiff said.

We turned into one of the creepy Stepford developments. A few of the homes had new residents living in them already, others were in a half-finished skeletal state, and some sat newly completed, with an open house sign on their front lawn. There were no trees to provide privacy, only freshly cut, well-behaved lawns. It was a smug, wonderful thing to drive around with Tiff, listening to her snobby jazz music and judging the crap out of these people.

When we got to her house, her parents said hello. They were in their pajamas watching a movie together. It was funny to see that, whenever I saw them at school functions or Tiff's concerts, they were so well-dressed. But tonight, our school superintendent, the hard ass who never gave us snow days, was wearing a flannel pajama set. Tiff's brother Robbie ambled down the stairs with his Gameboy, trailed by a wheezing pug.

Tiff nodded at the dog. "Say hi, Toby."

She asked her dad if she could get the fire pit going. He said yes, as long as she was careful. I helped her carry firewood from the garage to the yard. She set up the wood in the fire pit and lit a match.

"Oh wait, I forgot," she said. She went back inside, and brought out her backpack, the same one she used at school. She had packed it with marshmallows and graham crackers and chocolates. We looked around the yard for some decent sticks and then we got down to business. I love s'mores, though I always get antsy waiting for the marshmallow to cook. Usually I set the thing on fire and burn it to a black crisp. It tastes better that way anyway. Tiff, more patient, rotated her marshmallow until it reached a smooth, uniform golden brown.

"What's your middle name?" I pointed to the embroidered TSM initials on her backpack.

"Sun," she said.

"Like, s-u-n?"

"Yeah. Before I was adopted, I had a Korean name. Ji-sun Kim. My parents kept my Korean middle name, though I looked it up recently and I don't think Koreans have middle names. I think Ji-sun is my hyphenated first name. Anyway, Sun is still a sweet middle name to have."

"It's cool."

The wind changed and blew smoke in our direction. After we both had a brief coughing fit, she continued, "My uncle goes by his middle name, so for a while I thought I might do that. Beats stupid Tiffany. But I don't know. Sun McKee sounds ridiculous too, like a tropical drink."

"It does kind of make me think of Capri Sun," I said. My third marshmallow caught on fire and I let it completely char before blowing the flame out with a satisfying breath. "My middle name is Asian too. Well, Chinese."

"What is it?"

"Xuan." I spelled it out. "It's my grandfather's name. He died a year before I was born."

"Wait, so your middle initial is X?"

"Yeah."

"That's sick. You should use that more. Ellora X. Gao."

"Where would I use it?"

"I don't know, as your acting name when you go on auditions? On the top of Scantrons? Everywhere."

Maybe I would. Robbie opened the back door and shouted, "I want a s'more." Tiff shouted back, "Come make one yourself." He trudged out to the fire pit. They lightly bickered at each other, but I caught the tender way Tiff broke a Hershey bar and gave the larger half to her brother. She was so clearly the older sibling now, with her new buzz cut. Robbie still had a bowl cut. He ran back inside.

When we were full of marshmallows, we kept the fire going, and laid down in the grass next to each other. Out in the boonies, there were less lights and you could see more stars. The set up was such a romantic cliché, I almost giggled. I looked over at her and she appeared deep in thought. I wondered if it was possible she was also thinking about kissing.

"What are you thinking about?" I asked.

She hesitated. "Do you ever think it's weird that we're Asian, but the people who raise us are white?"

"What?" Besides the fact that this was not exactly the romantic answer I was hoping for, I thought it was a blunt thing to say. Sure, we both made jokes about being Asian and I often thought about being Asian in relation to my chances of landing acting roles, but it was almost shocking to hear her straight up call her parents and Brian white (most people opted for "Caucasian"). I mean, they were, as were all our teachers, and 95% of Parkview, and now that I thought of it, so were nearly all the musicians I listened to, but—"What do you mean by that?"

"Don't get me wrong, I love my parents, even when they're

being annoying, but sometimes I see Joyce Eng with her parents, and I feel like I missed out on learning something."

"I don't," I said quickly. "Joyce's parents are so strict and Christian. That would suck."

"Yeah, maybe you're right." She flashed a smile. "Never mind."

We were quiet again. She had tried to open up about something and I had shut her down before knowing what it was. Sometimes the closer your experience was to another person's, the heavier the small differences felt. I wanted to remind her that I'd been raised by someone Asian for the first ten years of my life. Though as time went on, Mom's influence had faded. I sat wearing Brian's jacket and tried to remember the sound of Mom's voice, or certain phrases she used in her speech, but missing her for so long had trampled my memories.

"Do you miss your real mother?" I asked. Instantly I knew this was the wrong thing to say.

"You mean my birth mother?"

"Yeah. Sorry, I didn't mean to imply that your parents weren't your real parents. I'm such a—"

She held up her hand. "It's cool. Just don't let my mom catch you saying that. She'd probably start crying."

"Really?"

"Yeah, we were watching some sitcom where twins were trying to find their biological parents and they kept saying to each other, 'we've got to find our real parents.' The third time one of them did it, my mom burst into tears and said, 'They already have real parents' and ran out of the room crying."

"Jesus."

"I don't think I miss her. My birth mother. Can you miss someone you've never met? Or don't remember meeting? I do think about her sometimes, though. Like, I wonder if she looks like me. And I doubt there were a lot of creative opportunities where she lived, but sometimes I wonder if I get my musical talent from her, because it's not from my parents.

"But most of the time, no. It's not like for you. I can't imagine if my mom left me at the age yours did. And to clarify, I'm talking about Carol McKee here."

"It's fine. We weren't that close."

Tiff sat up. "Yeah. See, I don't really believe you when you say stuff like that. You don't have to fake being tough."

"What?" I almost laughed. I surprised myself by adding, "That's what you do all the time."

"That's why I'm telling you not to do it."

Now I sat up too. "What are you saying? That your whole personality isn't real?"

"No." She grabbed her marshmallow stick and waved it around to emphasize her point. "Look, what you see is what you get with me. I'm not faking being somebody I'm not. But sometimes, yeah, I'm putting on a bit of an extra show. I feel pressure to be the entertainment. And you want to know why? Because it distracts people from hating me."

"Hating you? What are you talking about? Tiff, everybody loves you."

"Fine, not hate. Most people here aren't that homophobic. But some look at me with disgust. Or confusion. I don't like seeing that in their faces. And if I'm making them laugh, or if they're fawning over how I am the best musician Parkview High School has ever seen, I won't have to."

She stabbed a marshmallow with her stick and shoved it into the flame, forgoing her usual technique. I didn't really know what to say. Again, I felt a wide divide between our similar experiences.

I didn't have to say anything, Tiff was still talking. "There's this diner that my parents drag me and my brother to almost every Sunday morning. And every person in there is like, 60+.

The second my family comes in, everyone stares. Not in a blatantly racist 'get these Asians out of our fine establishment' way. It's more... we're on display at the zoo. 'Look at these nice parents and their two cute Asian boys.'"

We both laughed. She added, "I brought this up to my dad and he said, 'Don't be so conceited, no one is staring at you.' And then I thought maybe he's right, I am imagining it, but if I am, it's only because of other times when people definitely were staring at me. The whole thing makes me feel nuts. Does that kind of stuff happen to you?"

"Yeah, sometimes people are weird at my job. Men will ask me where I'm from and say I look exotic."

"Gross."

"Fuck Parkview," I said.

"For real," she said, her voice low. "Fuck. This. Place."

We high-fived over this and it felt great.

"I want to move to New York City. After graduation." I'd never voiced that out loud to someone before.

"Me too. I want to go to Julliard. Nowhere else. My dad doesn't like that either. He says I need a well-rounded arts education and I should apply to ten schools minimum." Tiff started putting out the fire. "That reminds me. I'm going to make you a copy of *Mingus Ah Um*. You need this album."

Current Music: Charles Mingus – "Fables of Faubus"

Tuesday, May 8th, 2001 | 6:53 p.m.

Our lunch table is going to see how the other half lives. Kendall had learned from her old crowd that Stacey Hayward's parents would be away and she was throwing a huuuuge party this weekend. Most of us had never gone to a party, nor been invited to one.

Alice rolled her eyes and said, "I was totally over partying by sophomore year."

Personally, I think she was just sour about still having the curfew. The fact that Alice would be unable to join is what persuaded me to go. She continues to give me the silent treatment and I dread lunch every day. Thinking about how she hates me keeps me up at night.

I've continued to sneak sips of Brian's whiskey to help sleep, though it has become harder, since he's not drinking as much lately. And yes, I know this isn't a good idea in the first place. Shout out to the anonymous person who left a passive-aggressive link to an article about how children of alcoholics are at higher risk of becoming problem drinkers themselves. I'm aware, I have things under control. Also, I'd never leave an anonymous comment. Show yourself, coward.

Current Music: Radiohead – "Morning Bell"

Friday, May 11th, 2001 | 11:54 p.m.

Remember when I told you about l'esprit de l'escalier? The French phrase for realizing the perfect comeback long after the moment has passed? I would say my whole damn life is l'esprit de l'escalier. I'm always coming up with something brilliant when it's too late. Once in a blue moon, however, I say something clever and tonight was one of those times. It helped that I had prepared in advance, practicing what I'd say when the occasion arrived, like some kind of demented monologue.

It was a busy Friday night on counter at Earl's House. As

usual, I was barely getting by. A man ordered a burger and asked, "Where are you from?"

I put on my widest customer service smile. In a fake, chipper voice, I said sweetly, "Where am I from? Look at me."

The man made direct eye contact, because he thought it might be a sexy moment or something, but instead, after checking to make sure Angie wasn't nearby, I leaned forward and altered my voice to a low and creepy whisper. "I am from nowhere. I am a motherless child who has never known her father. I root from a long line of brilliant, difficult, possibly mad Chinese women dating all the way back to 3000 B.C. My grandmother tricked my grandfather into leaving behind his homeland and everyone he knew, for somewhere halfway across the world. He did it, because he loved her and wanted to create a better life for their daughter. For his sacrifices, he died a prolonged and agonizing death of cancer before age fifty-five. She was struck down too, a few years later, by a lightning bolt to the brain. Her daughter grew up to be madder and even more dazzling. She abandoned her own child and left him under the tutelage of a Western man whose heart she had broken into a million pieces. But he was weak and took to drink. So now, I, the bitter urchin she forsook, walk alone in the world. And I have become the most powerful one of all, the daughter of the new millennium, who carries the fury of my ancestors in every cell of my soul. That, sir, is 'where I'm from.'"

You should have seen the look on his face.

"Um…sorry… um," he stuttered.

I switched back to the customer service voice. "Any fries with that?"

Current Music: Gorillaz – "Clint Eastwood"

Sunday, May 20th, 2001 | 6:49 p.m.

I'm alone, I've always been. Fuck. Bye.

Current Music: none

🔒 Saturday, May 26th, 2001 | 1:55 p.m.

Okay, the first thing I want to say is I'm okay. I realize that last post caused some concern and subsequently my not posting for nearly a week after caused greater concern. Slayer has already raked me over the coals. But I'm getting way ahead of myself.

It started with the party. Before I left, I took a strong swig of the cabinet whiskey. Pre-gaming is what it's called. Christopher picked everyone up. He said he was only interested in drinking cocktails, and when Kendall explained that where we were headed wasn't exactly a cocktail scene, he became our designated driver.

On the way, Dev and Christopher practiced for their big end of year debate on gun control.

"The right to bear arms," shouted Dev from the backseat. "It's the second amendment. You should read it, fool."

"I have read it," Christopher said. "Perhaps you need to re-read it. Like much of the Constitution, its wording is deliberately open and elastic, which was a brilliant and foresighted move by our forefathers who knew that our country would need a malleable document to change with the times."

I turned around and faced Dev. "What if someone pulled a Columbine on our school? Wouldn't you feel like an asshole screaming about guns guns guns in Debate Club?" The whiskey was working. I felt loosened up and more social, more sassy.

"Screaming? Nah, I give my opponents calm, well-articulated verbal beatdowns."

We rolled up to Stacey Hayward's house—mansion would be the more accurate word. From the street, I could hear the strains of an Eminem song. I hate to admit it, but I secretly love Eminem.

My geeky friends and I got out of the car and tried to look badass, like we belonged. We walked in a line, over the front lawn, as the house loomed larger and "The Real Slim Shady" got louder.

Dev continued to ramble about gun control. "My family has a right to defend themselves."

"Against what?" Kendall asked.

"Our own neighbors! My dad was out lawn-mowing and our neighbor starts yelling about the borders of his lawn. It ended with this asshole telling my dad to go back to his country."

"I'm sorry you have a racist neighbor, but I do not understand why this necessitates the purchase of a gun," Christopher said.

"What if that guy tried to break into our home?"

"Nobody breaks into anyone's homes here. There's like, hardly any crime ever. Maybe sometimes in The Pines," Kendall said.

I looked over at Christopher. His face betrayed nothing.

"Yo, there hasn't been a murder in Parkview since like, 1988," said Tiff. "Though that was one fucked up situation. Okay, get this: this guy, he kills his mom and his wife, and then, in his basement—"

"Tiff, I promise you don't have to share this one," I said.

We opened the door to the party.

Fun fact: when a bunch of tightly wound overachievers get a rare chance to cut loose, we cut so loose we completely ricochet out of control.

A quarter of the school packed that mansion. Dev and Kendall hit the keg immediately. I did too, if only because I didn't know what else to do. I gripped a red cup and drank from it frequently. Tiff didn't seem interested in drinking, but when some football guy ran up to her shouting, "McKee! I didn't know you partied!" and passed her a pipe, I watched as she smoked weed like a pro. She passed it to me and I tried my best to imitate her and coughed.

We moved to the kitchen, which easily fit twenty people. I leaned on the gigantic white marble island and kept taking nervous sips from my cup. Soon, I felt that feverish heat in my face again. I touched my cheek and Kendall said, "Don't worry, it looks like you're wearing blush." She passed me a drink she called a Long Island Iced tea. She held one too, and when Christopher asked, "What's in there?" she answered, "Vodka, tequila, and like, some other stuff?" "That's almost a cocktail," he said and took one. Wait, he was supposed to be the DD, I thought, but didn't say anything. As I kept drinking, to ease my unease, the less I cared about my anxiety until suddenly I was puking on the lawn. I didn't even remember walking outside. I heard some kids jeering, saying "Gross," but I didn't care. I counted to three over and over, and on each three I tried to snap myself into being sober. It wasn't working. I was fucked up, and I needed my friends to help me, but then I remembered they were fucked up too. I could die and they wouldn't care. Everything was murky from there. I heard Christopher shouting and Tiff saying we need to call an ambulance and someone else yelled don't you dare call the cops. I rode in the backseat of a car and the weight of my head nodding would briefly wake me up before it was dark again.

The next time I opened my eyes, I was in a hospital bed. A nurse and Christopher's mother Susan stood over me.

"Hey, sweetie," Susan said. "You're okay, it's going to be okay. But you sure gave everybody a real scare."

Why was I here? Why was she here? There was an IV in my arm, which freaked me out. Susan put a comforting hand on my shoulder to stop my thrashing. "Don't worry, we're going to get your mom here."

My cheeks were damp, I had been crying. "My mom?"

"Yes, you were crying out for her, you poor thing. Can you tell us your telephone number? We'll call her."

"You can't call her," I said.

"It's a little too late to worry about that," the nurse snapped. "You should have considered the consequences before."

Still drunk, I laughed darkly at the misunderstanding and mumbled my home number before passing out. When I woke up again, Brian sat next to me.

"Well, welcome back. How are you feeling?"

I didn't answer. I needed to sleep for a thousand years. My head hated me. Little specks of vomit were stuck to my t-shirt. I focused on the ceiling panels' florescent lights to avoid crying again. One flickered on and off.

"Hey, it's going to be all right," he finally said. "Let's see when you can get the hell out of here." He went to talk to the nurse. Shortly after, she took the IV out, Brian signed some paperwork, and I was cleared to leave.

Outside, the sun was coming up. The noise of the party still echoed in my head and contrasted with the silence of the drive home.

"Are you mad at me?" I asked.

"No."

"You look pissed off."

"I'm not mad," he said. "I feel guilty."

On the highway, as cars passed in the other direction, I thought about how cars were simply large metal containers carrying people from place to place. For some reason, I imagined all the cars transparently dissolving and leaving only seated groups of people zipping by at incredibly fast speeds. The image was so absurd I had to cover my mouth to suppress a goofy smile. What the hell was wrong with me? It was the most inappropriate time to laugh.

"Have you been drinking stuff of mine?" he asked.

There was no point in lying. "Yeah."

"That's what I thought. Well, actually, I thought you were pouring it down the sink, like you used to."

I'd done that in middle school, during the days of the Al-Anon list. I thought I'd been clever and he hadn't noticed. Apparently not.

He sighed. "We need to have a talk when we get back."

We got home and I waited on the couch while he made coffee. He sat down across from me and I could practically see the gears turning in his head. He was preparing to say something disciplinary.

"All right. I know kids drink. And I know you've seen me do some stupid things. That's my own business. But you cannot drink like that ever again. Do you understand?"

"Okay."

"You especially need to be careful."

"Why me, especially?"

"Because—you're Asian."

"Are you being racist right now?"

"No, I'm not being racist," he said. "Your mom told me about that. Some Asian people have an enzyme deficiency that makes it harder to break down alcohol. It's why she'd get red in the face and act loopy after a single glass of wine."

Oh.

"Well, I guess she wasn't able to keep up with you then," I said.

He glared at me. "I already said I feel guilty." He stood up and took his time getting coffee. When he sat back down, he said, "There's something else you should know. We're moving."

"What?"

"We're moving out of this apartment. On June 15th."

I didn't know if he was serious. That was in less than a month and during the last week of school. School. My friends.

"Relax," he said. "You're not going to have to change schools. It's a house in Random Knolls."

Random Knolls Circle was a very suburban-y development not far from Alice's. A lot of manicured lawns. I didn't want to live someplace like that. I was surprised Brian did.

"We're not doing that. I don't like changes like that." I could hear that I sounded bratty, and young, but I'd had no emotional time to prepare for this news.

"Look, I knew you'd get upset, but this is going to be a good thing. We'll have three times the space. You'll have a room that isn't the size of a closet. There's a yard, a garden."

"I don't care about a yard. I like the lights in the parking lot, I like it here."

"Then stay here," he said sharply. "Drop out of high school, take over the lease, and pay the rent. How's your job at Earl's House going?"

"Wow," I said, shaking my head. "I don't understand how you bought a house."

"I didn't. An older editor at the paper retired. He and his wife are going to travel the world for a year or two. Must be nice. They don't want to sell their house. I can rent it from him, at a fair price, until you go to college."

"When did you decide this?"

"Just now."

"Just now?"

"That's right. I told him I'd take a week to decide. I was going to see what you thought, but after last night, it's not up for discussion. We need a change around here."

"I don't need—"

"I need the change."

Maybe it was the idea of leaving my home that made me nauseous, or my hangover, but I ran to the bathroom thinking I might throw up. I didn't even heave. I stood up as straight as I could, all 5 feet and 3 inches of me, and returned to the living room.

"This is all I have of her now," I said. "Here. When she lived here. It's not fair."

"Yeah, well, life's not fair."

"It's not fair how you've decided everything about her. You threw out her stuff without asking me. And you're the only one who gets to talk about her and only when you can say something sarcastic or mean. If I try to talk about her in a real way, you shut down or get upset. It's ridiculous that I have to dance around your feelings. She was my mom. She was only your girlfriend of three years."

"That's not how it was," he said. "Think whatever you want about me now, but that's not how things were back then. I was all in."

"Then why didn't you do something? Why did you lie to me for so long about her being on a trip and act like everything was fine and throw pizza parties?"

"You were nine. I thought letting you be a kid was the right thing to do."

"I was ten and we could have been looking for her. Or before she left, you should have made her get professional help. You kept avoiding things and doing nothing."

I knew I'd struck a nerve. He didn't respond right away and

when he did, his voice was quiet and bitter.

"I wasn't doing nothing. It was very hard when she got sick. I was taking care of her while taking care of you. And I had my own"—he gestured around his head—"emotional problems. Not to get too poetic, but it's pretty hard to save someone from drowning if you don't know how to swim. I started to feel like it was my fault that she wasn't getting better. So, when she left that note, I thought if what she really needed was time away—fine. I didn't think she meant permanently. I thought it'd be like the last time."

"What last time?" I asked, feeling dread.

He hesitated, then he said, "When you were two-years-old, she left you with your grandmother for a month. I asked her why the hell would she do something like that, but she wouldn't talk about it anymore. She said she made a mistake and she thought you didn't remember."

I didn't, but I instantly knew it to be true, without any memories. The anxiety I felt every time Mom dropped me off at Grandma's, something within me feared she wouldn't come back, even if I couldn't grasp why. I fled to my room to lie down and nurse the rest of my hangover.

I had spent my entire life being well-behaved, controlled, perfect, but after the hospital, the entire house of cards threatened to collapse. I briefly thought *I want someone to take care of me*, before pushing that thought down. I couldn't think that, there wasn't anyone. Alice hated me. My other friends abandoned me at the hospital. Brian had confirmed every insecurity I'd ever had as to why he stuck around. Mom, I thought of myself crying for Mom. My mom who had left me, twice.

When I got up, I made the 6:49pm May 20th post that got everybody concerned. I'm getting too tired to write anymore, I'll continue tomorrow.

Current Music: Weezer – "Say It Ain't So"

🔒 Sunday, May 27th, 2001 | 5:00 p.m.

After spending Sunday night in a dark place, I woke up Monday morning to pouring rain. I decided to ride my bike anyway, and while packing my things, I imagined a car running me off the road and bringing an end to my sad self. From there, I indulged in an elaborate fantasy where everyone who has ever wronged me, or not loved me enough, gathered together at my funeral, collectively weeping.

As I maneuvered my bike down the stairs, I struggled more than usual, because I was distracted with picturing Alice's distraught face. My focus on the torment she would feel at my funeral was so all-encompassing that when I reached the last step, I was momentarily confused to see the actual Alice, standing in front of her car.

"Are you really going to ride your bike in this weather?"

I was speechless. Why was she here?

"And what were you thinking about just then?" she asked. "You had this weird smile on your face."

"Nothing," I said.

"Take your bike back upstairs. Hurry up, we're going to be late."

Alice had never once given me a ride to school. We drove for a few minutes until she said, "I'm sorry, okay? For the way I've been treating you. And for the mean stuff I said."

"I'm sorry too. For what I said."

"Tiff told me about the party. It was the first time we really talked since our thing ended. Are you okay?"

"I don't want to talk about the party. Everybody left me."

"What?"

"Christopher called his mom and everybody left me at the hospital with her. When I woke up, she was the only one there."

"Are you serious? That's not what happened. You must have completely blacked out."

"I don't know."

"Tiff said you collapsed in front of her. She said it was the scariest thing she'd ever seen. She wanted to call you an ambulance, but some assholes didn't want cops to bust the party. They literally blocked her from the phone. She and Christopher had to carry you to his car and drive to the nearest pay phone. They called 911 and his mom. They wanted to stay at the hospital until you woke up, but Christopher's mom told him to take Tiff home. Apparently, she got really mad and like, ordered him to do it, saying they both had gotten into enough trouble."

My friends had not abandoned me. "What happened to Dev and Kendall?"

"That's what you're asking? I don't know, they must have gotten a ride home from someone else." There was another long silence. Alice sighed and said, "I've always felt jealous of you."

"What?" The idea was ridiculous. Alice had everything compared to me. She was beautiful and outgoing. She had a rich family at home and numerous admirers at school. "Why?"

"You know what you want," she said.

"You told me I never say what I want, that I never speak up when—"

"You don't say what you want, but you know. You have goals. Sometimes it feels like you have some weird, mysterious inner life going on, and I have the sense that it will help you succeed more than any of us after high school, even Tiff, and because I'm a jealous monster, I'm not always happy for you about it."

"Alice, I don't know what I'm doing any more than you do."

"I'm not really good at anything," she continued. "I'm going to be someone that peaks in high school. At our high school reunion, people will say, 'Oh, what happened to her, she was kinda hot.'"

"That's not true."

"It is true. Those are the only things I'm good at. Looking kinda hot. Getting people to sleep with me. Being thin. It really hurt when Tiff called things off. I had started thinking how nice it was to date someone who had been my friend first, some-one who liked qualities about me beyond my looks. Someone I could laugh with. Just being around her and her confidence makes me feel better about myself."

"Yeah." I thought about the s'mores night with Tiff and decided to change the subject. "I'm sorry for what I said about your eating. I want to help you. I've wanted to help you for a long time."

"You wouldn't get it."

"I'd like to try. I don't have an eating disorder, but I know what it's like to feel bad about yourself."

"Actually, are you sure about that? Because I've watched you eat, I watch everybody eat. You eat the same thing almost every day. And remember that time at Denny's when you sent back an entire plate of pancakes because you had asked for no butter and there was butter on it? There was like, the tiniest pad of butter touching one bit of pancake and you got so upset and sent it back. That was a really rude thing to do, by the way."

I forced myself to move the conversation along, not get stuck in embarrassment. "I don't do things like that to be thin. I want to have control."

She laughed that short shriek laugh. "What do you think I'm doing? It's not just about being thin. I've seen you looking at me like I'm an after school special. My mom does that too. You want a reason. You want to hear that I'm doing this because my dad's barely in my life, or because of what happened with Mike, or 'the media.' And it is those things, but it's also not. I can't put the thoughts in my head into words without cheapening them, but they're really complex." She pounded the steering wheel in frustration, accidentally honking the horn. "That's so embarrassing to say."

I almost suggested she start writing, except I wasn't sure that was the solution either. Writing about everything, as I have done for months now, has brought me closer to articulating my feelings, but not completely. There was still so much for which language was completely inadequate. Yeah, I know that sounds pretentious.

"I don't think it's embarrassing at all," was all I said.

We got to school and walked into Mrs. Ross' class together. Tiff noticed and asked, "So... are you two... cool again?"

I looked at Alice. "Yeah," she said. I nodded in agreement.

"Good," said Tiff. "Peace in the Middle East." She flashed a peace sign and returned her attention to Mrs. Ross, who was starting class.

Everyone was weird with me about the party for the first ten minutes of lunch. There were a lot of shifty eyes and mumbled um are you okay's and then it was back to business as usual. The rest of the week, I stayed offline, simply because I was busy. With the AP exam two weeks away, we got the study group back together in the nick of time. We crammed two nights in a row, grilling each other on practice questions. I wasn't settling for anything less than a perfect 5. On Friday, Alice's monthlong curfew lifted and we continued rekindling our friendship by celebrating at North by Northwest.

On Saturday, I worked at Earl's House and when I got home, Brian greeted me with, "Jesus Christ, there you are."

"I was at work." I gestured at my uniform. "What's wrong?"

"One of your 'Internet friends' called. She sounded very worked up about you."

There was only one person it could be. "British?"

"Yeah. When I asked what was wrong, she got cagey and hung up. After last weekend, I thought—I don't know what I thought. What the hell is going on with you lately?"

I didn't say anything. The idea that Slayer had spoken to Brian blew my mind. I couldn't handle my two worlds colliding. Brian left and I signed online, saw that Slayer was on AIM, messaged "??? I'm home now. Also, that wasn't cool?" and signed off.

Five minutes later, the phone rang.

"Hello?" I said.

"Ellie!" She shouted my name so loud I had to move the phone away from my ear. "You can't make a post like that and go offline," she continued. "'I'm alone... Fuck. Bye.' I know us LiveJournal girls are dramatic, but don't you think that was a bit much? What happened?"

"A lot."

"A lot?"

"I got drunk at this party and had to go to the hospital. Also, Brian's pretty mad at me and you calling and acting weird didn't exactly help that situation. Why did you call?"

"Well, after you made that disturbing post, and you didn't post anything more, and you didn't comment on anyone else's journals either, and you weren't on AIM, people flipped out. I'm the only one with your number, so I called. Brian said you weren't home. I must have sounded nervous, because he asked if you were okay or if you hadn't shown up to school. I said I wouldn't know because I didn't go to your school, I knew you from LiveJournal."

"Slayer, what the f—"

"Sorry! I really thought something had happened to you. And what did you mean you got drunk and went to the hospital? By the way, I'm the one who left the anonymous comment about children of problem drinkers. Go ahead and get mad. Clearly, I was right. What happened?"

I sighed. "It's a long story."

"Well, this is a long-distance call, but I've got time."

"I'll write about it," I said. "Ugh, I can't believe you told Brian about LiveJournal. Someone from my real life!"

"I'm not from your real life?"

"Okay, fair point."

"Real life or not, people care about you there. Go check the comments, you'll see."

She hung up. I signed back online and went to Sunday, May 20th's post. There was comment after comment. I mean not thousands or anything, but more than usual. At first people gave the usual replies that my more sad sack material receives. "<3" "I relate to this" "i've been there" After a few days went by, some of my friends started commenting, "has anyone heard from Elora [sic] lately" and "she's been really depressed lately… I hope nothing happened." The last comment was from Slayer, a few minutes ago: "Hey everyone, just talked to Ellie. She's okay and she'll update soon."

So now we're all caught up. I'm sorry I got everyone worried. Still, I'm really moved.

I've never met any of you. And yet, you care.

Current Music: Fiona Apple – "I Know"

Junior prom was coming up. After some lunch table debate about whether we were even going to prom (Should we hold an "anti-prom" instead? Etc. etc.), we have decided to attend. Dev asked Kendall to prom and she said yes. He's pretty stoked about that. In an unexpected turn of events, Christopher asked me to be his prom date.

"Really?" I asked. "I thought your mom was cool. You don't have to pretend—"

"No, no, that's not it. Let me explain. I have always regretted that we live in the North and do not have debutante balls," he said.

There were some puzzled looks around the table. He explained, "It's a fancy party where rich Southern families announce that their daughters are of good breeding and have reached marriageable age."

"Oh god," Alice said.

"I know, a bit regressive," Christopher said. "But one's fantasies are not always aligned with one's politics. I've always had a vision of myself dressed to the nines in some centuries-old country club, proudly escorting an awkward young debutante as she's formally introduced to society."

He offered his hand to me, as if we might get up from the lunch table and ballroom dance right then and there.

"I'm afraid the Parkview High School junior prom, held in a 3-Star Marriott Hotel Conference Center will be the closest I get to seeing this fantasy realized."

I rolled my eyes and shook Christopher's hand. We were going to prom together, I guess.

Alice loudly announced that she was taking herself to prom. Tiff, however, was taking things one step further and running for prom queen. Everybody loved the idea. It was doubtful that she would win, but the idea of her "hacking" the prom royalty system was hilarious. Like most high schools, our prom kings and queens were usually popular football and cheerleading types. To be a nominee, you needed to get fifty signatures from your classmates, with the final vote happening at prom itself. She got the signatures easily.

"If you really wanted to be daring, you would have run for prom king," Alice said quietly.

Tiff gave her a sharp look. I wasn't sure what that was about. There were still some ripples between them.

"The administration would not go for that," Kendall said.

Tiff pointed at her in a way that said, "That's correct." Then she added, "I've got to ease them into the idea. First, I'm gonna have a sweet, sweet victory next week, and then next year, maybe I'll go after the senior Prom King title and be the only student in history to win both." She flashed the shock rock sign at us and went to turn her nomination form in.

Current Music: Third Eye Blind – "Semi-Charmed Life"

Wednesday, June 6th, 2001 | 6:30 p.m.

I got to school early, nobody was in the nook yet. Mrs. Ross stood outside her classroom, doing nothing. She does that sometimes. She'll look up and down the hallway, swinging her arms, like she's waiting for something to happen. She's such a kook, I love it.

"Ellora!" she said.

"Um, hi Mrs. Ross."

"What are you going to do your final paper on?"

"The History of Conformity in the American Suburbs."

Mrs. Ross widened her eyes and nodded in an exaggerated, cartoonish way. "Big topic. Remember this is supposed to be twenty pages."

"I'll stick to my main points."

"I'm sure you will. Mr. Krasner and I were just talking about you. We're both very impressed by your writing. He raved about the paper you turned in on Ralph Ellison's *Invisible Man*. You have a lot of talent. I want you to know that."

I accepted her compliment awkwardly, the way I accept all compliments, but hearing this really made my heart sing. My two favorite teachers thought I had talent when I wrote serious papers about important topics. I know some of you have complimented my writing in the comments, but that's just me writing LiveJournal stuff.

Current Music: Radiohead – "Motion Picture Soundtrack"

Sunday, June 11th, 2001 | 4:05 p.m.

We did prom our way. Everyone met at Alice's and we took loads of pictures. Then it was off to the hotel. Alice had completed her Louise Brooks transformation with a sequin-y silver flapper dress and antique hairpiece. Tiff wore a crumpled suit with a red tie, and when I asked her about it, she said it was an homage to Marty McFly's outfit in *Back to the Future*. The part where he inadvertently invents rock 'n' roll at the "Enchantment Under the Sea" dance is one of her favorite movie scenes. I'd taken cinematic inspiration as well. I wore a white frilly dress from Goodwill that resembled the dresses the Lisbon sisters wear to prom in *The Virgin Suicides*. No, I'd never be a blonde mysterious beauty, but I could make the look my own and I liked the dress. My ridiculous highlights had grown out and faded too, thank god. Christopher gave a wide-eyed nod of approval when he saw me, I imagined my white dress fit nicely into his Southern Debutante fantasy. His own outfit involved a ruffled white shirt that was more 1700s Rococo than Southern gentleman.

Prom was pretty boring in the beginning. A lot of standing around while the DJ played the worst songs. We awkwardly group danced together and when a slow jam came on, we mockingly slow danced with each other. Christopher had some ballroom dancing moves he wanted to try out, but he had to lower his standards because his dance partner was me. There would be no box stepping or tango spins with this klutz.

"Where'd you learn this stuff, the Internet?" I asked.

Christopher looked at me like I'd said something crass. Like, how dare I imply that he hadn't been born with the waltz in his blood? Once he realized I was the most uncoordinated person in the history of the earth, and that his skills would be lost on a Christina Aguilera song, he gave up. We strutted around obnoxiously and that was a whole lot more fun.

There was a big box where you submitted your vote for Prom King and Prom Queen. There were three nominees for Prom King and four for Queen. One of Tiff's fellow nominees, I noted, was Jenny Porter. I checked the box next to Tiff's name with real zest. I didn't really know who to vote for Prom King, I wished I could vote her for it all, as the one true ruler of our school, but I didn't want my vote to get thrown out. I picked Devin Riley, because while he was a meathead football guy, he always seemed goofy and nice.

A photographer had set up a portrait studio for couples and we lined up to take a group photo. The six of us crammed together to fit against a backdrop made for two people.

"Will there be anyone else joining you?" the photographer

asked snidely. Whatever dude, our pictures were awesome.

At 9 p.m., it was time for the big moment. The reveal of Prom King and Prom Queen. Tiff stood up there, smug in her Marty McFly suit, so pleased to simply disrupt the status quo, that I think she was the most shocked of all when Mr. Tolley announced that she had won in a landslide. I hadn't expected it either. People liked Tiff, sure, but people were cheering wildly, and this was no *Carrie* moment, their enthusiasm was genuine. I realized that, with the exception of a few popular kids who really loved high school, everyone considered themselves outsiders. I had thought my friends and I were special, and while we did have demographic identities that made Parkview a more hostile place for us than others, at the end of the day, everyone in this town felt they didn't fit in, so they all wanted to champion this well-liked person who seemingly wore her differences so well.

Devin Riley was announced as Prom King and he made an aww shucks face. After Prom King and Queen were crowned, the insufferable tradition was for the winners to pick a song and dance to it. Since most years the Prom King and Queen were a couple, they'd slow dance to their selection while the entire class watched like it was their freaking wedding or something.

As everyone continued to applaud, Tolley ushered Tiff and Devin over to the DJ booth to pick their song. She and Devin awkwardly discussed this, and I worried for her until I saw them both nodding and grinning. Tiff leaned in and told the DJ their selection.

They had picked Ace of Base's "The Sign," everyone's favorite elementary school jam. The already cheering crowd completely lost their shit. Tiff and Devin strutted out arm-in-arm to the cocky opening instrumental riff. It was almost hard to believe they hadn't planned this ahead of time. The crowd

parted for them and formed a circle, but instead of slow dancing, when they reached the center of the room, they split apart
and started lip synching the first verse to each other like they
were doing karaoke.

The whole room joined in for the chorus. Besides being nos-
talgia-bait for our younger selves, when I heard my entire class
scream, "But where do you belong?" to each other, I realized
that we had re-interpreted this song as a universal anthem for
the teenage quest for identity.

Tiff and Devin hammed it up in the second verse and
lip-synched lines to members of the crowd. For a football quar-
terback, Devin acted like a huge dork. I'm pretty sure I caught
Tiff making eye contact with Mal for a few lyrics, before winking and turning her back to her in a real "you dumped the
prom queen" kiss off.

During the instrumental break, Tiff and Devin dance bat-
tled. They took their jackets off and started swinging them
around like helicopters, to whistles from the crowd. Before the
song's last chorus, there was a beat drop, and the DJ paused
the track for a few seconds to stir an even greater build-up.
Tiff screamed "MODULATION!" like the true band nerd she
was and everyone rushed the center for the final key-changed
chorus.

The prom chaperones called for order. Devin went to
dance with his girlfriend, and Tiff walked over to Alice and
me. The whole school was high on her win, what they saw
as the outsider's movie moment victory, the gay kid's triumphant acceptance, however and whatever anyone wanted to
project on her. That certainly was how Alice saw it, she was
sobbing tears of joy, and I had too, until I saw Tiff's smug
and disappointed smile. I remembered our campfire conversation and wondered if for her, the win, the dance, was not a
cause for celebration. Maybe it had only been one more way to

entertain, one more way to make herself palatable to everyone, while hiding herself deeper. Still, she hugged me and Alice. The song ended and the whole school erupted in applause, but in that moment, it was really the three of us alone on our island, honoring our magical and difficult year. Tiff pulled away and her smile over that was genuine.

The whole gang slept over at Alice's that night. I woke up early that morning, while everyone was still asleep. I had shared Alice's bed with her. Tiff was on the couch. Christopher was on the other couch. Dev and Kendall were sleeping on the floor, half cuddling. My friends looked so childlike in their sleep, I felt a rush of protective love for them.

I knew that once everyone got up we'd probably go to Denny's and rehash the prom, especially Tiff's victory. A part of me didn't want that. I wanted to contemplate the events quietly to myself, and yes, there was an itch to get home to write them down. I packed up my things, and gently nudged Alice.

"Hey," she said, half-asleep.

"I'm going to go," I said. "Last night was the best night ever. Tell everyone I had to leave early and didn't want to wake them up."

She nodded. I hugged her tightly from her bed. When I got home, a soft early morning light came through the windows and cast a golden glow on taped up moving boxes in the living room.

I went back to sleep for a few hours and awoke to the sound of packing tape being pulled from its dispenser. I hated that noise. I wandered out into the living room where Brian was taping up more boxes. He looked up but didn't say anything.

I cleared my throat. "I've accepted the idea that we're moving. I was upset about it before because you sprung the news on me. I need time to emotionally prepare for big changes like that. But I am prepared now and I think it will be okay."

He squinted like I had spoken a foreign language, then resumed taping boxes. I returned to my room and started to scope out what I needed to pack. My simple clothes, my books, my tower of cassette tapes. The magazine collages would be stripped from the walls. My room wasn't much, but I liked it and I would miss it. It had been my own little world of comfort and imagination, while also being a place of great sadness. At my lowest, I'd spent hours in my bed, wrapped under the covers, trapped in my head. When I turned around, Brian held two folded boxes.

"Start with these," he said. "I'll pick up some more this afternoon. You're going to need two boxes for your damn tape collection alone."

Current Music: Belle & Sebastian – "Lazy Line Painter Jane"

Wednesday, June 20th, 2001 | 6:30 p.m.

We moved. I haven't written in over a week because I was busy with that and finishing the school year. Things between Brian and I are still not great. We talked to each other during the move, but it was only to get things done.

At least we're not arguing and I haven't seen him drink at all. We didn't move that horrible couch with us, and he hasn't picked up his drinking and depression routine on a new one. This might be because he has a girlfriend now. Yes, you heard that right, an actual girlfriend. The woman from the coffee shop.

I met her this past weekend, the first in the new house. I was eating breakfast and she came downstairs to make coffee.

"Hi," she said. "You're Ellora, right?"

"Yeah."

"Sarah." I shook her hand. "It's nice to finally meet you."

She smiled and it felt genuine, but I appreciated that she didn't try to have an extended conversation before walking upstairs.

Oh, I almost forgot to mention the sweetest thing about this new place: it has an ethernet connection. No more worrying about tying up the phone and the Internet speed is waaayyy better. After an unsuccessful campaign to move the computer into my bedroom, it was moved into a small guest room, or "the computer room" as Brian calls it. He sounded ancient calling it that, though I do like the idea of the computer living it up in its own space, just waiting for my return.

Current Music: Jamiroquai – "Virtual Insanity"

🔒 Saturday, June 23rd, 2001 | 11:40 p.m.

We went to Alice's house for an end of school year celebration. After doing the same things we always did (wander around Blockbuster, argue about what movie to rent, and hunker down to watch it in the basement), we decided to hit the pool for a late-night swim. I loved the electric blue lights that lit the pool. And I loved diving into the deep end and swimming all the way to the other side without coming up for a single breath.

Alice lounged on a jelly chair. Its lime green plastic nearly glowed in the dark. "Enjoy tonight, nerds. I'm going to camp for the entire summer, so this is the only pool time you get."

"What?" I said.

"You didn't tell us about this," Tiff said. "Where? When?"

"In Massachusetts, near Boston. I'm leaving next weekend and I won't be back until the week before school starts."

This was a shock. Tiff was also going to summer camp, some elite music camp in Michigan, but not until mid-July. I'd already felt loneliness at the prospect of Tiff being gone for a month, but now, with this bombshell announcement, I realized I'd be spending a good chunk of the summer alone. This was so at odds with the summer I'd imagined for myself, the first one in years where I'd finally have friends to idle long days away with.

Later, while Christopher went inside to use the bathroom, and Dev and Kendall canoodled at the other end of the pool, Alice swam over to me and Tiff.

"I can't believe you'll be gone all summer," I said. "When were you going to tell us?"

"Yeah, I thought we planned a 4th of July thing," added Tiff. "What camp are you going to anyway?"

Alice stared at the bottom of the pool. "It's a camp for eating disorders."

We said nothing.

"It's not really camp, obviously. It's rehab. Don't say anything to the others."

I had so many questions, but before either Tiff or I could say anything, Alice dived underwater and away from us. I watched her outline ripple along the bottom of the pool, until she emerged next to Kendall and Dev.

"Break it up, break it up," she teased, splashing water on them. "Get a room."

Current Music: Mazzy Star – "Fade Into You"

I thought Alice would hang out with us every night until she left, but when I asked her to hang out earlier in the week, she said she was busy packing and when the next night I asked her the same thing she said she was still packing, and then the next night she admitted that she was depressed and didn't want to see anyone. I feared she was going to leave without saying goodbye, but last night she asked Tiff and I if we wanted to come over for a bit.

I headed to her house after work. Tiff was already there and Alice was in a low mood. I didn't know whether she had asked her parents for help, or if they finally convinced her to get help, or whether rehab was something she had even fully consented to, but the portion of my mind that always worried about her and wondered whether I should be doing more to help her, could rest. It was in someone else's hands now.

Tiff tried to lighten the mood with a funny story, but I could tell her heart wasn't in it. Neither of us asked Alice how she felt, or why she had decided to go, and maybe that was the right thing to do. Maybe it was the wrong thing. I asked if she was going to be able to call us, or if we would be able to call her. She said that they were going to be restrictive about phone calls, and she'd probably be limited to calling her family. But she could receive mail at an address, which she gave us. Tiff and I promised to write. We hugged her three times before we left, but it still felt inadequate. Everything I'd done for Alice had always been a little inadequate.

Current Music: Ani DiFranco – "Independence Day"

Wednesday, July 4th, 2001 | 11:14 p.m.

On the Fourth of July, Tiff and I got a cookie cake from Steadmans and had them draw the Union Jack on it. We ate it in the parking lot while sitting on the hood of her car. Other people crowded around their own cars with food and drink. This was the best place in town to watch the fireworks.

"I wonder how Alice is doing," Tiff said.

"Me too."

"You think they let her out of her room to celebrate the Fourth?"

"She's not locked in a cell or anything like that. I checked the website. It's a fancy place." I also had initially envisioned a bleak psychiatric hospital à la *Girl, Interrupted*, with Alice playing some combo of Angelina Jolie's character and Winona Ryder's, but when I searched the address, the site loaded pictures of a mansion in the woods. Further scrolling revealed a beautiful cozy living room with a fake fireplace and grand piano. There were tennis courts.

"I'm going to New York to look at colleges the weekend after next," Tiff said. "I only care about Julliard, but my parents are going to make me look at NYU and Columbia too."

"That's cool." We only had two more weekends together and I tried to hide my disappointment about her spending one of them out of town.

"I think you should come with me."

I stared at her.

"I already asked my parents if you could and they said yes. Don't worry about money. They'll pay for our meals and everything."

I shook my head. "I can't accept that."

"Why? It's not a big deal for them. All you have to do in exchange is act semi-interested in a balanced liberal arts education at NYU or Columbia, and I'll pretend you're being a good influence on me."

"I don't know."

"They were excited I wanted to bring a friend. They like you."

"Let's keep it that way." I cringed picturing Christopher's mother, who probably thought I was an alcoholic train wreck. "I don't want to be a mooch."

"Yo, I know you want to see NYC. You said that's where you want to live after high school. You're always talking about what your favorite musicians or writers are doing in New York. We'll have fun. C'mon, get over your hang up about accepting anyone's help or whatever your deal is. You're going to love it."

I knew I'd love it. "I don't know," I said again. "I don't even know if I'd be able to get the days off work. Can I think about it?"

"Sure. Just let me know in the next few days."

The fireworks began to loud applause. Tiff cut another piece of our Union Jack cake and took a bite. I didn't understand how she could eat during the fireworks. There was no way I would have been able to comfortably digest with all that noise.

"You know what, no," Tiff said, and for a second I thought she was rescinding the whole trip until she added, "I'm not going to let you be a little bitch about this."

"What? I am not a little bitch!"

I was laughing, but Tiff wasn't.

"Request the days off work tomorrow." She shouted to be heard over the fireworks. "We're going to New York."

Current Music: The Beach Boys – "I Know There's An Answer"

Brian got home from work and asked if I wanted to go to the Erie Canal. We hadn't gone there in years, but I said yes, because I figured there was something he wanted to talk about and I anxiously wanted to get it over with. Moving had turned out to be okay, but I didn't want more surprises or changes to my routine.

At the canal, people walked and biked and rollerbladed down a path that runs parallel to the water. Brian and I sat in the park grass. We didn't talk. We hadn't talked much in the last month.

We watched the lift bridge instead. As a tall boat approached, bells went off and traffic halted. The bridge raised vertically until the boat passed and then it lowered again. When traffic resumed, three boys walked onto the bridge and jumped. I was nervous they were going to get hurt, but they were fine. They laughed and swam to shore to jump again.

"Remember when we used to feed the ducks here?" Brian asked.

"Yeah."

"Guess that's not allowed anymore."

Three feet away, a big PLEASE DON'T FEED THE DUCKS sign stared at us.

"So, uh, what exactly are we doing here?" I asked.

I watched him concentrate very hard, preparing to make some big speech.

"After your trip to the hospital, I did a lot of thinking," he said. "I haven't done a great job as your guardian. Not recently, not when you were in junior high school, maybe not ever. I want to change that." There was a brief pause before he added, "I think what you actually need is a parent."

I snorted. "I don't need a parent."

"I figured you'd say something like that. Let's pretend you did. How could I do better?"

"Stop drinking." It was such a relief to finally say it.

"I figured you'd also mention that. I haven't had a drink in almost two months."

"Yeah, but you've done things like that before. You'll stop drinking for a while, but then something happens and you get really depressed and go back to it."

He winced. "I can't promise anything about the depression. It comes on like a cold. I think you know how that feels yourself."

"Yeah."

"But the drinking stuff, that's not going to happen anymore. Passing out outside the apartment. Or every night in front of the television."

I looked at him skeptically.

"I've started seeing a counselor—a therapist." He said it quickly, as though admitting it embarrassed him.

"Is it helping?"

"I don't know. Maybe. I'm pretty stuck in my ways. It would have been easier if I'd started when I was your age. That's why I'm bringing it up. I think you should see someone too. We've discussed this before."

"If by 'discussed' you mean you threatened to send me to a doctor for acting like Mom, then yeah, we did," I said. "And my answer's still no, I'm good." We sat quietly for a few seconds until a thought occurred. "Did your therapist put you up to this?"

"Up to what?"

"Making a big heartwarming speech about how you want to be my pseudo-dad?"

"No," he said. "Okay, I did work with her on a plan for how to talk with you—"

"Wow—"

"But it was my idea, because I want to fix things. I know you're going through something. You can't understand this now, but this little tough guy act is what's getting you through. Once you get to be my age, your feelings will catch up to you and you won't know how to handle them. It doesn't have to be that way. Not for you. So, get this chip off your shoulder and tell me what you want me to do."

"Tell you what to do?" I lost it. "You know you do the bare minimum, right? Food. Shelter. You didn't even do the food part once, but I took care of it. I always take care of things. I know you didn't sign up for this, but it's a little late to decide you want to be some kind of parent figure. And I shouldn't have to tell you how to be one."

I shot up off the grass and ran to sulk on a bench closer to the canal. He got up too. I thought he was going to get in the car and drive away, but slowly, he walked over and sat next to me on the other side of the bench.

"So, this is it?" he asked. "We'll avoid each other like roommates who don't get along until you leave for college?"

I shrugged.

"Well, that makes me sad."

If he'd said something similar a couple years ago, maybe I would've felt differently, but what was the point now? This weekend I was going to be in New York City with Tiff. I couldn't imagine what it was going to be like, but I could see that my future, the one where I finally got out of Parkview, and left behind Brian and memories of my mom, while not here yet, was within sight.

"How would you know if I need parents?" I asked. "You don't even talk to your own parents."

"Yeah, that's true."

"Why?"

"It's complicated. That's not what we're here to talk about."

"What about your sister? Do you talk to her?"

"Not really. No."

There was another silence.

"You want to know what you can do better? You can stop keeping secrets," I said. "Stop lying and hiding things."

"Fine. Ellora, what do you want to know?"

"I want to understand why you act certain ways. Ways that stress me out."

"You're going to have to be more specific."

"The day you told me my mom wasn't on a trip. Why were you upset? It wasn't just because of her."

He looked away. He didn't like remembering it either.

"Why did you flip out on my friend's dad? Why don't you talk to your family? I need to know. There's never anyone else around. It's lonely." I'm lonely, I wanted to say.

"I know that. And I'm sorry, but I've burned those bridges." I waited for him to say more. "When I was a kid, my parents had an ugly and drawn-out divorce. They fought constantly, sometimes one of them would run off. Then they'd get back together and try to make it work by going on a long vacation. Or they'd attend some new age-y couples retreat. My sister's eight years older than me, so she checked out and spent most of her time with her boyfriend. That meant my parents were always dumping me with their hippie friends. And one of them, he—he was someone they should not have left me alone with. He was someone children shouldn't be left alone with. Do you understand what I'm saying?"

His voice choked and I felt horrible. "Brian—"

"It's all right." He closed his eyes. "I'm all right. I'm not going to act like that day you were talking about, okay? Just give me a minute."

I stared out at the canal and listened to him take deep,

deliberate breaths until we both sat in silence.

"Did you tell them?" I asked quietly. "Your parents."

"No. No, I didn't tell anyone." He took one more of those counted, long breaths, then he continued. "A few years later, they finally—thankfully—got divorced, but by then I had flipped the script. I got into every kind of trouble I could. Drugs, getting arrested. You name it. I said hateful things to them. Any goodwill left between us was destroyed."

There was another long pause. "So, you don't talk to them at all anymore?" I asked. "What about your sister? What about that time your mom called?"

"I was never close to my sister growing up because she was so much older. She's a rich lawyer married to some asshole stockbroker in New York. I haven't seen her since their wedding. The last time we talked was when I needed her help to file for your guardianship. As for my parents, well, by the time I graduated college, I had matured and so had they. They reached out and wanted to make amends. Both of them, separately, from their new marriages. They asked me to visit over the holidays. That sort of thing. But I didn't want to.

"And I didn't need to, once I met you and your mom. Well, actually, I wasn't sure about you." He smiled. "Oh, don't roll your eyes, you weren't exactly my biggest fan at first either.

"It just seemed like a lot to take on, her having a kid. After years of not caring about myself, I'd met someone who made me really want to live. I was worried you'd limit what she and I could do. Also, being around a kid inevitably makes you think of your own childhood memories, and for the reasons I just told you, that was not a path I wanted to go down.

"But a life with her meant a life with you too, so I had to man up and take on new responsibilities. No one was more surprised than me when that turned out to be okay. I got a kick out of talking to you and hearing you discover new ideas about things. I still do, even though half the time now I think you're just saying things to piss me off. And the other stuff—about my own memories—quieted down when I realized I could protect you, the way I wish I had been. It made me feel a lot better.

"I started to think things would be good. It wasn't the wild life I imagined living with her, but there was a lot about it that I loved. I loved being here and walking along the water. She usually looked so stylish, but whenever we went to the canal, she'd tie her hair up in a ponytail and wear this dorky sun visor, like we were going on a serious hike. I teased her about that. She and I talked endlessly on those walks. I wanted to hear every thought she'd ever had and tell her every thought I'd had. You'd skip ahead, in your own little world. Independent already. If you got too far ahead, she'd laugh and swear and take off after you. And I'd watch her run after you, her ponytail bobbing up and down until she caught up and steered you back to us, and I'd think—my family, finally."

It sounded like he was holding back tears again, but by then I was struggling not to cry too.

"But she already had a family she loved. She loved her parents, your grandparents, and losing them had been hard on her. She was often not in a great mental space, but I—incorrectly—romanticized it at the time. I thought we were two fucked up people who were going to save each other. Then she got really sick, and I realized there was nothing romantic about it and no one was going to save anyone."

He turned to me. "I'm sorry I lied to you when she left. I don't think it would have changed how things turned out, but I shouldn't have made up that vacation story."

I watched the boys jump off the bridge and into the canal for the fourth time. I had thought they were my age, but when I looked closer I saw they were not even in high school yet. People around me were already becoming younger than me, which made sense because I had always felt old.

"You asked about the time my mother called," he said.

"Yeah. I thought maybe someone had died."

His voice took on a mean, sarcastic tone. "No, she was calling because she'd learned some horrible news. An old friend, someone she hadn't talked to in years, had been arrested for child molestation. She said his name and the name of his wife and she had the nerve to ask if I remembered him. I was so angry. She couldn't bring herself to ask the real question because she already knew the answer. She started crying and said, 'We took you there all the time.'"

"What did you say?"

"Nothing. I hung up." I watched his face and sensed he was considering what feelings were appropriate to share with me. Finally, he said, "A better person would forgive her, but I'm not."

There was something powerful in the cruel way he said that. I knew that holding bitterness was bad. It certainly hadn't made him happy. But I saw its allure and I wondered if I was headed down the same path. I was a year ago. Now I wasn't sure. I was friends with Kendall again. The other day, Jenny Porter came into Earl's House and I was surprised at how much I didn't give a shit. If I could forgive them, then maybe I could forgive people who had hurt me much more.

"Will you forgive her?" Brian asked, reading my mind. "If she tries to get in touch with you? Tomorrow? Ten years from now?"

"I don't know."

We sat looking out at the canal for a few minutes more until he said, "Let's go" and we got back in the car to head home. He kept nervously glancing over at me. I didn't know what to say. I was glad he had told me what he told me, but it was heavy and I felt spent.

I noticed a pile of CDs at my feet. They weren't the usual abrasive noise artists that I knew Brian listened to. They were more singer-songwriter types. One of them was an artist I'd been meaning to check out for months. I picked it up and scanned the song titles on the back.

"Is this yours?" I asked.

"They're all Sarah's. That one's good though."

"Elliott Smith. I've heard the name, but I don't know any songs."

"You'll like him. Put it on."

There aren't many albums that I love on first listen, but *XO* drew me in immediately. The first track started as another lo-fi indie song with a guy singing and playing guitar. I thought that was going to be the gist of it, but then, halfway through, the song bloomed to an unexpected place, like the electricity coming on. His voice was beautiful, almost too beautiful, but I heard the bottled-up rage in it. Anger sung quietly cut deeper than anger shouted.

"What do you think?" Brian asked, but with a smirk. He could tell I loved it.

"His voice," I said.

He nodded and missed the turn into the development where we lived, and when I started to protest, he said, "What?" facetiously and kept driving.

We drove out to the more rural part of town, where Tiff lived. We didn't say anything, or talk about the songs, we only listened together. The sun went down, and in the dark, from far away, the new suburban housing developments on plowed land looked less ugly. From the road, the houses resembled lonely candles. And Elliott Smith's singing comforted me, while simultaneously being a stand-in for my own voice, articulating the feelings I couldn't.

By the time we got home, we had listened to the whole

album twice. Brian watched the way I carefully placed the CD back in its jewel case, making sure the text was straight and perfectly aligned. I set it back on the floor with the others.

"I know you don't need a parent," he said. "But I'd like to finally be there for you. If it's too late for that, well, I'm in no place to judge. I hope it's not though."

This time he didn't pressure me to respond. He went inside on his own, which left me sitting in the car by myself, with the time and space to decide.

Current Music: Elliott Smith – "Waltz #2"

Monday, July 16th, 2001 | 09:06 p.m.

I left with the McKees at the crack of dawn to reach the city by mid-day and tour colleges in the afternoon. As we got closer, it was thrilling to see the New York skyline flicker in front of my eyes, like I'd seen in movies.

Dr. McKee parked in a garage, and when we walked out onto the street, I couldn't stop grinning. New York City, I was in New York City, I sang over and over in my head.

"Whoa! Look at that smile," said a man. "Someone's having a good day."

Normally I wouldn't like a toothy stranger talking to me, but he was right. I looked to see if Tiff was having the same thrilled reaction. As usual, she displayed considerably more cool. She carried her trumpet the whole time.

"Is it really necessary to lug that thing all day?" her dad asked.

"Yeah," said Tiff.

"You plan on leading a marching band down 5th Avenue?"

"Maybe." Perhaps she hoped that when we arrived at Julliard, people would see her and think she was already a student in attendance. Or maybe, she was hoping to run into one of her jazz heroes and impress them with an impromptu audition.

The plan was Columbia and Julliard today, and then NYU in the morning before driving back to Parkview. Columbia looked like a brochure-perfect campus dropped right into Manhattan. There was an auditorium orientation for prospective students followed by a guided campus tour. I imagined myself on the green quad, writing my college papers on a portable retro typewriter. People would see that and think wow, she looks so interesting, and rush to talk to me.

"So, what did you think?" Dr. McKee asked us both. We walked through the campus gates and back onto another busy Manhattan street.

"I loved it!" I said. "The required core curriculum, especially. I know the tour guide said students complain, but personally, I believe that everyone needs a well-rounded, mandated diet of the liberal arts."

Tiff raised her eyebrows in a way that said, "please dial back your performance."

To get from Columbia to Julliard, we descended into the subway. On the packed train, I gazed at the subway map and daydreamed. When I returned to New York on my own, I pledged to ride every line out to the very end. I'd explore every borough—Manhattan, the Bronx, Brooklyn, Staten Island, and especially Queens, to see where Mom had spent her early childhood years.

"Remember our emergency plan," Mrs. McKee said. "If we get separated on the subway, you get off at the next stop and wait for us. You hear me, Robbie?"

"Yeah," he whined, his Gameboy in hand, as usual. He

didn't seem to care one bit that we were in New York City.

When the doors opened, Tiff's parents both gently touched her back to guide her off the train. She didn't even notice, they'd probably been doing that since she was a little kid, but I remembered how she had used that same caring and protective gesture on me that day leaving school, and I nearly teared up. While my feelings for her still felt unresolved, I'd accepted her feelings for me were likely platonic. But lately, that friendship felt deeper. I wanted very much to remain close to my crew after high school, yet when I thought of Alice, faraway in posh rehab, I wasn't sure about our future. As we walked side by side in New York City, I sensed that Tiff and I, however, were going to be friends for a long time.

I loved watching her tour Lincoln Center and Julliard, the way her eyes lit up for the buildings and auditoriums, the famous alum's photos on the wall. There was an acting school at Julliard, but I actually agreed with Tiff's dad. I wanted a more traditional college experience. I was excited about NYU tomorrow and asking about the acting school there, the Tisch School of the Arts.

After the tour, Tiff wanted to explore the school and facilities on her own, so we followed her until her brother complained he was bored. We rode the subway further downtown, to check into our hotel. Her parents and brother were staying in one room, and Tiff and I had an adjoining room. When her mom handed her a room key, Tiff winked at me in a way that said, "We are totally sneaking out tonight when everyone's gone to sleep."

Dr. McKee wanted to go to a Mexican place for dinner, "a real hole in the wall" that he remembered from his own college days. You went up to a tiny counter and ordered your food. It was so good. I'd never had a real taco, only Taco Bell and crap like that.

Later, we walked around Greenwich Village, occasionally ducking into shops to browse. While Mrs. McKee and Robbie were still in a store, Tiff and I stepped outside to find her dad staring wistfully out at the street.

"You pining for your lost youth, Dad?" Tiff asked. "When you used to hang out with Bob Dylan?"

"I did not 'hang out' with Dylan. I went to a party once and he was there."

"Tell Ellie how you used to be cool."

Dr. McKee playfully cuffed her on the back of her head and deadpanned, "Ellora, I used to be very cool," which threw her into a snort of laughter. I knew that she and her parents had serious conflicts about her identity that ran much deeper than disagreements over where she should go to college, but today they were getting along okay.

In our hotel room, Tiff and I surfed the kajillion television channels offered until we figured her parents had gone to sleep. We carefully snuck down to the lobby and stepped outside. New York City was ours now. She asked where I thought we should go, and I noticed that we'd passed the perimeter of Washington Square Park on our way to the hotel. I was pretty sure I'd be able to lead us back there.

We headed north. Walking alone in New York City at night, without adults, was a next level of thrill.

"Remember what I said about the diner?" Tiff asked.

"Yeah." I remembered the diner she went to every Sunday, where the old people stared at her adoptive family.

"People stare less here." She smiled in a way that felt free.

I'd led us correctly to the park, and as we entered the south entrance, there was something in the air. I don't know whether it was the summer heat, or the energy of the people, or the live music we could already hear, but we both grinned at each other. Tiff grabbed my arm, linked it in hers, and we started running towards the arch.

In Washington Square Park, my mind was overstimulated by people watching and fantasizing. I watched couples cuddle and wondered if I could find love more easily here than I had in Parkview. Or maybe, New York could transform me into someone effortlessly fashionable, like the many intimidating twentysomethings who waltzed by.

Near the fountain, a trio of old men on drums, upright bass, and piano played jazz standards. They had wheeled a whole upright piano into the park.

After watching them for a while, Tiff said, "I'm going to ask if I can jump in for a song." She was still carrying her trumpet.

"Really?" I asked. This wasn't jazz band, or even Juilliard students. These guys were octogenarians and they looked grumpy.

"Really."

When the next song ended, Tiff jumped up to talk to the piano player. He didn't look enthused, but as always, she was persuasive. She took her trumpet out of its case. The pianist turned to the other players and they deliberated.

"So, this little cat here wants to play with us," the bassist finally said. A small crowd had gathered. He turned to Tiff. "Let's see what you got." Then he addressed the audience again. "Think y'all will recognize this one."

I didn't think Tiff would play the avant-garde jazz she preferred. She knew she had to cater to a more mainstream audience. Still, I was surprised when the band launched into the opening riff of "Hello Dolly," a song I knew was popularized by none other than Louis Armstrong.

Tiff announced her arrival by playing the chorus with the confidence of the most seasoned player. The bassist laughed, pleased to discover she was no amateur, and said, "All right, all right." The pianist nodded his approval and the drummer kept steady time. The crowd grew as people wandered over, drawn by Tiff's warm trumpet sound, the recognizable song, and the spectacle of a teenager jamming with a bunch of senior citizens.

Even in the darkness, I could see Tiff's eyes sparkle. She was exactly where she wanted to be. All eyes were on her, but this wasn't like her prom win. This time, she wasn't dancing for anyone, she had control of the whole crowd and they were dancing for her. And what a crowd it was. This wasn't homogenous Parkview. I stood among the young, the old, every race, every sexuality. The freaks and geeks and artsy weirdos. Our people. I watched two guys start dancing together, and I imagined some scenario where after the song ended, they'd decide to get a drink and ultimately, fall in love. Silly, but it seemed possible. There was magic bottled up in the summer city evening, and Tiff had lit a spark to it.

"This band is great," someone said.

"Who's the kid?" asked another.

For a moment, it felt like I was watching myself in a movie. I was framed in a medium shot, smiling at Tiff. And as the camera slowly zoomed in, I answered, "One of the best people in the whole world."

Current Music: none

Friday, July 20th, 2001 | 5:03 p.m.

I had a lot of false starts writing my first letter to Alice. It's strange, I write so easily to strangers here, but writing something personal to a friend I see in my day-to-day real life, well, it was harder. Did I ask how things were going? Or did I pretend she was not where she was? Did I write about me? And if I wrote about me, if I wrote about my trip to NYC with Tiff, for example, I didn't want to make her feel left out, or like I was trying to make her feel left out.

Tiff saved the day when she came up with a great idea of what to mail Alice. We got each other cracking up, discussing the sheer ridiculousness of it. She was leaving for music camp in a few days and I'd be alone for four weeks. We went over to her house and grabbed Tiff's digital camera.

"Shouldn't you be posing or something, like a goofy pose?" I asked.

"No, it should be stiff, no facial expression. Think: action figures of ourselves," Tiff said.

We took the pictures of each other and then I went to work. I downloaded the old trial version of Paint Shop Pro to her computer and test printed one page.

Tiff held out the printed page of her arm next to her own arm. "Not big enough. This has got to be to scale."

"Any bigger and it's going to look pixelated. I don't think your camera is hi-res enough to print these this large."

"Whatever, can't you just make it work?" She jumped around, almost childlike in her excitement.

I scaled the photos as large as I felt comfortable with, a size that still retained the image's integrity, and then we got down to the business of printing. The life-size printouts took eighteen pages of paper for each of us, and we scotch taped them together on the floor while laughing. Ultimately, some pixelation was unavoidable and the color from my knees down was faded because we'd run low on ink.

We carefully folded them into a legal-size envelope and headed to the post office. We paid extra postage for it to arrive sooner, that's how excited we were for Alice to get this package ASAP. I imagined her lounging in that luxurious area I'd seen on the website, the one with the fake fireplace. They'd distribute the day's mail and she'd open this envelope from us and slowly pull out our pages. She'd unfold and unfold them, while the other girls in her program stared, until she finally revealed the two gigantic life-size cutouts of us. We hadn't even written a letter with it, just a pink post-it note that Tiff had immaturely placed over my cutout's crotch area. It read, "Hey Alice, we got your back. Love, Tiff and Ellie."

Current Music: Kate Bush – "Hounds of Love"

Tuesday, July 31st, 2001 | 1:10 p.m.

Haven't posted in a while because LiveJournal was down again. Is it having more downtime lately, or am I imagining things? I've been having morbid thoughts about how LiveJournal might end. I predict the eventual downfall will come about in one or more of the following ways:

A) Loss of control: LiveJournal suddenly has more users than it can handle and/or has some sort of server crash. This results in severely increased downtime, slowness, and other malfunctions. LiveJournal users get frustrated and move on to something else.

B) Selling out: LiveJournal gets arrogant and sells itself to a bigger company. This results in new limitations and restrictions. Certain services become no longer available. Ugly advertising banners are added. LiveJournal users get pissed off and move on to something else.

C) Competition: Some bigger and better site comes along for journals and weblogs. A new trend. LiveJournal users move on to this new shinier toy.

Current Music: Radiohead – "Life in a Glass House"

Saturday, August 4th, 2001 | 10:43 p.m.

I wasn't sure where Brian and I left things after that drive listening to Elliott Smith. After that conversation by the canal, where he told me his whole life story, I thought, wow, now that I've seen the "real" Brian, this openly hurt person, things would never be the same. His sarcastic front is over, he will now only communicate in intensely emotional ways. A few days later, I was surprised to find we were back at our usual bickering. It was also sort of a relief. Slayer's right, you can't be radiating at 100 all the time.

But things aren't exactly the same. As promised, he's trying to be a more parental force in my life. We have cooked a few dinners, and I went to an outdoor concert with him and his girlfriend Sarah. We played a freaking board game the other day, I couldn't believe it.

Last weekend, he asked, "Is there a structured activity you'd like to do today?"

"Structured activity? Is that a phrase from therapy?"

"Please, just work with me here."

"I want to get my license." As soon as I said it out loud, I realized it was true. "Teach me how to drive."

I drove to Earl's House today, with Brian in the passenger seat. It was my first time driving on real roads after practicing in a parking lot. The lessons have been slow going, I was uncoordinated as always.

"Not sure you're ready for night driving just yet," he said. "I'll pick you up when your shift ends."

On my lunch break, I read a book at one of the picnic tables.

Angie came outside to smoke.

"Did you know that a Starbucks is opening at the four corners?" she asked.

I shook my head.

"North by Northwest is screwed."

She was right, but since I planned to leave for New York City in almost exactly one year, what the hell did I care if corporations took over Parkview? Let them have it. I knew sharing that thought would be rude, but I wasn't sure what small talk to insert instead. Sometimes, I was still at such a loss over what to say to people I didn't know well.

She sighed. "Okay, spill. What do you want to be when you grow up? You obviously aren't planning to work here forever."

"I want to be an actress," I said. "I plan to major in theatre, with a backup second major in psychology because there aren't many roles for Asian people."

I prepared for her to mention Lucy Liu, or tell me I had a bad attitude, or express doubt that I'd exude stage charisma when I struggled to speak to customers. Instead, she surprised me by saying, "Yeah, you're right." She added, "There's not many good roles on television for women like us. Not many good roles for women period. Half the time we're playing the dead girl or a nagging wife. You're going to have to change things. Change Hollywood. Write and star in your own movie. Make it so good people can't ignore you."

Of course Angie would think that, she was a natural leader. During her tenure as an Earl's House manager, she had nearly doubled the restaurant's monthly revenue. As for me, it seemed unlikely I would be revolutionizing the Hollywood studio system anytime soon. I was taking film studies as an elective in the fall and the final project was directing your own short movie. I planned to act in it as well, but making a student film was one thing, convincing bigwig producers to give you massive budgets was another.

"That sounds hard," I said. "I'd rather audition for roles that are already out there. That's competitive enough."

"Yeah, it will be hard. That's why you don't want to do it alone," she continued. "You've got to find friends who get what you're doing, and you get them. You'll help each other out."

It wasn't Tiff and Alice I thought about in that moment. It was Slayer and all of you, on LiveJournal. I imagined LiveJournal communities becoming filmmaking communities or writing communities once we became adults and pursued "real art."

"What's your generation called?" Angie asked. "Generation Y?"

"Yeah, I guess."

"The media says people of my generation, Generation X, are worthless slackers, with no direction. *Reality Bites*? Hated that movie, didn't relate at all. I work my ass off. People just like to hate the younger generation. Well, I'm not going to do that to you. Keep doing what you're doing and don't listen to the old geezers who doubt you." She put out her cigarette on the picnic table's ash tray.

"What do you want to be when you grow up?" I blurted out. She gave me a sharp look. "I mean, I know you're, like, already grown up, but what do you really want to do? Unless you actually like Earl's House, which is cool too, I'm just saying you could do anything you want."

Angie whistled. "Wow, Ellora."

She went inside. I congratulated myself on putting my foot in my mouth yet again. I was about to go down a negative thought spiral when Angie threw open the back door.

"Okay, this stays between you and me, but I want to start my own restaurant," she said. "It's what I do in my downtime.

Create the menu, plan the decor, look for investors. It's about time this town had a nice place to eat." And with that, she slammed the door closed again, but not before I caught her smile.

Current Music: Radiohead – "Lift"

Thursday, August 9th, 2001 | 1:09 p.m.

I got a postcard back from Alice. It was addressed to both Tiff and me, but mailed to my address, since Tiff was away at camp.

"You nerds" was all it said. She'd drawn a big heart at the bottom though.

Current Music: Elliott Smith – "Say Yes"

Saturday, August 11th, 2001 | 6:49 p.m.

I was in the computer room, chatting on AIM with friends and researching how to write in screenplay format, when Brian knocked. The door was already open.

"Hey, why don't you help me in the garden today?"

The previous owners had kept an expansive vegetable garden in the backyard and he had taken an interest in maintaining it. I was glad he was manically taking up hobbies, but this one was a hard pass for me.

"I'm busy right now."

"I think you've seen the last page on the Internet. C'mon, time to be among living things for a change."

I reluctantly followed him outside. I'd never gardened before and it was about as unpleasant as I'd imagined. Touching dirt, carrying heavy bags of mulch, being out in the sun for hours? No thanks, I'm an indoor kid. There were a million bugs and it was all very disgusting.

"Is it cool if I go inside now?" It had barely been an hour. "This is not for me."

"What? You don't think this is great?" He grabbed a spray bottle to water the plants. "You could grow everything you need here. You'd never need the outside world."

"Please don't try to feed us solely on things from this garden," I said, alarmed. "And I'm pretty sure you bought those seeds you planted from a store, so it isn't like you're living *Walden* out here."

I expected this reference to go over his head, but he immediately shot back, "Thoreau dropped his laundry off at his mother's house. Did you know that, smartass?"

I didn't, but I made a mental note to look this up later. (It appears he was correct.)

He aimed the spray bottle at me and spritzed me with water. "Go in, if you want."

I debated whether or not to go inside. My mind wandered, it opened new browser windows to other thoughts and subjects. I watched Brian water the plants with a weird, intense concentration and suddenly, I felt like a jerk. These manic family activities were not solely for my benefit. Or rather, they were, in the way that meant the most to me. He was keeping busy to distract himself from drinking. Last week, Sarah had brought over this thing called a juicer. You throw vegetables and fruits down a chute, then it grinds them up into juice. It's horribly messy and makes a terrible noise and he'd been running it multiple times a day.

"I changed my mind," I said. "I can stay out here and help."

I spent the entire afternoon helping him with the garden. After planting some vegetable rows, we did some weeding. At first, it was frustrating. I'd pull at the weeds and snap them in half. Brian handed me a tool and said I needed to dig around them first. I've got to admit it was really satisfying when I started to pull them up by the entire roots, like, damn, I got you fuckers.

He had purchased a few more plants already in pots. He kept those inside, near a window that brought good light.

"Pick one of these. It'll be yours," he said. "But you've got to be the one to take care of it every day."

I picked a small cacti thing because I figured it needed the least amount of watering. I wasn't changing my ways completely.

Current Music: Oasis – "Don't Look Back In Anger"

Sunday August 25th, 2001 | 11:07 p.m.

I've neglected LiveJournal again. I've been busy working nearly full-time at Earl's House, or working on my screenplay, or helping Brian with the garden, or he's helping me learn driving.

On Wednesday though, Tiff's coming home from camp. And then on Friday, Alice returns. I'm nervous. I want things to be as they are, except she's cured. She wrote in a letter that she wants to hang out the first weekend she's back, so that's reassuring at least.

Current Music: Aaliyah – "We Need a Resolution" (RIP Aaliyah)

Sunday, September 2nd, 2001 | 8:53 p.m.

Every Labor Day weekend, the city shuts down the circular highway that runs through its heart. It's a big deal, old people who walk laps around the mall take their act outside for a day, serious cyclists hit the loop in bicycle gear like they're doing a triathlon, and food carts set up to sell hot dogs and fried dough like it's a carnival. Tiff picked me up and we made plans to meet Alice there. She couldn't stop chattering about camp, and how for four weeks straight she got to do what she loved with people who loved it as much as she did. And—she'd had a romance, with some foxy violinist. Remember how I told you camp is a prime place for hookups?

"Are you two going to um, keep dating?" I asked.

"Nah, she lives in Portland, Oregon. I don't know when I'm going to see her again. A long-distance relationship could hold back my career."

Tiff parked on a city side street and we walked to the closed inner loop. We'd picked Exit 32 as the spot to meet Alice, but she hadn't arrived yet. Tiff skateboarded around, idling. I could tell she was anxious about seeing her again too. And then Alice appeared, my great and frustrating friend who had been gone the entire summer. She walked right onto a highway.

"Hey, nerds." She smiled at us and I smiled back, but I felt crushed because she looked almost the same as when she left. A little healthier, maybe, but she was still way too thin, which was hard not to notice when she wore a tank top and short shorts. Still, she was back and she was alive. The three of us went in for a strong three-way hug.

Tiff had brought her digital camera so that we could take pictures of each other on the empty highway. Other groups were doing the same thing. Alice held out the camera with her arm and tried to take a photo that got the three of us in it, but she kept cropping someone out or skimming the top of our heads, so we finally caved and asked someone to take our picture.

"Tiff, take a photo of this," I said and lay face down on the asphalt. "Goodbye cruel world."

My dark humored friends liked that one, so the next series of pictures was us lying down dramatically in the middle of the empty highway pretending to end it all. Onlookers shook their heads in disgust.

"Why am I not surprised to see you three causing trouble out here? As per usual," called a familiar voice.

It was Mrs. Ross. She was there with her husband and their college-aged son. The three of us screamed and ran to hug her. She asked us about our summer and we gave standard answers. She asked if we were going to keep up the study group for senior year's AP Government & Politics. We said definitely.

"Can we still camp out in the nook before school starts, even if we're not in your class anymore?" I asked.

She feigned annoyance. "Do I have any choice in the matter?"

"Nope," said Tiff.

Later, Tiff ran off to buy fried dough, and I sat on the highway shoulder with Alice.

"So, do you want to know what it was like?" she asked.

"Yes," I said tentatively. "I mean, whatever you feel comfortable sharing. I looked at the website. It seemed nice."

"Oh, it was baller, but it was still a prison. We couldn't leave except for scheduled trips. My whole day was planned out for me. A full schedule of therapies I had to go to. Group therapy, and individual therapy, and then art therapy, and even movement therapy. We did yoga, have you ever heard of that?"

"Yeah, I think so."

"And you almost never got alone time, because some of the

girls had suicide issues too."

"Did you make any friends?"

"Yeah. At first, I was ready to hate everybody, but…" Her voice got quiet. "They're all really brave and beautiful."

"You're really brave and beautiful."

"Ew," she said. "Don't you get corny on me now too."

"Are you feeling better?"

She shrugged and said, "I don't know," which wasn't the most encouraging answer. I don't know why I felt this anxiety over everyone getting better, but I did. Maybe because I wanted the same thing for me. We stretched our legs out and I stared at our feet next to each other.

"What?" she asked.

"I thought," I said. "I thought I could save you."

Alice rolled her eyes. "Do you realize you have delusions of grandeur?"

"The possibility has crossed my mind, yes."

"Ellie, my parents sent me to one of the top eating disorder rehabs in the country. It cost more than a year of private college tuition, as my mom loves to remind me. And I'm still not really better. What do you think you could have done?"

I figured she'd sneer at this answer too, but I said it anyway. I was done with not saying what I feel. "Yeah, but those people don't love you."

She didn't roll her eyes this time. She simply said back, sincerely, "Well, I love you, too."

Current Music: Hedwig and the Angry Inch (Original Cast Recording) – "Wicked Little Town (Reprise)"

Thursday, September 6th, 2001 | 4:53 p.m.

First day of school. We're seniors. I thought about everything that happened last year and it felt like an entire lifetime. What could this year bring?

It was good to get the gang back together at lunch. Dev and Kendall had fully cemented their relationship. I saw Christopher a couple times over the summer, but it was good to know he'd be a daily presence in my life again. Dev discussed his plans for comedy club. And Alice announced she was starting a club of her own.

"A Gay-Straight Alliance," she said. She passed out printed packets with information about similar student groups around the country and read from one of them. "We welcome LGBT students, their straight allies, and those who are questioning, to meet and talk about issues at home, at school, and in the world."

I looked at the readings. I'd always thought my friends and I, boldly declaring ourselves as gay or bi, were highly evolved, and we were, but only around school. To the wider world, maybe we looked a little rigid. It appeared there were more ways to define yourself and soon there'd be more still. Tiff was examining those printouts pretty closely too.

"It would really mean a lot to me if you all joined," Alice said. "It will be on Monday, so it shouldn't conflict with jazz band, debate club, play rehearsals, comedy club, or my appointments."

On Wednesdays and Fridays, Alice had special permission to leave school early to continue attending outpatient eating disorder treatment.

Christopher made an audible groan. "I suppose you think this club will be a support group for the fragile gay youth of Parkview."

"Well, I also want us to take action," Alice said. "Protest against Bush and the anti-gay legislation of his administration.

But yes, Christopher, some emotional support might be nice. Not everyone's as secure with themselves as you are, or appear to be. And we're lucky we have each other. Some of our classmates might feel like they're all alone."

Christopher remained unconvinced, probably thinking about how a teenage Oscar Wilde would never have partaken in a Gay-Straight Alliance.

Tiff set down the printouts. "Christopher," she said. She put her arm around him. "Think about how great this will look on your college applications. To be able to say you were one of the founders of the first club for LGBT students in Parkview High School's history."

He sighed. "Touché. You have my full attention."

Current Music: The Strokes – "Last Nite"

Tuesday, September 11th, 2001 | 11:03 p.m.

All the melodramatic things you worry about in your life suddenly seem irrelevant when the World Trade Center is nothing but rubble. I cannot comprehend that something of this magnitude has just happened. Remember when I told you about Mr. Greenwell, the sophomore year history teacher who told us nothing we've experienced in our lifetime will make the history books? I'm going to take a stab in the dark and say I think this one is going in. And maybe what happens next too. People are already talking about retaliation.

The rumors began in choir. Right before choir started, Ana Newton, always a bit dramatic, ran into class shouting, "WE'RE BEING ATTACKED." Mrs. Carlson-Clark shushed us and insisted that we not let "whatever silly little thing is happening distract us from singing." Yeah, she clearly made the wrong call on that one.

By next period, it was all everyone was talking about. Mr. Krasner ducked into AP Politics and Government.

"I'm giving every classroom an update on the situation," he said. "The World Trade Center is completely gone."

"Like, gone gone?" someone asked.

"Yes, two planes crashed into both towers and they have collapsed. There's no report yet on the number of casualties, but it's likely to be in the thousands."

A television was wheeled into the room and I spent the remainder of the day watching from various rooms and televisions. During lunch, Alice, Tiff, and I snuck into watch with Mrs. Ross. She put her hand over her mouth as we watched footage of one of the towers collapsing and it was unnerving to see her so visibly shaken.

Rather ridiculously, I was scheduled at Earl's House that night, so I had to go there after school. My coworkers kept talking about what happened, kept trying to make some big statement and predict what might happen next. I didn't mind that so much, I was doing the same. What I couldn't believe was that customers were still coming in, like nothing was happening.

How could anyone do anything but stay at home glued to the television? That was what I went to do straight after my shift. Sarah was over, watching the replay of Dubya receiving the news. He looked genuinely terrified.

Brian walked in, holding the phone. "Where have you been?"

"Work," I said.

"Who the hell needed to eat at Earl's House tonight?"

"Right? That's what I thought."

He turned to Sarah. "I finally got through. Phone lines are

back up."

"What did she say?"

"He's fine, he's at home. He doesn't work in the towers, but he was in the area when it happened."

He went to put the phone back in the other room and I followed him.

"You talked to your sister," I said.

"Yeah. Her husband works on Wall Street."

"How did it go?"

"All right. Cordial."

"You think you'll talk again?"

"Maybe. I should probably check up on her after things calm down." I must have looked a little too optimistic about him reconnecting with one of his family members because he added, "Stop worrying about me, focus on yourself. You ready for the test?"

I had my driver's test scheduled in two weeks. "I guess."

"How about we do a practice test this weekend?"

I nodded. I'd begun to really like those lessons. Once I became more confident, and needed less immediate instruction, we'd talk while I drove. And we'd talk about real things: my friends, mental health stuff, even Mom.

After watching some of the news with him and Sarah, I went upstairs to check LiveJournal and saw the weird controversy about Michelle's recent post. She had posted some artsy self-portraits with fake blood and broken glass. Her caption: *we are all broken today*. Dozens of angry commenters accused her of being tasteless when "so many lives were lost today and real blood was shed." Then there were some comments attacking those comments, saying things like "how dare u people try to censor Michelle's art" or "everyone has their own emotional response to this tragedy." I'm not going to give my opinion on the matter, but I've got to say, this wasn't the conversation I expected to be dominating my Friends page today.

Current Music: none

Thursday, September 13th, 2001 | 4:03 p.m.

When I got to the nook, Dev looked pissed. Kendall was consoling him. Christopher and Alice were already there, Tiff wasn't yet. Nobody was saying anything.

"What's going on?" I asked.

"My neighbor's son called me a terrorist," Dev said. "I told him 'I'm Indian, you dumb motherfucker. That's not even in the Middle East.'"

"Even if it was, that would still be a totally unacceptable thing to say," Alice said.

"Yeah."

"Reconsidering your membership to the Republican party, Dev?" Christopher asked.

"Chris, shut the fuck up," Dev said.

We all agreed that now wasn't the time for that.

The new AP Government & Politics teacher is no Mrs. Ross. She's around thirty, bottle blonde, and from the first day of class, it was clear she was a budding Young Republican.

Today, she said, "People have been questioning Bush's legitimacy since the inauguration and the unnecessary drama of the 2000 election. But, after the horrors of Tuesday, September 11th, no one will question that he's the president now."

The way she said, "no one will question that he's the president now" was deeply chilling.

Later, as we walked to lunch, Tiff confessed, "I know it's not what's important right now, but I can't stop thinking about when we were in New York."

"Yeah, I've thought about that too," I said.

"We'll still be able to go to college there, right?"

"I hope so, I don't know."

While I'd read that colleges didn't plan to shut down, I couldn't deny that things in NYC must be drastically changed from when we were there. It actually feels like the whole world is forever changed.

Current Music: Radiohead – "The Tourist"

Sunday, September 15th, 2001 | 1:19 p.m.

Everyone keeps making September 11th about themselves and I suppose I'm no different. First, in response to my recent conversation with Tiff, I want to say: screw terrorism, I'm going to New York after graduation, one way or another.

The other thing I've been thinking about was Mom. Somewhere, Mom was out there, and she had heard about the Sept 11th attacks. I was having this bit of shared experience with her, and everyone else in the world. I wondered if she thought about me that day too, if there was a connection between our brains, the way I always thought there was.

Last night I stayed online until 2 a.m. reading about the role of genetics in mental illness. It was complicated, genetics played a role, but there were a lot of different variables. People have multiple diagnoses or their diagnoses change. One thing that was interesting to learn was how it's not always as simple as parent has bipolar disorder, therefore, kid has bipolar disorder. Sometimes both parent and offspring struggle with mental illness, but they have different symptoms and diagnoses. Reading that rang true for me, when I thought about my own brain and compared it to memories of how Mom acted. It was freeing to feel that whatever challenges I face will be uniquely my own. And her decision to leave, while mental illness may have been a factor, and it may have made day-to-day life challenging for her, including the part that involved taking care of me, it wasn't the reason she left. There are plenty of mentally ill parents who don't abandon their children. It was a choice she made, a choice I may never understand, but a choice that was hers to own. As my choices will be mine.

I sound more confident than I actually am. So much about her still feels unresolved. Maybe it will always feel that way. It's like holding water in my hands. I go along thinking I'm fine without her, she's been gone almost half my life now, and then I notice all the water has seeped out and a great grief washes over me. Yesterday, when we were out doing the practice drivers test, I told Brian I was strongly considering his offer to finally see a therapist.

Sometimes it's easiest to just remember how much I loved her as a younger Ellora. Those times we sat quietly together in public, not talking much, simply being together. Or when we walked along the canal, and she ran to catch me. She would wrap me in her arms and ask, "Where's my favorite explorer going?" Or when she cut my hair and looked at me with love in her face, which in that moment, I hope I reflected back to her.

Current Music: Fiona Apple – "Across the Universe"

Friday, September 21st, 2001 | 7:37 p.m.

I've decided to put my LiveJournal on hiatus. Consider this

a break, not goodbye. I might change my mind and be back next week. But right now, everyone's writing about September 11th and Michelle's controversial post and the backlash to the backlash about her post. Yadda yadda yadda. It's too much. I want time away to reflect before I speak.

Everyone's saying the United States is going to retaliate, that we're going to war. If that ends up being the case, my friends and I might organize a protest at school. Maybe I'll return to write about that, but maybe not, because a curious thing is happening: people at school are getting LiveJournals. During lunch, Kendall mentioned she was thinking of starting one and I nearly choked on my peanut butter sandwich (yes, I still eat those every day). Look, I said it in my very first entry, I don't want people from my school reading this. And if LiveJournal catches on at Parkview High School, the risk is too great. Time to shut this club down.

But I'm not disappearing. Pleeeassee, I could never fully disconnect. I still plan to talk with my Internet friends via email and AIM and the phone. Some of you are as important to me as my "real life" friends, you are my real life, even if I don't see you day-to-day. Maybe someday I will. Keep in touch, you rogues, even if I won't be regularly reading your journals for a while.

Speaking of our journals, I want to amend something I said earlier. Remember when I said how much it meant to hear Mrs. Ross and Mr. Krasner compliment my writing? It still does, but I don't believe anymore that important writing has to be about famous books or the history of the American suburbs. Those topics aren't more worthy to write about than what I've been writing about the whole time—my life. Sure, LiveJournal is a little silly, and I'll always make fun of how dramatic we all are on here, but our thoughts and our stories have always been important.

On AIM last night, Slayer said that while she supported my decision to go on hiatus, people might worry about me. They'll remember the alcohol incident. They'll want to know that I'm doing okay. She said a few of you have even been comforted by my posts during your own hard times. That amazes me. Like I said, it's totally possible I'll be yammering here again someday or making noise on whatever comes next after LiveJournal inevitably shuts down. But in case it's a longer break, I'll leave you with this final image:

Picture me running a marathon. I never run, or do any serious exercise, so please suspend your disbelief. Also, since I've never shown you a picture of me, you might just have to picture yourself instead. I'm not going to list my current music for this final entry either. You get to pick this one. It can be any song you want. Happy, sad, angry. I recommend it at least have a good beat.

Okay, you have your music now and you're running, running, running. It's hard and there's pain along the way. Sometimes you don't know what it's for, or whether it's worth it. I can't promise you it will get better, because sometimes it gets better, but other times it gets worse and then it gets better again. It does, however, get different. If you keep jogging, you won't be in the same spot forever, and the scenery will change. And sometimes in your run, there will be parts where you get it so right. You'll be in your groove and you will hit every mark you want to hit and it will feel great and—this I can promise you—you deserve it. That joy has always been rightfully yours. But still you have to keep moving. Things must go on and might get dark again. It's so unknown and you don't even know what you're running towards, or if it's worth it. But I ask you to keep at it, keep going. Even at my lowest, I've always felt curiosity for this world, its oddness and beauty and ugliness. There's always a chance to see new places, learn new ideas, and meet new people. Or discover new aspects of people I already love. That's why I keep going, and I know that every step of the way I'll be making art to make sense of it, and so will you.

And in the meantime, why not reach out and let people in a little?

LOG OFF|

Acknowledgments

Saturday, March 9th, 2024 | 7:54 a.m.

Current Mood: grateful
Current Music: Fiona Apple – "I Want You to Love Me"

Name: Kristen Felicetti
Location: Rochester, NY
Who is the first person you want to thank? Lucy K Shaw.
You really only need one person to believe in a book to make
it happen and you're the one. Thank you for the endless time,
love, enthusiasm, and brilliance you have shown this book.
Working with you has been one of the most rewarding and
fun experiences of my life.
Who is the most visionary designer in the game? Tim
Vienckowski. Love to see us back on our bullshit. Thank you
for designing the book's exterior and interior to perfection,
and for being my friend and great collaborator for over ten
years and many projects.
Who made this novel's incredible cover illustration?
Jinhwa Jang. Thank you for bringing the world of this novel
to visual life.
What is the most iconic publishing house to be part of?
Shabby Doll House. Thank you to Caroline Rayner, Sebastian

Castillo, and Oscar d'Artois. And speaking of which...

What's the best poetry book of the year? *The Island* by Oscar d'Artois

What's the best writing group of all time? Wordswordswords. Much love to Alex Marden, Ben Weger, Brigid Marz, and Cara Neil Warner. Honored to kick things off and be the first to publish a book. Y'all are next.

Who were the first people to read this novel? My Writing By Writers workshop—Anna Ferrandou Sawyer, Ella Mei Yon, Katiy Heath, Michael Narkunski, and our fearless leader T Kira Māhealani Madden. I'm so happy we met. I'm ride or die for your work.

Where's the best place to hold a workshop? A literature-themed hotel on the coast of Oregon. Shoutout to my Tin House workshop crew—Angie Gentile, Cassie Duncanson, Joni Whitworth, Lauren Spinabelli, Ray Stoeve, and our captain Nina LaCour, for being the first people to read an early excerpt. TMI 4ever.

What's one of the most nerve-wracking aspects of the publishing process? Asking for blurbs. Thank you to Bud Smith, Chelsea Hodson, and T Kira Māhealani Madden for generously writing such nice things about this novel.

Where was an early excerpt of this novel published? *Vol. 1 Brooklyn*. Thank you Tobias Carroll.

We're getting to the end, any other people to thank? My family and friends, who have cheered on and supported this book, and me, in countless ways. I particularly want to thank Lois Farningham, Dave Hannon, Joy Pierce, and the Indoor Kids I grew up with—Sue Spang, Colleen O'Connor, Caitlin Pratt, Chris Adams, and Lisa Hillengas.

One last thing. Do you have a significant other? Yes.

If so, what is your significant other's name? Philip Pierce. I love you.

Kristen Felicetti is a writer and the founding editor-in-chief of *The Bushwick Review*. She is based in Rochester, NY. *Log Off* is her first book.

🌐 kristenfelicetti.com
📷 @kris10felicetti

For the secret liner notes
to this book, visit:
shabbydollhouse.com/LogOn

Made in the USA
Middletown, DE
22 May 2024

54484744R10177